NIGHTRISE

NIGHTRISE

Jim Kelly

CRÈME de la CRIME

This first world edition published 2012
in Great Britain and 2013 in the USA by
Crème de la Crime, an imprint of
SEVERN HOUSE PUBLISHERS LTD of
Salatin House, 19 Cedar Road, Sutton, Surrey, SM2 5DA.
Trade paperback edition first published
in Great Britain and the USA 2013 by
SEVERN HOUSE PUBLISHERS LTD.

British Library Cataloguing in Publication Data

Kelly, Jim, 1957-
  Nightrise.
  1. Dryden, Philip (Fictitious character)–Fiction.
  2. Journalists–England–Fens, The–Fiction.
  3. Fathers–Death–Fiction. 4. Murder–Investigation–
  England–Fens, The–Fiction. 5. Detective and mystery
  stories.
  I. Title
  823.9'2-dc23

ISBN-13: 978-1-78029-033-1 (cased)
ISBN-13: 978-1-78029-533-6 (trade paper)

All Severn House titles are printed on acid-free paper.

Severn House Publishers support The Forest Stewardship Council [FSC],
the leading international forest certification organisation. All our titles that
are printed on Greenpeace-approved FSC-certified paper carry the FSC logo.

MIX
Paper from
responsible sources
FSC
www.fsc.org   FSC® C013056

Typeset by Palimpsest Book Production Ltd.,
Falkirk, Stirlingshire, Scotland.
Printed and bound in Great Britain by
TJ International Ltd, Padstow, Cornwall.

For Jenny Burgoyne
Who, despite being part of the family, has kept an objective and
professional eye on the text of this novel – her tenth such assignment.

ACKNOWLEDGEMENTS

I would like to thank Faith Evans, my agent, Kate Lyall Grant, my publisher at Severn House, and Sara Porter, my editor, for their support and skill in bringing about the 'return of Philip Dryden'. Here in Ely I have again relied on my volunteer team, led by Jenny Burgoyne, who provided the text with its first thorough edit. Rowan Haysom helped me improve the plot and kept the characters in line, and Midge Gillies, my wife, provided a free consulting service on plot and motive, as well as double-checking the script. My daughter Rosa continues to provide proof of the magic of books.

Three specific debts need to be acknowledged. The National Post Office Museum and Archive at Mount Pleasant, London, was extremely helpful and welcoming.

A personal thanks must be extended to Albert Howard-Murphy, at the Coroner's Office, Merseyside Police, for tirelessly helping me to understand technical details. *Nightrise* would have never been written without his expertise.

The spark that provided the inspiration for the book lies with a building – *The Little Chapel in the Fen*. Despite my descriptions it does not lie beneath the waters of Adventurers' Mere. It still stands and holds a harvest festival on the first Sunday of October every year. If any reader feels they would like to help it survive in the decades to come please send a cheque, made out to 'Prior Fen Chapel Upware' to the Hon. Treasurer, c/o Chapel Farm, River Bank, Nr Upware, Ely, Cambs. CB7 5YJ

ONE

Thursday

Philip Dryden walked to the window of his wife's third-floor room at Ely's Princess of Wales' Hospital. The view north was uninterrupted, as if he was looking out to sea, the flat fen fields stretching to the edge of his vision. Early morning but already sun-drenched and humid, the heat burning off the rain that had fallen overnight; the few shadows retreating under hedgerows and solitary trees. Dryden thought he could actually hear things growing out there: creaking green shoots reaching out like a time-lapse film. Nothing else moved; not a cow, not a sheep, not a tractor. But the sky was alive, a cloud the size of a housing estate heading away towards the coast.

He made an effort to live in the moment, to let the joy run through his veins. Bending at the knees he lowered his six-foot-two-inch frame until he could insinuate an arm under the child sleeping in the cot by the window. He held his son of seven days easily – one hand behind the head, which was soft with a sheen of dark hair, the other encircling the narrow hips. He turned him to look out of the window.

A Ford Capri stood in a wide open space in the car park, emblazoned with a hand-painted sign which read:

Humphrey H Holt, licensed taxi. Ely 556335.

The cab's lights flashed once in recognition, then twice.

'That's Humph,' said Dryden to his son. 'Well, that's the car he lives in, but same thing.' The baby was lost in a profound sleep, the limbs as loose as a puppet with the strings cut.

The window was open, providing some relief from the damp heat. It had been a steam-room summer, furnace by day, rain after dark, and the sky often broiling with fair-weather storm clouds. There was loose talk that malaria was back in the Fens and the locals wondered if they'd all end up living in the tropics.

The Tropic of Cauliflower.

Dryden turned back to his wife Laura; she was asleep, as deeply unconscious as her son. He studied her skin, still pale despite her Italian tan, after the caesarean which had brought his son into the world.

Thursday's child has far to go.

It was a miracle she was here, that the boy was here, that he was here. Laura had been badly injured in a car accident a decade earlier – trapped in a coma for more than two years. She would never completely recover. They'd been told a child was impossible. They'd never be free of the repercussions of that single second of screeching tyres, or the impact of the car meeting water. But the baby had come. This version of the future had always seemed impossible. Now that he was living in it Dryden took every opportunity to slow time down, to prolong the moment.

He looked away from the baby's face to the cab, alerted by the sound of a door opening – the familiar grate of rust on rust. Humph prized himself out of the driver's door like a self-propelling cork, then circled the Capri, delicate dancer's steps expertly balancing the seventeen-stone torso, a spinning top of flesh and bone encased in a tight-fitting Ipswich Town tracksuit. The fingers of both small, delicate hands fluttered as if offering aerodynamic support, giving the impression that his feet only just touched the ground.

Dryden turned his son's head, as if he were awake, to watch Humph's early morning exercise routine. 'Once round, twice round and three times round,' said Dryden, as the cabbie circled the cab.

His voice was a surprise, deeper than his thin frame suggested: gravel-gutted, as if speaking from a larger, fleshier version of himself. You would have had to know him very well to discern that he was smiling: his face was usually immobile, as if carved in stone on some cathedral tomb, or peering from an illuminated manuscript. Or – given the black, unruly close-cropped hair – a figure in the Bayeux Tapestry, offering a parchment to a king. A face looking out from the past.

Putting the child back in the cot he rearranged a wooden

articulated eel and a series of glittery fish. A fen boy's watery
playthings.

The cabbie paused in his exercise routine, leaned against the
side of the Capri with one hand and threw open the passenger-
side door with the other. A dog leapt out, a shifting wraithlike
apparition of grey limbs, suddenly at an almost impossible speed
racing over the concrete, turning and twisting as if following
some arcane and invisible pattern. Then it stopped, the greyhound's head looking back at Humph as the cabbie produced a
green tennis ball and a yellow plastic chucker: the ball flew; the
dog flew faster, catching it before it bounced and dropping it at
the cabbie's feet where the ball's momentum carried it on, out
of Humph's scrambling reach, so that he had to totter after it.

Laura stirred in the bed and opened her eyes: they were brown,
with a slight caste in the right. Instantly awake, she brought both
hands up, then down, so that the bed rippled. She had this ability
to come out of sleep and pick up a thread of conversation she'd
left unfinished eight hours earlier.

'Yes – I want to get out of this bed!' The face was immediately
animated, the eyes luminous, the full lips parted to reveal large
white teeth. 'Today – Philip. Today,' she added. Her speech was
quick, the voice quite deep, even syrupy. But the consonants
were dulled, as if she might be deaf, each word tending to be
built round a solid dominating vowel. The disability was one of
the few that had seemed to deepen in the years since she'd
emerged from the coma.

'It must be today – yes?' she asked again. 'This room. I must
see *something* that is not in this room. Anything.'

Since the birth they'd been treating her for high blood pressure.
They were reluctant to send her home because of her medical
history – the accident, the coma, the bouts of fatigue. But for
forty-eight hours her vital signs had been returning to normal.
The doctor would judge this morning. Until then she must stay
in bed.

'Please.' She held out her hands, and Dryden gave her the
child.

She studied his face as if reading a map. 'Jude?' she offered.

'Too biblical,' said Dryden. Their son had no name. In the womb
they'd called it 'touchwood' for luck. Now, faced with the reality

of the boy, they'd struggled to find the right note. 'And there's the echo of Judas – a model of treachery, selfishness, and materialistic greed.'

'A child of his time,' she said.

'Not Humph,' said Dryden.

'Not Humph,' she said, looking to the window and missing the shadow of disappointment which crossed Dryden's face. The whole process of naming was oddly disquieting. He felt that the child didn't properly exist unless they could name him – but by naming him they'd somehow capture who he was, and that was too great a responsibility. Dryden was waiting for the child to give them a hint about who he was, a flicker of attitude, or character. So far he was a bundle of bodily functions.

They'd dismissed all the obvious names – her father was Gaetano, which would be memorable, and a tribute to her Italian roots, but difficult in the Fens. It would end up shortened to something ugly – Tano, maybe. Dryden's father had been Jack. But Dryden's father had died young – at thirty-five – swept away in the floods of 1977. The tragedy seemed to taint the name.

'We're going home,' said Laura, looking at the baby. 'To a *house*!'

During Laura's long illness Dryden had lived alone on a boat on the river. He'd left his Fleet Street reporter's job on *The News* and got a job on the local paper – *The Crow* – to be near his wife, walking away from his career. Once Laura was well enough to leave hospital they'd lived together on the boat, converted to accommodate a wheelchair, hoist and a specially adapted shower. There wasn't room for a child. They'd used Laura's savings to buy a house on the fen with a distant view of the ruined farmhouse in which Dryden had been born. But domesticity repelled Dryden, who'd come to like his footloose life. He said he'd sell the boat, but he kept forgetting to put the advert in the paper.

'Humph said he'd run us to the house in the cab,' he said. 'He's going to tie tin cans to the back.'

They'd lived out at the new house for a month. But tonight would be special.

'Will you carry me over the threshold?'

'I'm not carrying Humph.' Dryden squinted at the battered car. 'He's tied a ribbon to the aerial.'

'That will make all the difference,' she said.

She had a point. The cab had seen better days. Even the fluffy dice attached to the rear-view mirror were dusty and threadbare. The exhaust wasn't shot, it was dead and buried.

'For the child he can be a godfather – yes? *Padrino.*'

'He's got some champagne too,' said Dryden.

'But only little bottles?' she said.

'Yup. Only little bottles.'

Humph's car had its own minibar: the glove compartment, crammed with miniature spirits and wines. The cabbie's principal daytime duty was acting as Dryden's unofficial chauffeur. His real money came in late-night runs picking up nightclub bouncers from Newmarket and Cambridge, and working unsocial hours for a Stansted Airport minicab firm. He had regular customers – mainly academics at the university or execs at Silicon Fen's bio-tech and IT companies. They saved him the miniature bottles of spirits dished out in business class on the long-haul flights. His glove compartment looked like a bonded warehouse in Lilliput.

'But he should exercise more,' said Laura. 'I will write him a programme – a fitness programme. He can take the boy for walks in the pushchair.'

Laura found it difficult to approve of Humph. There was something unsettling about a grown man who lived in a car.

'He's been round the cab three times.' Dryden walked to the window. 'He's back in it now, mind. Oh, no, he's out again.'

The cabbie tottered twenty feet from the Capri and opened a book, looking up at the sky.

'Ah,' said Dryden. 'Clouds. The latest collection.' The cab was littered with I-SPY books – fifties and sixties dog-eared copies. Humph was a dedicated 'spotter' and had worked his way through the classics: I-SPY churches, I-SPY Trees, I-SPY creepy-crawlies, I-SPY pub signs (a particular favourite). Such obsessions were a diversion from the reality of his life: a messy divorce, two girls he didn't see, an inability to be still.

It had been the cabbie's own idea to collect clouds but there'd been no book. So he'd parked outside the library and Dryden had got him a textbook. Fifty different cloud types were listed and he'd already ticked off ten, then run into the complexities of identifying objects which changed their shape as you watched. It was proving as troublesome to name clouds as it was children.

'He's stuck,' said Dryden, enjoying the moment. 'He said he saw a cloud in the night, an hour after sunset – like a rainbow, but brighter, cloud-shaped. I reckon he'd been in the glove compartment.'

The cabbie stood stock still studying a single cloud, a billowing chef's hat, a cathedral of water drops. He looked between the page of the book and sky repeatedly as if one or other image might re-form itself to provide a match.

Another vehicle entered the empty car park. Police markings, just through the car wash. It parked right next to the Capri, and the driver's window slid down. Humph nodded then turned towards the hospital, beckoning Dryden with a small, delicate hand.

TWO

The hospital swimming pool was one of the few remaining parts of the original buildings, built in the 1940s to care for wounded RAF pilots and crew. Hydrotherapy had been offered to burns victims, their skin taut and raw, frightened to touch the world, but enticed by the cool embrace of the water. Dryden always imagined the pool back in that first summer of the war – young men being lowered into the water by hoist. Two walls of the building were made of glass doors which could be opened on to a lawn. He'd seen pictures of patients set out on chairs, swaddled in bandages, limbs stiff and awkward, watching bombers overhead bound for Germany. Today there was just a single woman in the water, in a black one-piece swimsuit, cutting efficiently through the pool, notching up languid lengths.

A coffee machine stood by the exit to the changing rooms with a set of cheap plastic chairs. Dryden took one and watched Detective Sergeant Stan Cherry struggle with coins to get two black teas. DS Cherry was the local coroner's officer: bluff, a northerner who'd never lost his accent, a few years from retirement, stiff-jointed. Cherry's skin was like a baby's – pink and shiny, and almost completely without lines on his round face.

'There you go, my man,' said Cherry, passing Dryden a plastic cup. 'Get yourself on the outside of that.'

Dryden watched the swimmer turn, her body an agile corkscrew. He was in no hurry to find out what Cherry wanted. He was very rarely in a hurry for anything, nurturing his natural inclination to be an observer, letting it deepen and flourish. When he watched ticking clocks he made a conscious effort to try and slow down the second hand.

Cherry's mobile rang but he killed it without looking at the screen. The little tactic made Dryden uneasy, creating a small frisson of anxiety. What was so important about what he had to say to Dryden? Then Cherry smiled inappropriately. He'd built a career on being jovial and he clearly wasn't going to let being a coroner's officer stop him now.

'I've got some bad news, Philip.' Dryden had covered many inquests in the last five years and Cherry was a good contact, a helpful officer. They were on first-name terms. It was the kind of mannered friendship which can mean nothing. 'Well – startling more than bad,' Cherry went on. He took a breath: 'Look.' He leaned forward and fixed his watery eyes on Dryden's. 'It's about your father.'

Consulting a notebook he gave Dryden the full name. 'John Philip Vincent.' Cherry looked for some sign of recognition but Dryden didn't flinch. 'I've got a body in the morgue, Philip. Male – roughly between sixty and seventy years of age. It might be his.'

His father had been swept from sight in an accident on the fen during the floods of 1977. They'd searched for the body but it had never been found. He'd always pictured white bones uncovered in some fenland ditch, or emerging in a fisherman's net. 'Bones?' he said.

Cherry shook his head impatiently. 'It's not that simple. There was an accident out on the road to Manea last week. You carried a paragraph in the paper: the car hit a dip, lost control, ended up in the ditch. There was a fire so we couldn't ID the driver. Well, we've got a name now. The name's John Philip Vincent Dryden. Born April 8, 1942.'

'There's been a mistake,' said Dryden, although the skin on his scalp had begun to crawl. 'Last week? This happened *last week.* You're saying Jack – my father, Jack Dryden – was alive this time last week?' Dryden shook his head, laughing. 'It's a common name,' he said. 'He's been dead thirty-five years.'

'We started with the vehicle, of course,' said Cherry. 'But there was some sort of problem at Swansea with the computer. We got the vehicle licence this week – and an address. He lived in town, Jubilee Estate, a rented house. Neighbours didn't know a thing – kept himself to himself. Old bloke – retired, solitary. A loner. Like I said – name of Jack Dryden. He didn't tell many people his surname, by the way – so just plain "Jack" to most. Local GP had his file, which went right back to London. Born in Hampstead – right? It's your Dad's records all right. We got his dental file too – a rough match, but nothing cut and dried. And fillings are post-1977, after your Dad went missing. So that doesn't prove owt.'

Dental records. It was one of those euphemisms that didn't work, because it just conjured up its own horrors.

'The fire was bad?' asked Dryden.

'If you want to know what I think,' said Cherry, 'I think this is ID theft. I think someone took the chance when your Dad went missing. There was no death certificate. So, officially, he's still alive unless your mum applied to have him certified dead?'

Dryden shrugged, then shook his head.

'See – that's got to be it. Somehow they got hold of his documents. If they got the birth certificate they could build a whole new ID. Like I say – got to be.'

But Dryden could see in Cherry's eyes that it hadn't *got to be*. That there was another solution.

Cherry leant forward and produced a passport in his hand like a magician.

Dryden flicked the stiff old-fashioned black wallet open. It was his father's – dated 1974. So, again, it didn't prove anything. It was thirty-eight years out of date. The corner wasn't clipped, so it had never been sent in for a replacement. 'This is crazy,' said Dryden. 'There must have been pictures in the house – up-to-date ones?'

'Nothing. There's nothing on the walls 'cept wallpaper. I think we're going to have to take a DNA swab – if you're OK with that. Can't see any other way forward. We can hardly ask his neighbours to identify any of your family snaps. They're a lifetime out of date.'

'Trade, profession – any work?'

'We're on to that, but it looks like he was some kind of tutor – you know, GCSEs, A-Levels, that kind of lark. Somewhere he'll have picture ID – bound to have. Then we might know. But it could take time and I'd rather, you know, rule out the *real* Jack Dryden.'

'What subjects did he teach?'

Cherry blinked, his good humour strained by Dryden's peremptory tone. 'Looks like biology, chemistry, maths. All the paperwork's in the house.'

His father had read natural sciences at Cambridge. They were his subjects. If someone had stolen his ID that was a hell of a coincidence. Dryden's heart was racing and he was glad he was sitting down. His father's death had always felt unfinished, insubstantial – not just because they'd never found the body. He'd always felt that his mother – the family – had kept something from him. The whole episode had the aura of a myth about it. It was that uncertainty that made him think of the other solution to the conundrum. 'Maybe it was Dad. Maybe he just didn't want to come back that day. Maybe he didn't want to come back to me and Mum. There was no body. Why's that impossible?' The coffee cup Dryden was holding had begun to vibrate. He held it in both hands. He pressed on: 'And he lived – *here*. In Ely?'

'Right. But not for long – just the last three years. And the bloke next door says he hardly ever went out – chip shop, that pub with the shutters – The Red, White and Blue. But before Ely the medical records say Peterborough until we get back to 'seventy-seven – then it's Ely again.'

Dryden felt dizzy, his mouth dry. He was thinking about that year – 1977. After his father's death, after the floods, after the inquest, they'd fled back to London. His mother had got a job teaching in a suburban comprehensive, swapping the farm at Burnt Fen for a faceless, nameless semi. He'd never understood why. Then he thought of one of those questions which make your heart freeze. 'Seven days ago, Stan – this accident. So it was a Thursday. Time?'

Cherry checked a notebook. 'Late rush hour – what passes for a rush hour in Manea. Call to nine-nine-nine timed at 9.08 a.m.'

An hour after Dryden's son was born. If it was his father then they'd been alive together on the same earth for those fleeting sixty minutes, unaware of each other. Grandson and grandfather.

Cherry produced a DNA swab kit. 'This way we'll know.'

'And the body?' asked Dryden.

'You don't want to see the body.'

THREE

The steep bank of the Old Bedford River ran like a slide rule across country: twenty-five feet of earth, holding the flowing water above the land, crossing a world turned upside down: rivers above the land, land below the distant sea. On the bank top cows grazed – the only living things likely to break the fen horizon. Dryden got Humph to park just below the electric pumping station at Welch's Dam – one of the many along the length of the artificial river. Beyond it, a mile distant over the marshland was the New Bedford – its twin. In the winter they'd open the sluices and flood the land between, creating a huge lake. But in summer rough pasture lay where only a few months before the winter storms had whipped up white horses.

Humph didn't move from the driver's chair, merely eyeing the bank top balefully.

'I need to show you something,' said Dryden, getting out and squatting down to eye-level, his angular frame folding like a deck chair.

'I thought you didn't like water.'

Which was half true. Dryden was drawn to water with the power of an emotional magnet, but he also lived in fear of it, as one might live in fear of the dark. It was a dramatic tension he knew might kill him one day. He always said it went back to an incident in his childhood when he'd been trapped under the winter ice on the river. But it felt deeper than that: something atavistic, like his eye colour.

'Can't I see it from 'ere?' asked Humph. 'The dog's tired.' He did want to know what it was that DS Stan Cherry had told Dryden but he didn't see why he had to get out of the cab to hear it.

Boudicca, the greyhound, barked in response, scrabbling at the back of the passenger-side seat.

'I'll take the dog,' said Dryden, flipping the seat forward, losing patience with Humph's laziness.

Wooden steps had been set into the bank up to the brink and a metal footbridge over the Old Bedford. The water was streaked with green algae and weed and a flotilla of swans headed towards the sea. There were no boats in sight but the wreck of one – fibreglass and covered in slime – lay just beneath the surface. Across the bridge a staggered gate led through a bird hide to a path with a view over the marshland, and of Ely cathedral in the far distance.

The dog ran south along the bank, taking the very slight bend in the great artificial river, leaning into the curve to pick up speed. As it ran it kicked up a miniature red sandstorm. To the north the bank ran straight until the eye lost it in a blue horizon. It was like standing on the lip of the world, thought Dryden: as if he'd reached the edge of the map.

He heard Humph's rasping breath before the cabbie appeared above the bank. There was a bench and the cabbie sat on it, his chest heaving, avoiding Dryden's eyes, looking along the bank at the receding form of Boudicca.

Dryden pointed at a stone cairn. Humph hauled himself up on to his feet and stood before it. There was a slate plaque which read:

IN MEMORY OF JOHN 'JACK' DRYDEN
LAST SEEN HERE ON JANUARY 22, 1977.
HE GAVE HIS LIFE IN THE BATTLE OF THE BANKS.

Humph would have looked at his feet if he could have seen them. He knew about the floods of 'seventy-seven. He'd been ten, and the school house at Black Horse Drove had been closed so he'd played on the edge of the village, watching the water level inch up the side of Tyler's Barn. The nationals had called it the 'battle of the banks' after the Army had been called in. Millions of sandbags, amphibious vehicles, trains loaded with rubble and sand. None of it had stopped the water.

'I didn't know,' he said. 'I thought . . .'

'No,' said Dryden, guessing the missing sentence. 'They never found the body. Mum had this put up.' He looked around. 'I've seen press cuttings, pictures taken that day, right here. It's like another world.'

One picture had shown the far bank, the one they'd parked beneath, water pouring through a gap the floodwaters had breached. White water blew over the bank tops, thundered through the breach – a noise people said could be heard in Ely, six miles east. On either side of the gap men stood, everyone in caps, the rain grey, the water grey, the sky low and lightless. No two-thirds sky to lift the spirits. Military lorries were parked along the bank, loaded with sandbags. In the river barges packed with cement were ready to push into the breach. It was the day after the accident and some of the men held their caps to their chests as if already at the funeral.

'They held an inquest at Reach – the old school house,' said Dryden. He'd been there, in the front row, more curious than moved. 'There was a witness over here, where we're standing, and he said he was watching Dad – Dad and his mate, a bloke called Boyle. They were checking the bank. A kind of night watch, although there was still a little dusk left. Then they heard this wrenching noise – you can't imagine it, can you? What a thousand tonnes of earth just sliding away sounds like. I always remember what he said – that witness: *And then they just sort of went away from us.* I guess they did. They were lit on the bank by an arc lamp and then they were gone, but for a second they saw them moving away, out of the light.'

The dog was back, hurtling straight past them, heading north.

'Nobody ever saw him again,' said Dryden.

Humph pursed his baby-lips, aware that saying anything was likely to be inappropriate, but impelled to say something. 'Nothing?'

'Just his watch. He'd taken it off and left it with one of the overseers – for safe keeping while he filled sandbags.' The thought opened up an emotion in Dryden. 'I loved that watch as a kid. Roman face – classic – but with a compass set in the middle. I've never seen another. My uncle's got it.'

'What happened to the other bloke – Boyle?'

'Survived. I couldn't think it at the time, but that made it worse. He was at the inquest, although he didn't have much to say. He left – left the Fens, tried to find a new life. That's the problem with surviving, I guess. You end up being this constant reminder to everyone of the dead.' Dryden pointed to the distant smudge of a village in the mid-distance. 'Boyle was washed up over there, near the bridge. He couldn't remember anything. Came round looking up at the sky with a stomach full of sea water.'

'But there was a search?' prompted Humph. 'For . . .' He looked at the memorial stone, not wanting to use the word 'father'. 'For Jack?'

'He went into the water holding some loops of heavy rope they'd used to snare cattle. The coroner said he might have got caught up, dragged down. When he said that the men all nodded, as if they knew the truth. I thought it sounded right too, as if he'd been tangled with a serpent, a fen eel.

'When the water finally fell away there was mud, of course – mud everywhere. So we thought he'd be in the mud and he'd stay there. Buried. But if he'd got free of the rope he'd have been swept north – the current was running with the tide then, and the body might have got round the sluices at Denver. Then there's the sea. That's what I always hoped – that he'd just got taken out to sea. Like he'd been diluted. I used to think that on the beach sometimes, and when I swim. That I can sort of feel him around me. I'd sink my head under and listen. He had a voice like that – a rumble, bit like mine, gravelly, like stones being turned over by the tide.'

Humph nodded, appalled at the thought.

Dryden looked up, letting the sky lift his mood. A single wisp of cumulus sliding past at speed, changing shape. That was Humph's problem, of course – that clouds weren't fixed even if you could name them.

The cabbie flexed his hands, wondering if they could go now. 'I'm sorry,' he said again. He didn't really like making emotional contact with anyone, and had always understood Dryden to be the same. He strongly suspected that this rare breach of their unspoken etiquette was going to get worse, not better. The warm plastic interior of the Capri beckoned.

Dryden looked at him, puzzled, then disappointed. 'I didn't bring you here to tell you that,' he said. Humph looked away, embarrassed to see that his friend's eyes were flooded with tears.

'Stan Cherry – the coroner's officer. He said there was an accident out on the Manea Road. A car crashed, caught fire. They didn't give the name out because they couldn't trace the vehicle licence to start with. In fact, we ran a paragraph in the paper – I wrote it. Asking for someone to come forward. He must be missing: missed. Someone's father, someone's son. That kind of thing. The body was destroyed, charred. They've got a name now. John Philip Vincent Dryden.' Dryden took out the piece of paper. 'This is his address. It's 500 yards away from yours, on the Jubilee.'

He walked to the memorial and put a hand on the smooth slate.

Humph's head moved from side to side like one of the nodding dogs he had on the back sill of the Capri. 'Yeah, but it's not him, is it? It can't be him. Is that what Cherry said – that they think it's him?'

'No. He thinks it's ID theft. But I wonder. It might be Dad. There was no body. I don't know what he had on him when he was swept away – driving licence, I guess. Wallet – some cash. I don't know . . .' Dryden threw his hands out wide as his voice rose almost to a shout. 'No death certificate. Mum and I went to see the registrar after the inquest but he wouldn't issue one without a body. So he could have just picked up his life again. The farm was in Mum's name, and the bank account. So it could be him, Humph. Maybe it is him.'

Humph took a step back and almost fell over, his hand searching for the bench again.

'Question is, why?' said Dryden. 'Why leave us? Mum and me. Why didn't he come back? *How* didn't he come back? What did he do – just walk out of the water into another life?' An image had been haunting Dryden since he'd talked to Cherry. A scene from *Beowulf*, perhaps – a man, only half-human, walking out of the mere, dripping mud.

Humph's shoulders sagged, unequal to the task of finding an answer. Then he had it. 'Amnesia,' he said.

There was just a trace of something lighter in Dryden's voice when he answered. 'But how does that work? He gets washed up – he can't remember who he is. But every copper in the Fens, every medic, every doctor, *everyone* knew we were looking for him. His mate was alive, so maybe he was too. There was hope. It's not like we weren't looking.'

Humph was speechless. This was the problem with getting involved in conversations. You made a perfectly reasonable suggestion and then got pilloried for it.

'Cherry said there was no point in a visual ID because of the condition of the body,' said Dryden.

Humph nodded, agreeing.

'I said I didn't care. I want to be sure, so I'm going to see him – tomorrow. I'd like you to come with me.'

Humph felt oddly elated at the request. It included him but he didn't have to do anything. Above all, say anything. Then he remembered something and he couldn't stop himself articulating the thought. 'I was going to suggest Jack – for the boy. It's a good name. Solid, honest.'

He turned away, beginning the long trek back to the car.

FOUR

Dryden got out of the Capri while it was still trundling to a stop on the rank. Looking up and down Market Street he tried to breathe in the everydayness of the scene: a queue waiting for the Littleport bus, loaded down like refugees with market-day shopping; one of the waiters at the Indian restaurant cleaning a plate-glass window; a parrot in a cage hung outside one of the barber shops. From Market Square came the sound of a busker and the gentle hum of the cooling unit on top of the mobile fish stall.

He watched Humph positioning earphones on his small, neat round head. The Capri was the tenth cab in the line so – even on market day – he had a half-hour wait. In his copious spare time Humph learnt obscure European languages from tapes. This year it was Estonian. Any language would do, as long as there was very little chance of him actually having to use it. Every Christmas he'd fly out to the chosen country to try out what he'd learnt. Then he'd bin the books, the tapes, and pick a new language. Dryden suspected the routine was designed to ensure he avoided the long shadow cast by other people's happy festive holidays.

There was a scrum of women round the fresh flower stand on Market Square. Dryden got a cup of tea in a plastic cup from the mobile café emblazoned with its name: Big Business. He stood sipping the tannic liquid, looking down Fore Hill, and over the riverside willows. The image of the burnt-out white van on the Manea Road, the driver reduced to carbon, refused to fade. He gulped the tea, convinced he could taste something like ashes on his tongue.

The Crow's offices were next to a jewellers'. All the watches and clocks showed exactly the same time – 10.14 – and Dryden was pretty sure that hadn't always been the case – that they'd been recalibrated for market day. Which was an oddly touching affectation because he always felt that one of the things he loved about Ely and the Black Fens which surrounded the little city was that time didn't seem to matter that much. You could go and sit right now in one of the steamy cafés around the market stalls and listen to conversations which were set in 1950, or 1970, or 1930 – as if the intervening decades had never happened. Dialogue peppered with the lazy East Country accent, complaints about bus routes which ran once a week, cess pits and reservoirs, irrigators and flash floods, peat so dry it was covering the kitchen table with red powder, and the wind – always the wind: turning the new wind generators, shaking windows in frames, drying washing cracking on the line.

So what was the point in resetting the minute hands on clocks?

As he pushed open the door to *The Crow*'s reception he heard the cathedral strike the quarter hour. Jean, the paper's deaf receptionist, beamed at him from behind the counter where she was serving a gaggle of women, clearly in off the fen for market day. Jean's face was constantly in a state of tension – the intelligence and empathy in her eyes saving her from the brittle, irritable lines of the skin, which she'd strained for a lifetime to hear the words of others.

She adjusted both her hearing aids and fiddled with a control at her belt as all the women talked at once. They'd come to put an advert in the paper to sell three children's prams but they hadn't agreed the wording and so they were doing it now – by committee. Dryden loved market day for these people. Dressed in clothes that were out of date – always – and never coordinated, so a ten-year-old shell suit, thirty-year-old leather brogues, a sixties shopping bag, a Victorian umbrella. And they always seemed to smell of fresh air. There were only six women but they took up most of the space. Fen people were of many shapes but generally only one size.

He was going to flee up the narrow, uncarpeted stairs to the newsroom but Jean pointed towards the small office set aside for interviews with members of the public who called in with news stories – or what they thought were news stories. One woman, in Dryden's first week on *The Crow*, had called to inform them that her husband had grown a potato in the shape of a newborn baby. They'd eaten it, but taken a photo. Dryden had humoured her, taken the picture up to the news desk, and been quietly appalled to see it on the front of the paper that week. It had prompted an avalanche of readers' letters and a series of lookalike vegetable pictures which had been wildly popular. It was the first time in his career that Dryden had doubted his news sense.

A young couple sat behind the single desk in the interview room. He was black, West African by descent, perhaps thirty years old, with hands that were pale on the palm-side. He said his name was Yoruba, David Yoruba. He introduced the woman beside him as his wife, Gill. She was white – fen-white – with the kind of skin that light seems to shine through, and she was crying, two steady trickles from both eyes, into a damp ball of tissue she pressed to her face. Could tears smell? Dryden thought he could smell salt on the air. She moved the tissue around her mouth and to both eyes. Extravagant grief, thought Dryden, African grief: certainly the mannerism was un-English, and he wondered if she'd learnt it from her husband or his family.

Yoruba gave him a letter on headed notepaper: West Fen District Council. His hands were very large and muscular but they shook – or rather, juddered – as if mechanically flawed. The text was brutally short. 'You should read this first, perhaps,' he said, the diction clear and sonorous, with an educated edge.

Dear Mr Yoruba,

We regret to inform you that we are unable to comply with your request for the return of the body of child XXY/678 – 13. You will be aware that on 18 June at the Princess of Wales Hospital in Ely, Mrs Gillian May Yoruba signed form B34 – a copy of which is attached. The burial of the child was therefore undertaken, at her request, on 20 June at Manea Cemetery. Exhumation is not possible in this case. However, I have been instructed by the legal department to examine whether, on this occasion, there are grounds for compensation. You will receive a letter, in due course, from the council clerk.

May I take this opportunity to express our condolences at your loss.

Yours, etc.

The letter had a reference number and was dated three days previously.

'I was so ill,' said Gill Yoruba, 'I just signed. David wasn't there. I don't blame him. I couldn't think.' Her jaw shuddered as she took a breath and dabbed at the corners of her mouth and eyes, then swabbed her forehead. Her husband looked down at his hands as if he blamed himself nonetheless.

'I don't understand,' said Dryden. 'I'm sorry.' He wasn't comfortable in this room, with its compressed emotion. The urge to walk out was almost overwhelming.

'I was in Yarl's Wood. The government detention centre.'

'For illegal immigrants?'

'Asylum seekers,' said Yoruba, smiling. 'I left my home – Niger – because I upset the government.' He spread his hands wide. 'This is a very easy thing to do.' He smiled again, and Dryden detected a sense of resilience in this young man. 'I cannot go back. Well, let's say I do not want to go back. I met Gill. We were married – in March, at St Withburga's.'

Despite the weight of sadness in the room he constructed another smile and Dryden knew it was for the memory of the church and its great wooden roof adorned with angels. The first time he'd seen it Dryden had thought, for a moment, that a flock of birds had got into the building and were trapped beneath the beams.

'They do not accept our marriage as a legal one,' added Yoruba, sliding an arm around his wife's shoulders. 'They believe we have faked our emotions, so to speak, and that the marriage is a sham. They doubt – in short – our love. I have twenty-one days to gather statements from friends to prove our case.' His eyes widened at the thought of such a nonsense. 'They let me out of custody for this, but not for the birth of my daughter. She arrived early. Too early. She was born but lived only for a few minutes. *Then* they let me out.'

The tragedy in that simple statement seemed, finally, to suck all the air out of the room. It had no windows, just plasterboard walls, but it was open at the top, like a public toilet.

'But the child . . .' suggested Dryden. 'Wasn't she proof?'

'No. The birth was only days after the marriage. The lawyer – their lawyer – explained to me. And he spoke very slowly so that I would understand. The child is *immaterial*.'

'I held her,' said the woman. 'I didn't want to give her a name until David came.' She seemed to implode at the thought of the nameless child, sinking back in her chair, but she carried on talking, her chin down. 'When they came the next day I said I had no money, that David was in the jail. That our families would not help – would not know, because I would not tell them.' A flash of anger made her look ten years younger. 'I have no family now. So I signed the form.'

'The council buried our daughter, Mr Dryden,' said Yoruba.

'And now they won't give her body back?' prompted Dryden.

'That is correct. I have some part-time work and access to some funds that I placed overseas before leaving Niger. We can afford to give her a grave where we can visit. I think that is important. And we have a name – at last, we have a name.'

They exchanged a glance and Dryden felt his skin prickle with anxiety.

'I have been there – to this cemetery at Manea – but they say the . . .' He couldn't go on, his jaw set murderously straight. He filled a barrel-chest with air. 'They say the public graves are unmarked. There is only an area, beyond some trees, where they keep rubbish. I left flowers there.'

'And they won't explain why you can't have your daughter's body?'

'They won't,' he said. 'I've asked many times. They are not bad people, Mr Dryden – I can see that. But they won't say, or can't say. Something is very wrong.'

Dryden took the letter. The touch of the paper gave him a thrill because writing this had been a mistake. It posed more questions than it provided answers, but most clearly it betrayed weakness – in the offer of condolence and the hint that compensation might be paid. The implication of the letter was clear – *in this case*, this sole case, the body could not be exhumed. Why? He felt a surge of pride in his trade because he knew he could get the answer.

'I'll make some calls,' said Dryden, taking the letter. 'Can I make a copy?'

'Do you have children?' she asked, nodding.

'Yes. A son – newborn.' They all smiled. Which was when he

realized he couldn't tell them his name. He wondered what he would feel if his son had died.

'Aque,' she said, and for a moment Dryden didn't understand and it must have shown in his eyes. 'That was the name we gave her.'

FIVE

The south-facing room was flooded with light through *The Crow*'s second-floor bay window, frosted with a design of the paper's crest: a bird in heraldic form with the motto: *Bene agendo numquam deffessus*. Never weary of doing good. The news editor, Bill Bracken, may have been weary but it was hard to tell as he was asleep, head back in his captain's chair. Where an air of excitement and feverish activity should have hung in the air there was instead the stale aroma of Bracken's sweaty shirt. There was still twenty-four hours until the deadline for the main weekly paper, *The Crow*, and the news editor had never taken personal responsibility for the quality of the news coverage. If the paper read like a not very interesting section of the telephone directory he didn't lose sleep; Dryden did.

It didn't look like it, it didn't feel like it, but *The Crow* was a newspaper in transition. The editor – Septimus Henry Kew – had decided to step down. In theory he was still in the post but for the last six months he had done nothing but read the final proofs before letting it go to press. The paper's owners, a group of local businessmen, were struggling to find a replacement. Interviews were being held – sporadically – in a room at The Lamb Hotel. Rumours were circulating that the outcome of this process might not be the appointment of a new editor, but the closure of the paper. *The Crow*'s modest circulation had been on the decline for fifteen years. The local population had been on the increase for precisely the same period. It was as if there were two worlds in one town: in one the readers were faithful to *The Crow* but dying off; in the other they were happily multiplying but didn't know *The Crow* existed.

Dryden sat at his desk and switched on his new laptop iMac. It was time for calls: the ritual round-robin of regular checks with police, fire, ambulance, coastguard, county police. Then he'd surf the BBC websites and local radio. But first he took out the address the police had given him for Jack Dryden – an old council house, half a mile from where he was sitting. He'd see the body tomorrow. Telling Humph what had happened had helped relieve the tension but it hadn't been the catharsis he'd hoped for. It was like shouting down a well, except there was no echo. He'd tell Laura later, but he felt he should let her have the joy of going home unsullied.

He wanted to speak to someone now. It was as if he had some emotional GPS in his head that needed to make contact with satellites before he knew where he was. Or who he was. The first time he'd flown abroad, as a teenager – a trip to Spain from university, pre-mobile phones, pre-text messages – he'd stood in the departure hall at Gatwick asking himself the key question: he was leaving the country, who should he tell? He'd rung his mother – at the new farm, back in the Fens after twenty years in London – just to let her know, as if she was some unpaid official at passport control. And when he'd returned he'd rung her again to say he was back. Reconnecting his emotional GPS.

Beyond his immediate family, Laura and the baby, there were only two people left – two lonely satellites – and they lived together, circled each other.

His aunt picked up the phone.

'It's Philip.' His uncle, Roger Stutton, was his mother's only brother. Con, Roger's wife, had always been there in Dryden's life. The couple lived on a remote farm at Buskeybay, out on the fen. The farm, which they'd bought soon after getting married, had never been a success. Over the years they'd sold off land, leased plots, started a car-breaking business, tried to keep ahead of the remortgage payments. None of these disappointments had been grave enough to rob Con of a kind of frontier optimism.

'How's Laura – and the baby?' His aunt's voice contained a sustained power.

'Fine. Can I pop by – tomorrow, perhaps?' Dryden heard dogs in the background and the farmhouse door grating on the tiled floor of the entrance hall. 'I've got some news – nothing awful. It's about Dad. Just a bit of the past that's come back to haunt us.' He'd realized, too late, that he couldn't just say it on the phone.

'Jack? What on earth could have happened?' asked Con. 'Philip, he's been dead more than thirty years.' Dryden often sensed an undercurrent of irritation when he spoke to his aunt.

'I'll tell you when I see you.' Face-to-face he'd ask them questions. Had Jack been happy? Was there any reason he'd want to walk away from his life? Why had his mother taken him away, to London, a world away from the farm at Burnt Fen?

There was a silence.

'OK,' she said finally. 'Do you want to talk to Roger? He's just back from the post office and now he's going fishing on the lake.' A door slammed.

Suddenly Roger was there on the other end of the phone. 'Philip. I was just thinking about you.' He laughed to himself, unhurried, happy to let Dryden fill in the silence.

'I was just saying to Con – I'll be over, tomorrow. We can talk then.' Dryden imagined them at the other end of the line, exchanging glances, his aunt shrugging.

'OK. I see. Very mysterious.' It was odd how satisfying a conversation so banal could be. Perhaps it was some deep-rooted connection he was making between similar gene pools. 'Come to think of it I have a mystery for *you* – but it can wait till tomorrow too.'

'Fine. You're going out in the eel boat? Be careful on the water,' said Dryden.

'Right. Yes. I am,' he said. 'Tomorrow then?'

'Tomorrow.'

Dryden rang off. He could see his uncle now, standing by the phone, the same slightly Edwardian straight back as his mother, the pepper-and-salt hair, but most of all the scientist's mind – always collecting detail, building hypotheses.

The lake, Adventurers' Mere, had been created two years ago by the deliberate re-flooding of part of the Fens. Not so much a lake at all, a true mere – an inland sea: more than fifty square miles, the far side only just visible in fine light. The original plan had been for marsh and fen, and a little open water. But then a toxic partnership of global recession and global warming had resulted in something quite different. To save money the government decided to simply re-flood the fen, creating a brackish inland mere. It was stocked with eel and zander, tench and pike; open to fishermen by licence. Roger had one of the few commercial licences given – another attempt to bring in cash.

But it was the eel that had been the big success. Dryden had been out with Roger laying the wicker traps and nets. Lifting them – usually at night by torch light – was an oddly Gothic experience. The traps coming up out of the oily water, the eel glistening, shivering with movement, coiling and lunging. Roger ran the catch out to the Cambridge restaurants, and the coastal 'Chelsea-set' pubs of the north Norfolk coast.

The thought made Dryden hungry so he fished in his coat pocket and found a pork pie he'd stowed away a few days earlier and a packet of Hula Hoops. He survived largely on such snacks – a bad habit picked up during Laura's long illness. The new house promised hot meals around a table. He'd miss the al fresco pies.

He started calls. First up was county police headquarters at Milton – a faceless MFI block on the outskirts of Cambridge. They had two items on the press list. First, a sit-in at Whitemoor Prison. More than fifty prisoners were refusing to leave the canteen building due to changes in the menu. Dryden sympathized. He'd been in several prisons to interview inmates and they all said the same thing: that the way to survive a long sentence, and nobody at Whitemoor was in for less than four years, was to make each day predictable. Routine was the prisoners' salvation. Routine days flew by. The same food, the same view, the same people, the same TV programmes, the football results. Routine. Anything which cut into that made time slow down. The menu was a key milestone en route to the day they walked out of prison. Every Monday's shepherd's pie, every Tuesday's curry, was mentally ticked off as one less they'd have to eat before going home.

The enemy of routine was change.

He had decent contacts in the Prison Officers' Association so he'd make a call, see if he could flesh out the story. It might even make the nationals if the menu changes were actually interesting. He could see it now: *Prisoners Riot Over Cauliflower Cheese.*

Second item on the police press list was an unspecified 'incident' on Feltwell Anchor – a large, inaccessible area of farming land now on the far north coast of the new mere. The unspecified incident was at a place known only as Eau Fen.

Most of the area was farmed by one of the big agri-businesses which grew salad crops for the supermarkets. Acres – thousands of acres – of black soil crocheted with seedlings.

'What kind of incident?' asked Dryden, watching the news editor wake up like a baby, out-of-focus eyes fixing finally on the office cat. It was a few minutes to eleven and the Fenman Bar opposite would be opening its doors at any moment. Bracken called it his 'city office' – and that's where he'd be until three. He began to struggle into his jacket, whistling tunelessly through fat lips.

There was no answer from the police control room to Dryden's question. 'I said, what kind . . .'

'The kind of incident where we can't tell the press any details. Ring later.' The line went dead.

Dryden loved it when officials – any kind of official – tried to be obstructive. Firstly, it made him more interested in what was happening. But mostly it meant that they almost always gave away more information than they ever imagined. That one line told Dryden something was up – and twenty-four hours before *The Crow*'s weekly deadline it made his blood course just that little bit faster.

He was on the line for the local police at Ely when Vee Hilgay came in. According to the National Union of Journalists Vee was the oldest trainee journalist under indenture in England – she was seventy-four. When *The Crow*'s last trainee had left for Fleet Street the paper's owners had decided to cut costs. They'd take on a part-time replacement, no qualifications necessary. Dryden knew Vee – she ran a local charity that helped the elderly get through the winter, which she'd founded with family money. She was tough, smart, political (Old Left), and streetwise. Dryden's mother had described her as 'effortlessly top drawer' – in other words old money, with manners to match. He knew she was bored running her charity so he offered her the job. She was a natural – not because of the qualities Dryden had recognized: the intellect, the dispassionate stance, the sheer bloody-mindedness; but because of the quality he hadn't known about – curiosity, both obsessive and boundless.

Vee produced a flask the size of one of the shells fired at the Somme and poured tea into a mug emblazoned with the face of

Tony Benn. She waved a notebook at Dryden. Vee had taught herself Pitman and got to eighty words a minute – more than good enough for the local magistrates court, which is where she'd spent the morning.

Dryden cupped a hand over the phone. 'Something's up – out on Feltwell Anchor. No one's talking . . .'

Dryden's call to Ely's police control room switched to an answerphone.

Both fire brigade and ambulance confirmed they were at Feltwell Anchor but could release no details. Dryden poured himself a coffee from the communal stewing pot and went over to the newsroom's wall map – fifteen feet by six, installed a decade earlier, it was like having a picture of his entire world as seen from space, with the pubs marked with little blue beer barrels. The only major alteration to the real world in the last decade had been the new mere which Dryden had – expertly – added to the map with a set of sky-blue marker pens.

Vee appeared beside him cradling her thermos cup. She ran on tea. Dryden had never seen her drink anything else except malt whisky.

'You can't get anything at all?' she asked, studying the map.

'Nothing. I might go out. Courts?'

'Good,' said Vee. She'd never pick up the hallmark cynicism of most journalists, but she'd developed an eye for a good story with ease. 'A flasher up on High Barns. Broad daylight mostly. Used to stand on the corner and shout "Look at me, I'm a teapot". Poor man.'

Vee put a finger on a lonely farmhouse on the map of Feltwell Anchor, very close to the edge of the mere Dryden had drawn, at the spot marked Eau Fen. 'One of my charity volunteers – a Mrs Dee – lives there. I've got a number.'

Mrs Dee was in her seventies but busy and sharp, a full-time carer for her husband who'd had a stroke. They'd sold most of the acreage to the agri-business but still had thirty acres for kale. She told Dryden she'd been out just after dawn when the over-night rain was still on the dark green leaves. She'd seen nothing then – just the automatic irrigator trundling over a distant field. Dryden asked her to go to the window and tell him what she saw now.

Dryden heard footsteps on a cool tiled floor. 'I'm looking south,' she said. 'Over the fen – there's a drove road there and the pickers are out. I can see the Portaloos.'

'Anything unusual?'

'There's a bunch of policemen taking a shower.'

'In the sense that . . .'

'In the sense that the irrigation gantry I mentioned is still shooting water over the fen, and these coppers – in uniform – are all over it, like blackbirds, getting wet.'

SIX

The Fens ran ahead of the cab like a chessboard landscape. The sun was well up so that the shadows were beginning to shrink back, the temperature already in the mid-seventies. Humidity, after the storm the night before, was high. They had all the windows open in the Capri but it didn't help. Boudicca hung her jaws open trying to catch some breeze in the back seat.

They came to a T-junction and the SatNav said right, but Humph turned left. Contradicting the talking routemaster was one of Humph's hobbies. 'What do you know,' said the cabbie under his breath, shaking his small, neat head. The voice of the SatNav was a woman's, modulated, Blue Peter English, no aspect of which had endeared it to Humph. 'So,' said Humph. 'Where,' and at this the cabbie waved a finger in the air, 'do we get the common phrase "on cloud nine"?'

Humph's attempts at conversation were maladroit at best. He'd sensed Dryden's darkening mood, perhaps also the dread he was feeling at the prospect of trying to identify his father's body at the morgue the following morning. This was Humph's way of trying to relieve the tension.

'You mean as in euphoric happiness?' asked Dryden.

Humph, dimly sensing he'd put a foot wrong, edged a finger between his Ipswich Town top and his chin.

'Give up,' said Dryden.

'International Cloud Atlas 1896,' said the cabbie. 'Introduced cloud classification. Number nine was cumulonimbus – the highest of all.' He gripped the steering wheel. 'Simple.'

Silence again, only deeper and heavier.

'There,' said Dryden, pointing an arm out of the open window across the fen where a line of police cars stood parked in a chain. They were four miles out of Ely, past the last hamlet, on a stretch of road which flew like an arrow towards Adventurers' Mere, the direction marked by a line of poplars which seemed to dip away towards the horizon with the curvature of the earth – an illusion, Dryden knew, but a powerful one.

Humph swung the cab on to the drove road and switched off the SatNav as it announced that it was re-computing its location. Three hundred yards ahead of them was a police checkpoint, at which stood an armed policeman in a flak jacket.

'Guns,' said Dryden, as Humph pulled up, kicking open the passenger-side door. 'Great.'

Leaning on the top of the cab he rang Jean at *The Crow* and told her to go round to the photographers on the High Street and get the paper's part-time picture editor, Mitch MacIntosh, out on the road. Mitch's business was wedding photos, but they paid him a retainer to take pictures of local news events – mostly 'smash-and-grab' cheque presentations or school Ofsted line-ups. Real news photography wasn't his forte: he had to battle an almost irrepressible urge to ask anyone in a picture to smile, even if they had just witnessed a fatal road crash. He also refused, point blank, to take any pictures if the subject, or object, was in motion. But even he could snap a stationary armed copper.

Dryden walked away from the cab, fields running out of sight on both sides, the road itself made of concrete sections, so that he altered his stride to miss the cracks.

The field to the east was dotted with salad crops and blue Portaloos and the two stationary mobile picking gantries. The workers, about sixty or seventy of them, cradled plastic cups, smoking, but not talking. Some peered into mobiles.

Dryden had often wondered what life as a migrant worker was like. Not the outdoor back-breaking part, the visitor-in-a-foreign-land part. As he walked towards them every single one of those distant faces turned towards him, watching, watchful, like a field of sunflowers following the sun.

The armed copper was on a mobile too. He held up a hand to stop Dryden in his tracks ten feet short of the squad car.

'Can I help, sir?' The tone of the voice was so divorced from the meaning of the sentence Dryden didn't understand what he'd said.

'Sorry?'

'You can't go any further, sir. Crime scene.'

Dryden flashed his library card. 'Press. *The Crow*. Philip Dryden – any chance of a word?'

A radio crackled and the officer turned away to talk.

Dryden peered ahead. A screen of willow trees blocked a view of the field beyond, and the blue surface of Adventurers' Mere. It was a big field, even bigger than the one in which the migrant pickers stood. Dryden, who'd been brought up on a farm less than ten miles away from this spot, estimated it was a hundred acres. He'd worked it out once – the size of an acre. A decent football field was ninety per cent of an acre so that's how he tried to see it – imagining football fields stretching out, like a picture he'd once seen of Hackney Marshes in the 1950s, crammed with Sunday-morning matches.

Through the close-planted trees he could see – and hear – an irrigation gantry: a metal frame 100 feet wide, set on six large wire-wheels. A hose connected it to a metal reel at the end of the field, roped up to one of the poplars which was pulling in the gantry, powered by water pressure, so that the whole operation was automatic. They'd had a much smaller version at Burnt Fen. He'd go out with his father before dawn and switch on the water supply, which would set the gantry in motion. They'd stand by for a few minutes, scanning the field with torches, then walk home to breakfast. By the time the sun was high enough to start burning off moisture the gantry would have crossed the field. They'd run the reel to the far end by tractor and then repeat the operation after sun set. The Burnt Fen gantry had been fifteen feet across – a toy compared with this monster, which emitted a swishing noise and a mechanical ticking from the reel, audible at half a mile.

Despite their witness' earlier report the gantry was devoid of policemen. But it was moving, and it was spraying water, creating a vast cloud of droplets like a mist. Inside the cloud there was an artificial rainbow, a broad, broken spectrum, a fragment of a great arc. In the hot mid-morning air Dryden could even feel the slightly cool, damp breeze blowing his way. And now he could see an ambulance crew, in Day-Glo jackets, by the field gate with a stretcher and paramedic gear. A group of uniformed police stood to one side smoking.

Out of the trees walked someone Dryden recognized: Detective

Inspector Tom Friday, one slightly lame foot dragging in the peat. DI Friday was the Ely division's senior detective, a man with a reputation for uninspired labour and patent honesty. Like most policemen he had a habit of acting older than he was: Dryden guessed he was mid-thirties, but his world weariness made him sound much older, as did the defeated shoulders and the skewed foot. Dryden had seen him on countless wet Saturdays watching one of his four sons playing local football. Up close Dryden saw that he was soaking wet.

'Don't say a sodding word,' he said.

The water ran out of his mousy hair into his eyes, and water brimmed over his shoes from inside.

'You grew up on a farm?' He readjusted his weight and one of his shoes made an obscene sucking sound.

Dryden nodded. He'd once been out on a job at one of the big agricultural processors with DI Friday. A worker had fallen in a machine and been killed. They'd had to wait while the sheds were evacuated and the plant shut down, so they'd swapped life stories: Dryden – organic farmer's son, Friday – copper's son. Dryden – brought up in the country and educated at home until moving to the city after his father's early death. Friday – brought up in King's Lynn and educated at the local grammar school. Both married. Now they both had kids. It wasn't the time or place to share the good news.

Taking silence for affirmation Friday nodded his head at the distant trundling gantry. 'We can't turn that bloody thing off. Any ideas?'

Dryden followed him back down the track and through the poplars. They came within fifty yards of the migrant workers. The faces turned their way, with not a smile in sight.

'Happy bunch,' said Dryden.

'Piecework. They're not earning. You and me, we've got salaries, pensions. They get cash at sundown. It's medieval. We could be hours yet. It's costing them a living. Poor sods have mouths to feed like you and me.'

Amongst the trees they passed the ambulance crew, one on a mobile, one on a radio, the other checking through the paramedic kits.

'You gonna tell me what's up?' asked Dryden.

'Nope. You turn the water off, I'll let you see. Fail – you can join the Glee Club back there for a cup of tea while we get someone out. This is one of Doggard's fields – could take hours.'

Doggard's was one of the big fen agricultural companies. They farmed thousands of acres. But the salad crop 'factory' was thirty-five miles away towards Peterborough.

The irrigation reel hummed, the hydraulic mechanism within clicking as it tugged in the hose and line on the distant gantry. Here, even on the edge of the field, they were in the droplet cloud, so that Dryden's skin was instantly moist and he could taste the slightly metallic water on his lips. The coolness was all-encompassing, like a blanket in reverse.

An articulated plastic water pipe ran away from the reel and Dryden followed it to a stopcock in the ditch: a hi-tech affair of dials and switches but the basic mechanics were simple. He cut the water supply. The reel fell instantly silent; the cloud of water spraying from the gantry seemed to implode, leaving behind dripping sprinklers. The gantry came to a shuddering halt fifty yards away. As the mist cleared they could see the distant mere beyond more clearly – a single boat in the mid-distance, no sail, flat in the water, like a miniature dredger. Even now, five years after the lake had been created, the sudden sight of it was a shock to Dryden, as if he'd glimpsed a distant make-believe mountain in a bank of clouds.

'Hoo-fucking-ray,' said Friday, stalking off, walking down a furrow between lettuces, his wet shoes picking up peat like sticky-toffee pudding.

It was still difficult to see the gantry in its lingering cloud. Water dripped from every nozzle on the 100-foot steel frame; a mathematical grid against the sky, perched on the six giant wheels, each square empty, each a picture frame without a picture: all except one. Out on the far end of one wing of the gantry there was a hanging object.

Dryden stopped dead. His heartbeat picked up and the sudden double-coldness of his skin made him feel like someone else's blood was flowing in his veins. He'd seen the gently swinging shape for a nanosecond before looking away, but some objects are so deeply buried in the human psyche as to need only that fleeting glimpse for instant recognition: the angular dart of the rat, the strange heft of an arm carrying a knife in the hand, the cold quartz-like stare of the dead eye. And this: the hanging man, hung from the neck, until dead.

He looked again. A corpse, the neck broken to give that tell-tale zigzag in the spine, water dripping from the legs, which had been tied together, the arms behind. It swung still, maintaining the momentum of the moving gantry. The creaking noise it made didn't come from the wet rope but from the shattered vertebrae of the neck.

Dryden watched his boots in the peat as he followed Friday's tracks. He didn't look again until he was standing beside the DI, the shadow of the hanging body moving over the furrows, the only sound the dripping water around them and that calcium creak of the broken bone.

As soon as he did look he was aware that this was a victim whose death had been designed to shock. In its own obscene way it was as much an advert as a billboard flogging the latest Hollywood blockbuster. The broken neck appeared cosmetic; the face was disfigured by a gunshot wound to the right of the right eye. Dryden counted six more wounds in the torso, each ripping through a pair of blue overalls and a white shirt. There was one other wound visible – in the knee of the left leg. The water that dripped from the bare feet was tinged red. It was like looking at meat hung in a butcher's fridge. Or roadkill. He thought then, as he often had, that he'd been lucky not to see his father's corpse – washed up, decayed, ugly. It was a shock, a fresh jolt, to realize that he might see it now. Burnt up, wasted and as ugly as this, possibly worse.

'Christ,' he said, his voice cracking, unsure what shocked him most: the corpse he could see, or the one he feared to see.

He noticed the dead man's hands then – orange paint under the fingernails, the skin torn but clean. And a smell – quite distinct, which might have come from the hands – of petrol. But not quite petrol; something more refined, lighter.

'Overkill,' said Friday, using his mobile to ring the paramedics. They could relax – it was recovery only, and he'd need to let forensics look at the field first. 'Looks like they strung him up and then had a bit of shooting practice.'

Dryden hadn't thought of that. The lynching first, then the desecration of the victim. He looked back to the edge of the field and the figures of the migrant workers. The silence was complete and intense. They, he thought, were the killer's audience.

The Crow's photographer, Mitch MacIntosh, emerged from the shadows on the far side of the field, loaded down with enough equipment for a Paris catwalk. He'd avoided the police cordon by negotiating a drove road that wasn't on the map. Having been born in the Fens sixty years ago he was a living atlas of dead ends and tracks.

'Who the fuck's that?' asked Friday.

'Our photographer. Sorry. He's unstoppable.'

Friday shrugged. 'Tell him to stop there.'

Dryden held up both hands and bellowed Mitch's name.

Mitch, a humourless Scot with a penchant for fake tam o'shanters, was a techno nerd and never knowingly without the latest gadget. He set up a tripod and began to fumble with a telephoto lens.

'Who found the victim?' asked Dryden, thinking he'd keep Friday talking because then Mitch would be able to give the picture scale by including some human figures. They couldn't print a shot of the corpse but they could show the gantry, the reel, the cloud of mist drifting.

So he repeated the question because Friday was pretending he hadn't heard.

'Gangmaster spotted him just after six when he got here. He's local – Commercial End.'

'And he couldn't stop the reel?'

'Nope. Said his job was to get that lot working – picking, packing. He'd never touched the irrigation gear.' Friday's eyes narrowed. 'It's clever. Brutal and clever. The gantry's moved on from the spot where he was hung up so it'll have sprayed water all over the forensics, betcha. Over the footprints. No fingerprints – it's like we're underwater. Tidy. So – like I said – gangs. And there's that stench of fuel you've so far pretended not to notice.'

'Petrol,' said Dryden.

'More like marine fuel,' said Friday. 'Which is why I'm not smoking. And that's not an official confirmation either, by the way. I'm not stupid. Nothing's on the record.' He let his eyes linger on the dead man's face. 'Maybe they did plan to torch it, then figured the gun shots were good enough.'

It wouldn't be the first gang killing in the Fens. Two years earlier a Portuguese migrant worker had been tied up and shot out at Wisbech – his body dumped in the tidal mud. He'd have stayed in the mud if someone hadn't spotted a hand sticking up at low tide. Six months earlier a bunch of Lithuanian workers at Lynn had fallen out over gambling debts. A frank exchange of views had ended in two dead – one of them fed into a hay baler. But Dryden wasn't alone in suspecting that the death rate was much higher than that. The Fens offered many advantages to organized crime – not just migrant workers but gangs operating out of the East Midlands and London. You could hide anything on this wide open landscape. Tucking a body away where no one would find it was like hiding an acorn in a forest.

The difference this time was that they'd wanted this body found. This body was a message: *don't mess with us.*

Friday tore his eyes away from the shattered face. 'Thanks for your help, but I need you off now.'

'Can I talk to that lot?' asked Dryden, noting the corpse's clothing before he was too far away to see: a badge on the overalls that looked like the local water authority – FRWA: Fen Rivers Water Authority. A gold link neck chain, a small key on the chain, a gold ring, the hair cut short but stylish, a tattoo on the neck – something in High German Gothic script. Teeth – good, white – maybe whitened. Shoes – leather, with expensive multicoloured laces.

'If you'd asked me I'd have said no,' said Friday. 'But as you didn't I won't notice till the bus gets here – I've got one out from Ely, we'll take 'em all back and get statements. And they're all pretending they don't speak English – how's your Polish?'

'*Nie mowie po polsku.*'

'Meaning?'

'I can't speak Polish.'

Typically, Humph's backlog of European languages did not include anything as useful as Polish.

Dryden took one last look at the shattered face. 'But it's a murder inquiry – right.' It was a statement, not a question.

Friday laughed. 'Well, he didn't trip over his fucking laces, did he?'

SEVEN

The glass room was the only one Dryden really liked at Flightpath Cottages. The two original farm workers' houses had been knocked into one, so there were two of everything: two front doors, two outdoor loos, two staircases. To create the glass room they'd knocked out the attic divide to make a single office, half of which was covered with an unbroken set of solar panels, the other half just reflective glass set in a wooden frame. Blinds controlled the heat and light, and flip-up Velux panels allowed air to pass through. He had them open now so that a breeze blew in. It was still in the mid-eighties and the humidity was high; storm clouds were appearing like ack-ack bursts on the horizon.

The dark side of the room held his filing system and a bunk, a printer for the laptop and a set of the big red cuttings books from his time on *The News*, the Fleet Street national he'd left after Laura's accident. On top of the books stood a framed picture of his father at Burnt Fen: 1976, the year before the flood that swept him away. Dryden walked to it now and turned it face down. He wasn't going to think about Jack Dryden again that day – he'd promised himself that. Tomorrow he'd touch the body: he'd know then. One single revealing touch of flesh on flesh.

The house stood on a very slight rise – he'd used a GPS to measure it at eight feet. Not much, but in the Black Fen, a lofty peak, which added several miles to the view from the glass room. He could just see the conning tower on the horizon at the US air base at Mildenhall, nearly thirteen miles away, and beyond that, in the sky, a heavily laden fuel tanker dropping down from the stratosphere, twin contrails looped behind like giant washing lines. Before the US airforce had arrived after the Second World War the area – on the edge of Thetford Forest – had been a testing range for military aircraft, originally in the years leading up to the First World War. The house had been on one flight path or another for nearly a century. It was pretty much a miracle it had never been blown up.

They'd expected aircraft noise, of course. The clue was in the name. But they'd been quietly appalled by the frequency of the military flights which seemed to shake the house several times an hour during daylight. Nightfall brought silence, but that wasn't going to be a big help trying to get a two-week-old child to sleep. They told each other at regular intervals that they'd get used to it, that the rumble would become background noise, white noise, that they'd simply blank out.

Dryden touched the space bar on the iMac laptop screen and brought the story he'd written on the Eau Fen murder back to life, picking up his mobile to hit the speed-dial for the news editor. Bracken was in the Fenman Bar, where he'd long been awarded the ultimate accolade – his own pint pot and a bar stool. He picked up Dryden's call on the second ring. The background noise was dominated by a fruit machine chugging out coins.

'Philip,' said Bracken. 'What ya got?'

Bracken's attitude to Dryden had altered over the years they'd worked together. Dryden's Fleet Street pedigree had put the news editor's back up in the early months, but he'd come to realize that the paper's success depended on its chief reporter's skills, and that made his own life easier. And it was clear Dryden's own ambitions were strictly limited – if he wanted a glittering career he could leave anytime and one of the nationals would have him back. If he'd wanted Bracken's job he'd have gone for it – and got it – long before now. The fact that the editor's job was up for grabs hadn't upset their relationship. Both of them thought the other one would never apply.

Dryden filled him in on what he had from the corpse found in the lettuce field.

'Corker,' said Bracken. Dryden heard a door clatter and then the unmistakable buzz of the outside world followed by the swift intake of a smoker's breath.

The next day was press day. Dryden would be in early to write up the splash and then attend a police press conference at Cambridge. Anything new he'd update by mobile or laptop. He didn't tell Bracken that he'd written the story already – that way he'd engineered himself time, which was the reporter's ultimate commodity. He'd need time tomorrow; time for the short journey over the fen to the morgue.

'What's exclusive?' asked Bracken. The news editor might be lazy, a borderline alcoholic and a poor operator under stress, but his instincts were sound. He'd spent twenty-five years on an evening paper in West Yorkshire and it had taught him the basics. Dryden had long ago decided that he'd treat Bracken as he was treated – with professional detachment.

'Gunshot wounds to the head and body. I think we can say "riddled", if you like. I asked Friday and he said any statement would be minus detail from the scene. So far there's been nothing in the official press statements. We'll see if that still holds tomorrow – if it does it's enough. Suggests gangland revenge – a touch of mystery. That do you?'

'ID?'

'None yet. Unlikely to be official before we go to press either way.'

'Perfect. We like brutal. Callous. Good words. Use 'em, or I'll use 'em for you.' Bracken laughed. 'Still – you know what's what.'

Dryden saw the dead man's face again – the right eye obscured by the gunshot wound. 'Pix?' he asked, trying to dislodge the image.

'Yeah – Mitch did OK,' said Bracken. 'Can't use the body but they covered it with a sheet and he got that. I love these fen coppers. Up north they'd have left it hanging there and we'd have been scuppered. He's sold a couple to PA for us – but we've got the best. Alf?'

Alf Walker was the local press association reporter. Dryden had rung him from the fen to give him two pars on the murder which he could put out to the nationals, regional dailies, and radio and TV. Alf had been out in his garden sketching a corncrake – an obsessive hobby, witnessed by the exquisite line drawings that peppered his shorthand notebook. The lineage fee would be paid to *The Crow* and divvied up at the end of the month. If the nationals wanted more they'd have to send their own staff out – which was unlikely, although the local evenings would be all over the story like a horse blanket by tomorrow's press conference.

Dryden rang off and immediately heard his son cry out from the bedroom below. He went to the stairs and called down to Laura in the kitchen that he'd see to it. One day soon, he sensed, the various chores associated with the child would become an issue. Child care, feeding, washing. But today, at least, they were competing for the jobs.

The child's room was a bedroom, not a nursery. For Dryden and Laura the Victorian nursery cast too long a shadow of malevolent sadness. So they'd gone for white walls, a chest of drawers, and the wooden cot. From the ceiling Dryden had hung an array of mobiles. But the biggest was outside 200 yards to the west – a wind-powered generator owned by the farm next door. At sunset it cast a shadow which came and went across the wall. The swish he could live with, but not the high-pitched mechanical squeak with each revolution.

The baby had fallen silent, his eyes switching from the left wall to the right wall, apparently mesmerized by the moving shadow. Dryden didn't break the line of sight, but moved backwards out of the door and climbed the stairs again to his desk.

He sat rereading the story on the Eau Fen murder, but not taking in the meaning, just checking the spelling, the syntax, the sound. Oddly, of all the stories he'd dealt with that day, the violent murder wasn't the one that had stayed with him.

He found the photocopy he'd made of the letter the council had sent the Yorubas about their daughter's burial. Reading it again he felt the familiar excitement of the chase: authority with its back to the wall, bluffing, trying to wriggle free. He had the council's head of media on his list of mobile contacts. The phone rang and he thought it was going to transfer to answerphone when it picked up: his name was David Dudley-Rice, public school, decent, about twice as smart as he let on. The voice would have been perfectly at home on the BBC World Service.

'Philip?'

Dryden outlined the Yorubas' case then read out the letter. He said he'd ring officially the next morning for a statement but he thought Dudley-Rice would appreciate the heads-up.

'I'll have something for you, but you should know this case isn't as straightforward as the Yorubas – poor people – may have implied.'

Classic first response, thought Dryden, implying that the family was not telling him the whole truth. A ploy designed to sow anxiety and mistrust. Dudley-Rice clearly knew the case well – a sure sign they'd been expecting trouble and felt exposed to the risk of trial by media.

'Right. But you've offered compensation – or at least the possibility of it – and that's taxpayers' money. So I'd like an explanation.'

'It is a personal matter, of course. We'd be very constrained in what we can say publicly.'

'Just reply in private to the Yorubas – they're happy for me to see any correspondence.'

There was a pause at the other end of the line and the sound of a car engine starting. Dryden leant back in his seat and caught the smell of cooking rising from the kitchen. A pungent garlic sauce, tomatoes, and something else disturbingly earthy and almost gravid: Jerusalem artichoke – gnarled and marbled, dug from the ground.

'Of course, our legal department is involved in this, Philip – just so you know. It all takes time. You know what lawyers are like. But perhaps we can say a bit. I'll try and get you an interview out at the cemetery – how does that sound?'

'Who with?'

'Cemetery warden knows the story – odd bloke. Mad on motorbikes. But he could help you if we give him the green light. Leave it with me.'

'I'll ring at nine, David. I'm going to run the letter, plus a story, so if you want anything to balance that out let me have it then. If not, we'll come back to you next week.'

'It would be nice to get a balanced story. Like I said, there are legal issues.'

'We're a newspaper, not a Christmas annual. Deadline's noon tomorrow.'

'Right. It's just there are issues of taste. Decency. It's not a . . .' He pretended to search for the word. 'Not a pretty story.'

'So you're up to speed on it. Why not tell me now.'

'Like I said – lawyers. And they go home at four thirty sharp. They charge treble rate after that. We'll talk tomorrow.'

Dryden cut the line and felt drained, as if the mouthpiece had sucked out what energy he had left for the day. Hadn't the Yorubas told him the name they'd chosen for the girl? How had he forgotten it?

A ship's bell rang from downstairs – one strike, barely audible. He'd taken it with him from the house boat. It was the signal for food.

Laura had laid a red-and-white checked tablecloth out for two plates of spaghetti vongole. Red wine, decanted into a jug. His wife's family had run a small café and restaurant in north London. She'd been brought up with the idea that food was part of family life.

Dryden sat and pushed a piece of paper across the table.

Laura had her first forkful poised. She scanned it. 'So. Well done, Philip.' It was Dryden's application for the post of editor of *The Crow*. 'I wondered,' she said.

'But you didn't say.'

Laura's own career as an actress had spluttered back into life after her recovery but had now ended. The speech disability refused to improve and she refused to accept bit parts which played to her condition. What she'd do next was something they hadn't talked about. For all her enthusiasm for the new house, and for being a mother, Dryden was sure she couldn't face life without a career.

'Your decision,' she said. 'The right decision. I thought – maybe – you'd want to go back to Fleet Street. We could all go. North London, maybe – not a suburb, the city. Hoxton. Hackney. I'm OK with that. I liked cities once.'

'It's not just my decision,' he said, putting his fork down. 'I like it out here. In the Fens. I want him to grow up here,' he said. 'In all this space, all this freedom.'

'All this sky,' she said. 'Me too. I like to see so far. There is a magic here – very good for childhood. For *im-ag-in-a-tion*.' She pronounced all five syllables to make it clear which word she meant, then picked up her plate. 'Let's eat outside.'

EIGHT

Friday

Vee Hilgay woke up with her head turned to the clock as she always did. It was two minutes to five, and the alarm was set for the hour. She was seventy-four years old and had never yet been woken by an alarm clock. Her life had so far contained more than its fair share of grief. She preferred not to lie awake and stew in the past. And she was aware that she'd had more than her fair share of privilege too. A wealthy childhood, university, health. So before the rhythmic electronic buzz had completed its cycle of six she was on her feet.

Her bedsit was large and modern: a German galley kitchen in steel, a Habitat desk, a bookcase handmade for the space and neatly filled – each volume drawn out to match the edge of the shelf; wooden chairs, no cushions, no *soft furnishings* – a linguistic couplet that made her physically sick. She wasn't a snob; in fact, she'd spent most of her life proving to herself that she wasn't – but she'd always been clear that taste wasn't the preserve of the rich or educated. In fact, alarmingly, the relationship seemed to be an inverse one.

The one window looked down on High Street and the cathedral buildings along its southern side. The street was thick with a summer's mist, that particular species which seems to sparkle with the promise of the sun that will burn it away. A scarab street-cleaner edged along the kerb, its light flashing silently. Someone was slumped in the doorway of Asda – legs out on the pavement, a brace of beer cans lying in the crotch. She tried to memorize the boots and trousers in case she saw him later in Oxfam. Somewhere she could hear the mist, condensed, running in a drainpipe.

She turned the radio on to BBC Radio Cambridgeshire. Watching the minute hand creep to the vertical she thought about the day ahead: press day. She needed to pick up the post from the Royal Mail depot, open the office, do a round of calls. Anything from police, fire or ambulance that she judged important she'd text to Dryden. She listened to the news looking out of the window. The mist was making a last effort to cling on: thickening, gathering itself, so that the Octagon Tower of the cathedral which had floated free had gone now, leaving just a hint of its great bulk hanging in the white sky. A flashing amber light crossed the street – one of the early waste disposal lorries taking away bins.

The news bulletin was made up with what, she knew, Dryden would have called 'twists' – running news stories kept alive by the latest, often minor developments. Top of the schedule was the Eau Fen killing: a police appeal for any information. No name for the victim but relatives now informed. Murder inquiry under way. But no details from the scene of crime. Second item: Environment Agency announce plan to purchase and flood Petit Fen – Phase 2 of the programme which had begun with Adventurers' Mere. Details contained in an application to the planning authority to include a visitor centre for water birds, but also three entry locks allowing pleasure boats on to the new lake. A spokesman for the National Trust was already condemning the scheme and calling for a return to the original vision for the region of a managed nature reserve of marsh, reed and water. Third item: vehicle shunt on the A10 at Streatham likely to cause major delays for commuter traffic heading for Cambridge. Then national news: a bomb in Damascus, a merger on Wall Street, Whitehall rows over cuts to the NHS. One thing new – a police appeal for information on a missing car, no registration: a black four-by-four last seen in the Lisle Lane multi-storey. Easy enough to spot as all its windows were shattered.

Then the weather. Sunny, hot, maybe a thunder storm. High humidity.

Vee took a camouflage jacket and let herself down the stairs into her office and out the door. She walked this way every morning and was always quietly thrilled when it offered up something different: the thick, untouched snow of February, a hoar frost in November making the willows look like the old Crystal Palace, a dazzling sunrise in May – right into her eyes, as if the sun wasn't rising at all, but hurtling towards her. This morning the first persistent mist of summer, thicker down by the river, dripping off the bankside trees.

She walked north on the tow path for exactly one mile, leaving the town. Beside her, arrowing in at a tangent to the river was the railway line from Lynn, set on the flood bank. The first train went by – three carriages packed, commuters reading newspapers by orange light. The rumble of the wheels spooked the wild horses – she heard the thudding hooves but saw nothing amongst the half-lit scrubland. The train disappeared into the mist as if plunging into a tunnel.

Crossing under the railway down a dripping pedestrian passageway she emerged in a meadow and climbed the bank. The sky was lighter here and she thought there'd be blue sky by six. Ahead she could see the gibbet by the railway. Vee had always thought it took a dark imagination to call it that, but not this morning. She could imagine a body dangling from the single arm. This gibbet had been put up for the post bag, to be ripped from its hook by the speeding mail train. She'd seen a picture in the sorting office from the fifties with a post bag swinging, waiting for the train. It stood now only because no one could be bothered to take it down.

A hundred yards further on the path joined the road and a sign said:

HIGHFLYER DEPOT

The sorting office was brick-built with a playful tower, mullioned windows and an arch leading into a hidden yard. The mainline ran down one side of the sorting shed, the branch line, which allowed for deliveries to the depot's own platform, encircled the site in a huge loop the shape of a noose. North, unseen, Vee heard the clanging alarm signals from a level crossing. The Fens was the land of level crossings – hundreds of them, operated remotely, beside abandoned signalmen's cottages. She always thought it made the place seem more secretive, as if you could only enter through a series of checkpoints.

There was a postman behind the glass in reception who heaved up a small sack before she could say good morning. 'Sheila wants a word,' he said. 'You can go up.'

He flipped up the counter. Vee took the sack which seemed unusually heavy and pushed her way through plastic-sheet double doors into the sorting office. The interior of the building was a Victorian throwback to match the facade. About twenty men stood at a series of wooden frames, each divided into pigeon holes. In a wooden chute letters piled up as they sorted them into the different 'walks' – the postmen's rounds, marked on the pigeon holes with their own tag: High Street West, Dunkirk, Bishops, Riverside, Caudle Fen. Another sorter took the letters from the pigeon holes and added them to mail bags hanging in a metal frame. A radio played the local commercial station.

Vee liked the room, which exuded the almost hypnotic aroma of authentic industry: machine oil, rubber and wood. The floor was worn parquet, the frames oak, the wooden chutes in old pine. The pigeon holes were marked in an exquisite gold copperplate. Vee knew that the post office had installed the latest technology – Optical Character Recognition – down at Cambridge, but that the low volumes they took through Ely meant it was pretty much better to do it by hand like they'd always done. There'd been a plan to mechanize back in the 1990s but that had been shelved in one of the perennial rounds of cuts. As Vee worked her way down the back of the sorting booths she passed an office, cut off by wire grilles, two men inside at desks, sorting registered mail.

An open metal staircase took her up to a mezzanine floor – a series of offices opening off an overseer's balcony. Sheila Petit's was the last in the row. She was one of several managers who shifted paper and monitored performance.

The sign on the door said: District Inspector – Eastern Fens.

The room was brutally functional except for a large framed aerial photograph of a set of farm buildings around a house on an open fen and a page of the *Cambridge Evening News* showing Petit toasting victory after the last district council elections. *Councillor* Petit was nominally an Independent, accepting the Tory Party whip. Unlike most independents she wasn't just a Tory in sheep's clothing. Vee had sat on the reporter's bench at enough meetings to know she was her own woman: liberal, broad-minded, tough.

The desk and chairs were MFI, a kettle and coffee-making kit on a table by a socket. But once the room had held some grandeur

– the ceiling was plastered and decorated, and a dado-rail ran around the walls. Sheila Petit was, like Vee, class with no cash. Vee, of course, was aristocracy – the daughter of a penniless knight. Sheila had humbler origins – a fact she liked to point out on her election leaflets. The daughter of a shopkeeper from Clacton, she'd seen her father's business fail and the family home repossessed. She'd escaped poverty by winning a scholarship to Clare College, Cambridge. There she'd met, then married, Arthur Petit. An only son of a long-established fen family, he came complete with a landed fortune. Vee had seen him once at a harvest festival out on the fen. He'd given out trophies for fishing – catching pike on the Little Ouse. He'd been as plump and self-satisfied as the first-prize fish, that rarity in the Fens, a gentleman farmer.

Petit stood by the open window, smoking, her arm bent up at the elbow, the hand flopped back. She had grey hair fashioned like a cycling helmet and robust teeth, and those peculiar good looks which in England are called 'handsome'.

'Vee. Sorry – bad morning. Needed this and I can't leave the office.' Vee guessed she was in her late sixties, early seventies but she'd embraced new technology – there was an iPhone on the desk top and a laptop beside the PC. 'Could you tell Dryden I'd like to see him,' Petit said, stubbing out the cigarette in an ash tray on the window ledge, which she then hid under the desk.

Vee didn't like being used as a messenger.

'He's not answering his phone,' said Petit.

'Reception's dodgy at the new house,' said Vee. 'He'll get it when he sets off.'

'I thought I saw him on that boat of his the other day. They've moved, have they?'

'A child.'

'Did you hear the radio?' asked Petit, switching tack. 'They've officially announced their intention to go-ahead.'

Petit headed up a campaign to stop the second phase of the fen re-flooding, a phase which would include her home and what had been the family estate – most of it remortgaged or sold off. The government planned to use compulsory purchase orders to brush aside objectors, or offer over-the-market prices to buy up parcels of land from others.

'Well, we knew it was coming. But we can stop it. There's some money – a donation. We can buy a piece of land which runs right across the fen. Put the ownership in a trust, tie it up legally. It'll take them years to mop it up.' She beamed. 'It's a form of sabotage. Totally legal, totally brilliant.'

There was something predatory about Petit's need to win the fight for Petit Fen – it wasn't just the family name, her husband's family, after all. It was personal – Vee understood that – but there was something else. She wondered if she was haunted by her own childhood – the moment her own home had been taken from her. Perhaps she was simply determined not to let it happen twice.

Vee still found it unseemly, this bitter tussle to own something, not for itself, but to keep it from others. Vee's childhood home, a rambling fortified house, had long gone in a deal with the National Trust. She'd been back once as a paying punter and found the experience oddly cold. It was the same place in which she'd spent her childhood but it wasn't in the same time – change the date and you alter the place. It was as simple as that for her.

'We can write this?' asked Vee.

'I'd prefer you to wait. Dryden and I usually have an arrangement.' She pressed a hand to her forehead as if she'd been suddenly struck down with a headache. Vee noticed that her finger fluttered slightly, a rare sign of frailty. She'd never seen this woman betray any indication of stress or anxiety. Suddenly she seemed overwhelmed by events.

'Next week's paper would be fine.' She took a breath, regaining herself. 'I can give him the detail – the amount, where it's come from, and what we can do with it. Well, maybe not the amount, as the donor's a bit shy. Anyway, we're initialling the sale tomorrow. So for now – *entre nous.*'

'All right.'

'Tell him to meet me Saturday evening, about six. A bunch of us are meeting, totally informal. Petit Fen – the old chapel. I can give him enough for a story. He knows the place.'

The phone went and Petit grabbed it, immediately engrossed in the call, her hand holding the packet of cigarettes as if she could suck the nicotine into her bloodstream through the cardboard.

Vee left. She knew the chapel on Petit Fen and it seemed like another world compared to this: the ringing phones, the blinking computer screens, the serried ranks of post office vans and lorries in the car park. Petit Fen was primeval, as if the earth had just been made. A brick chapel stood on a flood bank in the heart of the peat fields. The building always reminded her of the living quarters on Noah's Ark – just four walls and a pitched roof, as if the biblical boat had come to ground after the flood, sunk to its gunwales into the black earth.

NINE

S tefano's was one of Ely's best kept secrets, an authentic Italian restaurant hidden in an alleyway off the High Street. Laura had discovered it one evening waiting for Dryden to finish covering a council meeting. Starving, she'd ducked in out of the rain expecting cardboard pizza or floppy *farfalle*, only to discover a menu limited to home-made pasta dishes, each one made to order. And Dryden had discovered Stefano's other secrets – imported village wine from Liguria and a small roof terrace used by the staff for smoking, plus coffee that could accelerate your heartbeat after one minuscule cup. They knew Stefano now, and his English wife, and were allowed to take their morning coffees up on to the roof.

Laura ascended the spiral staircase into the open air, her son in a papoose on her back, hitched high on her shoulders so that his head lolled in the crook of her neck. Dryden sat on one of the aluminium seats, his feet up on the low balustrade, taking in the view over St Cross' Green to the long wall of the cathedral nave just fifty yards away. He often played echoes here, in this great bowl of stone created by the cathedral and the curving embrace of the old monastic buildings which formed one side of the High Street.

He always felt it held the magic of a theatre, as if the sound of applause had just died away.

Laura pulled up a chair and sat, swinging the papoose round so that the child was held to her chest, keeping level her small china cup of black coffee.

Head down, rearranging the baby's clothes, she said something Dryden couldn't understand because he hadn't seen her lips move. And they were outside so the sound was lost to the sky.

He tugged his ear.

'Do Not Ask,' she said pointedly, each word distinct.

One of the reasons she'd been keen to get out of hospital had been a long-arranged driving test. She'd left the child with friends in one of the High Street charity shops for the test – the first of the day, timed for eight. Dryden understood that Do Not Ask was Italian for Failed. Which was bad news: if they were going to live out at Flightpath Cottages she was trapped on the fen unless she could use the car. Either that or she did what they'd done that morning and Humph brought her into town with Dryden. She found that both humiliating and irritating. She valued little above her independence, a view only strengthened by the two long years in a hospital bed after her accident.

'What went wrong?'

'He didn't like Italian cars,' she said, making an effort to pronounce the sharp 'i' at the start of 'Italian'.

She had a Fiat 500, a stylish icon of her homeland she'd bought from an importer near Felixstowe. It was racing red with white-walled wheels.

'Or Italian driving?'

Laura had been taught how to drive by her uncle on the mountain roads of the Lunigiana. 'He said I drove too close to the . . .' She used her hand like a cleaver.

Dryden knocked back his coffee like vodka. 'The white line?'

She dismissed the truth of it. 'And my three-point turn is not up to standard.'

'Why?'

'I did it in one point.'

She watched his laugh, and Dryden felt she was gauging it, assessing his mood.

He checked his watch. They'd talked briefly the night before about his plan to visit the morgue and see the body of the man called Jack Dryden. Humph was due to pick him up at nine by the cathedral's West Door.

Taking both his hands over the table, she said, 'Please do not do this. We know what this means, Philip – dental records. Why . . .' She held both hands up, indicating the sides of a box, perhaps. 'Why have this memory?'

He checked the watch again. She took that as an answer.

'It will not be him,' she said. 'You will feel nothing.' She knew she was being cruel but she couldn't stop herself.

Out on St Cross' Green a group of school children were trying to put together what looked like a long, thin Chinese dragon, the head complete with fangs. There was a child inside each segment, while others held steel drums and Scout and Guide banners. The gathering looked like a dress rehearsal, lacking the buzz of the real event itself.

'The eel, for Eel Day,' said Laura, smiling. 'This Sunday.' It was one of the town's best celebrations – a parade, from the green down to the riverside, a crowd behind the giant eel, a band in front, then a fair and music. Like the fiesta in her home village in the mountains above Pontremoli, it was a celebration of community. 'We must take him,' she added, picking a flake of dried skin from the baby's scalp. In the past she'd complained about the lack of a community life in the Fens, in England. On bad days she wondered out loud if they could live in Italy.

'I have something to say.' She unpacked a notebook and a wad of A4 printed sheets curled into a tube. Laura had grown up as part of a large, loud, bickering family. Direct statements came naturally to her. Dryden loved her for it, but like most only-children found it difficult to confront issues. 'I talked to Katie.' Katie was her agent. 'I said I won't act. Not again. I said I have to write – scripts. The BBC's doing a new soap – Sky Farm, a kind of Emmerdale in the south, set near Norwich. They need storyliners?'

Dryden nodded. She'd acted in an ITV soap for years – Clyde Circus, a kind of suburban EastEnders. So she knew the ropes. Storyliners were like shop stewards for scriptwriters. Looking after the big picture, setting the parameters within which the writers worked, making sure characters stayed consistent, drawing all the threads together.

'She's got me a three-month trial. First episode is in January.'

'You'll be brilliant,' he said. He meant it, and she knew it, so her face relaxed with the smile.

'Thanks.'

She took a deep breath. 'It's three days a week in Norwich. Starting in December. Two days at home. Once we start filming it'll be four in Norwich, one at home. Sorry, it screws things up. I know.'

'Next driving test?'

'Ten days. I've put in for a whole load – several centres. I have to pass.'

On cue, the child cried.

'Childcare. We need a plan,' he said.

'We can make it work.'

'OK.'

They watched the dragon ducking and weaving on Palace Green.

'I read this last night,' said Laura. 'After you'd gone to sleep.' She turned the A4 pile around and Dryden saw that she'd downloaded a Home Office report: Migrant Workers and Crime in East of England. 'My first plot line.'

'Anything I don't know?' he said, touching the papers. The night before, over dinner, he'd told her about the murder on Eau Fen, and the silent audience of Polish pickers.

'The English are not a fair people,' said Laura. 'You do not like immigrants because they do not work – they *sponge*.' She smiled at the word. 'Then – they come only to work – and you do not like this either. They steal your jobs.'

'Whereas Italians organize bunting and hand out plates of pasta?'

'Sometimes they commit crime – more crime than the locals. Drink-driving is bad, and car theft. In many of these countries you do not need licences or MOT. Illegal gaming too – dogs, perhaps, hare coursing. To them it is perhaps not a crime. Or taking fish from the river without a licence.'

'But that's all small beer, right?'

'Small beer?'

'Ah. Forget that. Petty crime – nothing serious, nothing violent.'

'Yes. Little crimes.'

'But you'll want organized crime. Some decent Balkan villains in your plot. Some half-shaven tattooed psychopath called Drac.'

She laughed, shaking her head.

Down on St Cross' Green a little band of drummers began to pound out a beat so that the giant eel could dance. The sound seemed to captivate the baby, his eyes widening with each bass note. The eel began to writhe and dip, the movement practised enough to prompt screams from some of the younger children.

'Do you know the truth? Mostly this is the surprise to me because much more often the migrants are the victims, Philip.

People smuggling. Drugs. Illegal alcohol stills. Stolen goods. All this is organized by gangs. But the migrants are the *market*. They must take what they are given and not complain. This is what we do not see. They have to buy bad drugs . . .' She rubbed the tips of her fingers together as if indicating money. 'Adulterated – this is the word?'

'It is.'

'And cheap, bad alcohol. And second-hand clothes. And rotting meat. They must take what the gangs give them. If they want to come to this country without the proper papers they must pay too – very much money. Fortunes.'

Dryden's mobile rang. It was DI Friday. He stood and walked to the safety rail.

'Dryden. I've got you a name for the stiff on Eau Fen. Rory Setchey, aged fifty-four, married, two kids, teenagers. Fen Rivers Water Authority bailiff. Had been for twenty years.'

'Spell.'

'S.E.T.C.H.E.Y'

'Address?'

'Withheld.'

'Why?'

'Next question.'

'Can you tell me anything more?'

Friday sniffed. 'He had a boat – a water authority Hereward – and we can't find it. The ignition key was round his neck. You know the kind of boat?'

'Sure.' The Herewards stood out on the river. Wide, with a stand-up wheelhouse, an inboard engine, a small cabin in the stern.

'We need to find this boat. It's got to be out there – we've tried all the moorings, marinas, the lot. It'll be in some backwater out on the fen, which is where your readership comes in.'

'OK. I'll get it on the front in the splash for *The Crow*.'

'Great.'

'Any luck with the Poles?' Dryden knew Friday had interviewed all the migrant workers from Eau Fen.

'You're joking. They heard nothing, they saw nothing, and they said even less. But it isn't a coincidence, is it? We're pretty sure Setchey was killed somewhere else, then taken to

Eau Fen. Then hung up on the irrigator and shot full of holes. Why?'

Friday rang off before he got an answer.

Down on St Cross' Green the giant eel was moving, a sinuous dance over the grass, the drum beat thudding to a faster rhythm, its jaws wide open to reveal fairy-tale teeth dripping with blood.

TEN

The sky, clear blue, was motionless above the Capri, which moved beneath it in a straight line across The Great Soak – the flat silt fenlands of the west – en route for the morgue outside Peterborough. The only movement in the landscape, besides Humph's cab, came from the wind farms which seemed to shimmer on every horizon, the white blades catching the eye, turning with that graceful speed which always induced in Dryden a desire to sleep. As if they were eyelids falling.

Out here the soil was so light it was almost white, as if dressed with chalk – a stark contrast to the Black Fen which they'd left behind. The fields were either green with crops or bare – almost dazzlingly pale, with no shadows because there was virtually nothing to *throw* a shadow. Mid-morning and already the sun had that quality of bearing down, like a weight. Dryden wondered what unit of measurement could be invented for the heaviness of sunlight. Rays? No – beams.

The cabbie swung the Capri north at a T-junction, ignoring the SatNav's instruction to turn right, so that they were headed straight for a Magnox power station – a glittering knuckle of aluminium and blue, blowing its own smoke rings, creating small jet-black clouds which drifted, then vanished.

Dryden let the passing landscape paint pictures on his eyes, but the image in his mind was very different. He'd only ever seen a body 'laid out' once before – and that had been a stranger's. It had been at the chapel at River Bank – a hamlet now lost beneath the waters of Adventurers' Mere. Late October: he'd have been seven, no more. The church was four walls, a pitched roof. *The Little Chapel in the Fen* his mother called it, and he'd always taken the name as her own creation. He was shocked – on the day they buried her there – that the name was official, painted in amateurish gold letters on the wooden board above the preacher's pulpit.

He'd caught furtive glimpses of the body within the open casket, the candle-like skin, the strange see-through flesh, as if the dead man had been made of soap which the light could penetrate. He'd expected the body to move because of the wind. That was the sound he always recalled. Not the discordant singing of *Shall We Gather by the River*, or *We Plough the Fields and Scatter,* but the buffeting of the wind, as if they were in a boat at sea. The wind and the peat dust blown against the windows. That had been the sound that made the toddlers cry – a kind of whispering sizzle, like milk boiling over on the stove. And finally a gold light had gilded the body in its coffin and someone said – from the pulpit – that he looked like an angel.

Dryden blinked once, swapping that image from his memory for the image beyond the cab window. They'd arrived. The mortuary was on a trading estate beside the power station, surrounded, inexplicably, with a high wire-mesh fence through which the constant wind had laced several decades' worth of airborne litter. The result was oddly pleasing, as if some giant prayer wall had been thrown up by the living for the dead. The stiff north-easterly breeze made the litter vibrate, as if the fence was alive, almost sparkling; the colour and movement in sharp contrast to the mortuary building itself which was in brick, with a few dismal corporate flourishes – a stone shield over the door, a green lead roof with finials in gold, an incinerator chimney badly disguised as a bell tower.

Stepping over the threshold, Dryden felt worse. There was piped-in musak for the grieving – *Massenet* – and a reception desk decked with flowers that could have been in the lobby of a pharmaceutical company, perhaps, or an IT consultants. The receptionist, a young man in a dark suit, was listening to something else on headphones. But it wasn't the wildly inappropriate sense that this was the foyer of some ring-road motel that unsettled Dryden, it was the thought of what it was all designed to hide.

It wasn't death that was the problem. Dryden loved graveyards with their ranks of the dead, their elegiac sadness, the Gothic symbolism, and the hard yet comfortable benches. But morgues were different. There was no peace here: the bodies waited, sometimes for years, sometimes forever, before the final release. It was purgatory in brick.

The room they were shown to was eight foot square with metal walls. Why did everything have to be aluminium? It was as if they had to remind you constantly of the room you couldn't see: the metal pigeonhole drawers, the slickly oiled runners, the clatter of trolley wheels and the audible *pop* of doors, so tightly fitted, so secure, that when they opened and closed the air pressure changed. There was a single window eight feet up on one wall which, with an inexplicable flourish, was half blue glass, like the windows in *The Little Chapel in the Fen*. It was so deep-set you couldn't see out; the light was lambent, limping in to cast a flat, shadowless beam.

'It's not a good idea,' said Humph. 'They've said. You won't be able . . .' The sentence faded out with the idea. 'There's nothing to see,' he added, his light voice catching on the last word. The small plastic chair on which Humph sat was not visible: just the legs, slightly splayed. The cabbie was outside his comfort zone, an area slightly smaller than the Capri.

'I just need to finish this,' said Dryden, the acoustics in the room emphasizing the sharp, tinny consonants. 'I'll know.' He looked at his clasped hands.

Sgt Cherry came into the room and pulled up a chair, the legs screeching, although he didn't seem to notice. 'All right?' he asked, again oblivious to anyone's sensitivities.

'We'll have the DNA result in twenty-four hours. And there's the house where he lived. Maybe there is something there – something we missed. Maybe we all missed something. If it was your Dad you'd maybe know – the food he eats, the pictures he likes, the books. I can get you the key. It's a better bet than what's in there . . .' He nodded towards the door. 'All I'm saying is that you don't need to do this.'

Humph nodded at his feet.

Dryden said he'd still like to see the body.

So they'd been left in the waiting room. Twice Dryden decided that it wasn't a good idea and went to stand. Twice he sank back into the seat. Humph read a small book: *The Little Book of Trivia 2012*. Dryden might have gone when he stood the third time but as he rose the connecting door to the mortuary viewing room opened.

Sgt Cherry stood back as they entered. The room was no more than ten foot square; one wall was a glass sheet, beyond it an identical room containing a metal trolley, the body covered by a sheet. The shroud was blue, where Dryden had expected white.

'I'd like to be in the same room,' said Dryden.

'That's not possible,' said Cherry, and something in his voice persuaded Dryden that this wasn't red tape. There was a good reason for the glass wall.

Humph breathed in some of the air-conditioning and caught a note of lavender, and lemon, where he was searching for burnt flesh, singed bone and hair. A young woman in a lab coat entered the other room.

'Ready?' asked Cherry.

Dryden nodded but the speed of things made him feel sick. It was like a judicial hanging, as if they were rushing him now he was through the door, so he wouldn't buckle. The young woman quickly pulled back the sheet so that the face was revealed. They hadn't lied: there was nothing to identify.

Three seconds: 'That's enough,' said Dryden.

The woman covered the head again. Dryden put a hand to the dividing window, the fingers splayed, as if he could communicate by touch, but felt nothing. He hadn't recognized the face; he hadn't recognized it *as* a face.

'Fire's a terrible thing,' said Cherry.

'It's all right,' said Dryden. 'I should have listened. I can't say anything about that man. I can't say it's him, I can't say it isn't. I'm sorry.'

They shuffled out, Humph first, forgetting to hold the door open for the rest.

Dryden almost ran from the building, from the piped-in musak, the brushed aluminium. He hardly heard Cherry promise again to get him the key to the dead man's house. Then they were out under the sky and Dryden filled his lungs while Humph got them coffees from a café on wheels in the car park. Workers from the industrial estate sat around on plastic chairs. Dryden stood watching the litter vibrate in the prayer-wall fence. A page of *The Mirror* wrapped itself round his leg so he picked it up and walked over to the mesh and thrust it through. He wanted to say a prayer for the man he'd seen, whose body even now would be back in its aluminium drawer. But then he thought that if it *was* his father he didn't deserve a prayer.

ELEVEN

When Dryden got back to *The Crow* David Yoruba was in reception. He didn't see Dryden come through the door and so the reporter was able to observe him at rest: the straight back, the eyes forward, sat neatly on one of the squishy, threadbare sofas. Dryden was struck by a certain innate dignity in the man. His daughter had died, he was threatened with being sent back to a country he had – apparently – good reason to fear; he was a foreigner in a country increasingly wary of outsiders. And yet he was patient, calm, meticulously mannered. It seemed like an African virtue: dignity.

They shook hands and Yoruba eyed the interview cubicle in which they'd talked before. The memory of that made Dryden uncomfortable. 'The newsroom,' he said. 'It'll be chaos – but there's tea.'

They found themselves a quiet corner in the old clippings library. Dryden got Yoruba tea – black, no sugar. Did he have lemon? He did. Vee kept a little bottle of lemon juice on her desk which he stole. Yoruba sipped the acrid, scalding brew with relish.

'I've made some progress with your daughter,' said Dryden, aware he could have phrased that better but still unable to think how. 'The council will talk, but I have to wait – maybe twenty-four hours. It's all a ritual I'm afraid; they'll be considering their options.'

'Aque,' said Yoruba. 'My daughter's name.'

Dryden sipped his tea.

'I wanted to be honest with you, Mr Dryden.'

The implication was obvious and Yoruba had the decency to look away. 'I thought if I was honest I could ask a favour.' He smiled, the white teeth too large for the small mouth. 'I'm a journalist too,' he said. 'Like you. I worked in Niamey – the capital. I own the paper. I did own it – now the government owns it – although there is not much to covet. An office, two phone lines, broadband, PCs.'

They looked around and both laughed.

'But here is the difference,' said Yoruba. 'We have many governments – like buses in the English joke. You wait for years – then along come three or four. But all are bad. All pay lip service to the idea of the freedom of the press.'

Dryden nodded, aware he'd been fooled by this man at their first meeting. The sense of pity he felt for him now seemed misplaced. He'd once had power, great power, and wealth of a sort. He guessed that in Niger an office, any office, let alone one with telephone lines, was a rare asset.

'I wrote a story about our country's one great treasure – aluminium. The details do not matter. There are two mines – vast, owned by French companies. This story is about how these assets are sold cheaply to foreigners who pay bad wages and then export their profits tax-free. Not a new story in Africa, but an important story in my country.'

Yoruba paused and Dryden had to make a conscious effort to concentrate on his story. The single word 'aluminium' had taken him back to the morgue and he was struggling to dismiss the images that created.

'As I say, I wrote this story but I did not publish it. I waited for documents, certain documents, which would underpin the story. In the meantime, the government heard of my inquiries and they decided to act against me. This is not a pleasant prospect, you see – the knock on the door in the early hours, the ticking of the waiting engines. I was one step ahead of them. I fled. In the night, across the desert to the north, by car. Algeria, then France, then England.'

Yoruba had a rucksack. He pulled the ties and retrieved a single CD disk.

'This story – and those documents for which I waited – are on this disc. If I fail in my appeal and am flown home I wish you to try and print this story where you can – preferably one of the London papers with a website. It will be read in my country if it appears in *The Times*, the *Guardian*, the *Daily Telegraph* – but also the *Financial Times*. That would be best because it would hurt them the most. Also – AP has an office in London. They'll pick it up and run it in Paris. Does this make sense?'

'Yes,' said Dryden. 'They'll have questions.'

'Yes. The documents should contain all the answers. I understand that they won't want the story I wrote – not in that form. You – or perhaps a journalist in London – will have to build the story again from the documents. That's good – that's how it should be.

'I cannot help once I am on a flight back to Niamey. I will go from the airport to the police station – I know this police station and the cells under the street. If I stay there all is well. If I am transferred it has not gone well. I may not be seen again.'

He smiled, sipping his lemon tea, and Dryden had the very strong sense that he'd trained himself to do this – to enjoy this moment, despite what might lie ahead.

'How will I know about the appeal?' asked Dryden.

'Gill will ring.' He licked his lips and Dryden was aware he was contemplating a lie. 'There is one other option. If things look bleak we may disappear rather than return to Yarl's Wood. Again, I would wish to see this story published. In which case, I will send you a postcard – like this.'

From the rucksack he took a leather document case and retrieved a set of postcards. Gaudy Technicolor showed an African city – a few downtown high-rise banks and a hotel, surrounded by single-storey shanty towns. A flourish of blue handwriting was printed on the picture and read: Niamey.

'It will say nothing but if it is this card then please try to get the story into print as quickly as you can.'

'What do you mean, *disappear*?'

Yoruba placed the cup down and edged closer. 'This is Gill's idea. She thinks I should become a non-person. Take up a new identity.' He shook his head. 'But this is not cheap.' The thought seemed to break a spell so that he pushed his tea away. 'A terrible prospect anyway – to lose yourself. Your culture. Your homeland. I do not think I can do this.'

'You've tried to do this – to buy yourself a new identity?'

Yoruba licked his lower lip. 'Not yet. Maybe never. Gill wants this. For us, I know, but it is her dream. As I said – it is not cheap, and we are not rich. And I would never see my country again. My street, my family.'

He gave Dryden a new address – a council block for problem families on the edge of town – a temporary flat while his appeal was considered. Dryden said he would visit the cemetery at

Manea the next day to interview the cemetery warden about their daughter, then he'd get a message to him via Gill Yoruba's mobile.

They went back to reception and out into the street. As they stood on the pavement a crocodile of children from the local private school walked past.

'You know,' said Yoruba, 'at school, a good school, I learnt history. Always – in Russia, in France – the ultimate sentence for the powerful is exile, isn't it? I never did understand that. You're allowed to leave. Just go. You have your liberty still. But people say they would rather die. Rather languish in a cell. Rather face torture than exile. I begin to understand this now.'

He looked up at the cathedral's West Tower, the east side in full sunlight.

'Exile kills you alive.'

TWELVE

The Peking House stood on a corner in the Jubilee Estate. Not just a right-angled corner, an acute-angled corner, like New York's Flatiron building, like a ship's prow. The restaurant had plate-glass windows which had been curved to accommodate the narrow angle and had miraculously survived a decade of Saturday night drunks leaving The Merry Monk next door – the Jubilee's alternative to the Red, White and Blue. Dryden always took a table in the apex of the prow: with views back down two streets, and ahead down one which led out of the estate to the water meadows by the river, where wild horses grazed.

He looked at his plate: a celebration meal, marking publication of *The Crow*, and the end of the working week – usually sesame prawn toast, spring rolls, crispy duck, pancakes, plum sauce. But not today. The visit to the morgue had left an indelible image. He'd ordered egg fried rice, vegetable spring rolls, crackers. And beer: Chinese beer in iced cans. No crispy duck.

The restaurant had been Dryden's oasis since those first few weeks after Laura's crash. Humph had never been inside The Peking. He would eat his food *takeaway* in the car – even if it was only six feet from the door. The cabbie had quickly set himself the task of eating his way through the menu by number – irrespective of the food described. He'd had some very unusual meals as a result, and was on his second run through because they'd changed the menu last Christmas, or at least the numbers.

Dryden drained the can and noted that as he lowered it from his lips Sia Cheong Yew, the owner of the Peking, crossed over from the counter and put a fresh one in its place. Sia had become friends with Dryden in the same period – the weeks, months, and eventually years of Laura's coma. They had recognized in each other a determined lack of self-pity and the natural instincts of outsiders.

He pushed aside his plate and flipped up his iMac laptop, Googling the name of the Eau Fen victim – Rory Setchey.

Setchey's name got him two links to a website called FenFishing.

As a journalist he spent half his life trawling websites and he knew a professional job when he saw one: this had video, hyperlinks, the full www-works. Most of all it had webcams – a selection of six, on fen rivers. The business pitch was straightforward. Rory Setchey could guarantee you a fine day's fishing in one of England's few remaining wildernesses: carp, zander, pike, sea trout. Setchey – or one of the group of dedicated fishermen behind FenFishing – would take you to the secret places and you'd go home with a nice digital-sharp image for the mantelpiece, holding a scales-topping prize.

He flicked through the webcam options and chose a spot on the Little Ouse north of Isleham, not far from Flightpath Cottages. The image pixilated and re-set to give a clear view of the river between reeds, the water surface oily and disturbed by little whirlpools. A duck landed, water-skiing, before coming to rest like a flying boat. There was a houseboat in the distance, with permanent wooden boards set to link it with the riverbank, and a wind-generator turning in a blur. He thought he recognized the precise spot, a mile south of the inn at Brandon Creek.

Dryden considered how much money you'd have to earn from such a website to be able to afford to keep it running, updated, virus-free. Finally he togged through a series of pictures of Setchey at work – fly-fishing, gutting a fish for an open-air BBQ. The image of his face: outdoor-healthy, a wide smile, mocked the vision Dryden couldn't wash from his memory, with the single gunshot wound to the face.

He sent the website an email, identifying himself and the paper, saying he'd like to talk to someone.

Sia sat down and pulled the rings on two fresh cans. Dryden snapped shut the laptop. Not because he had any secrets from Sia but because his friend was a busy man – cooking, ordering, cleaning – and if he had time to sit down Dryden could make the time to talk.

'Radio says a murder – out on the fen,' said Sia.

'That's the splash,' said Dryden. 'Nasty.'

'And Humph said there was something else that I should ask,' said Sia, holding the ice-cold can to his lips, nodding out the window to the cab parked just a few feet away. Humph was eating, ferrying noodles to his mouth with chopsticks. 'Something about your father? He said you wouldn't say anything unless I asked. He was right, wasn't he?'

'Sorry,' said Dryden. 'It's just been a shock. It was good not talking about it. But he's right, I should. We thought Dad died in 'seventy-seven – the floods. Then I got this call.' He told him about the road accident, the burnt-out car, the body on the mortuary slab. 'They say it isn't him – that someone stole his name, documents, his life. I have this fear – this premonition – that it *is* him.' He looked out the window. 'He lived here, on the Jubilee.'

Someone came in for food so Sia went to serve them. In his carefully cultivated broken English he chatted to the woman, asking about her children, whose names he knew. His English was first class but he'd developed the pidgin version to make his customers feel at home.

'I don't know, like, how it works here,' said Sia, sitting down again, running a finger along a slim white scar that ran from his eyebrow to his chin. Dryden was pretty sure he hadn't picked up that wound in a kitchen. It gave his friend an edge of suppressed violence which was a considerable asset on the Jubilee Estate.

From the kitchen came the sound of his wife cooking.

'At home this couldn't happen – in Singapore,' said Sia. 'If you're dead they write it down. Everyone knows. You don't get to keep stuff – medical card, driving licence, passport. You need papers for a job – for a pension. You'd be a non-person without them. And it's not like they don't ask. Police, on the street, they ask; you try and leave the country, they ask. Everyone asks. It's like a national hobby. And they take all that away when you're dead. They send people round to collect it.' He laughed, draining the can. 'No exceptions.' He crushed the can.

'Yeah – same here, sort of,' said Dryden. 'You have to register a death. You get a certificate. But to do that if someone's died in an accident, or suddenly, you need the coroner to say it's OK. And how can he do that if there's no body? I guess this time he didn't say it was OK. So Dad was left . . .' He drained the can. 'In limbo.'

The beer was freeing up his memory. 'We did try. We went

to some office out at Swaffham Prior. The registrar saw us – a man called Trelaw. I'll never forget the name. It was on his door, and he made us wait, in this cold office with a cold grate. That winter was icy. And then, when we did get in, he said no, we couldn't have the death certificate – we needed the body. I think Mum just gave up.'

Now that he'd unpacked the memory there was more of it than he'd expected. 'I can see him now. Trelaw. A big man, one of those men whose bones seem to show through they're so big, like an elephant, with the skin hung between. He had this big black fountain pen, and he held it like a child holds a crayon.' He shook his head, amazed he'd been able to reach back for the image.

'And when we went he stood up and he shook her hand, and then he shook mine, and he said: "I'm sorry for your loss". Nobody else had included me until then. I think that's why I remember him. Mum didn't speak – afterwards, on the way home. I think it was a blow. If she'd got the certificate she could have moved on, got on with her life, my life, but it was like we were caught – like one of those fossil flies petrified in amber.'

He hadn't noticed the squad car pulling up outside behind Humph's cab. A uniformed PC, short with glasses, appeared by Dryden's table, weighed down by a Hi-Vis jacket.

'Mr Dryden?'

He placed a single golden Yale key on the tablecloth. It was bright and new and appeared to emit its own light.

'Compliments of Sergeant Cherry,' he added.

THIRTEEN

The Jubilee Estate smelt of burnt tyres and newly mown grass. Late afternoon; the sun pressing down, driving the shadows under parked cars and around the trunks of the cherry trees, planted with military precision along the freshly cut verges. The flag of St George hung from a bedroom window; an Action Man hanging from a tangled parachute which had caught in the overhead phone lines.

He made Humph walk, leaving the cab outside his own house. Leopold Street looked just like all the others they'd just strolled down. When Dryden got to the front gate Humph wasn't in sight behind him so he waited, studying the house. Sweat broke out on his skin. What was it about housing estates that seemed to make them radiate their own heat? It was all that concrete, tarmac and brick. The house was mid-terrace, sixties, with asymmetrical windows of differing sizes which made its ugliness almost heroic. The garden was lawn, neat but perfunctory. The houses on either side were even uglier thanks to various Homebase affectations: a carriage lamp over the door on the right, a pair of giant plastic butterflies over the other.

Humph came round the far corner, mopping his face theatrically with a white handkerchief. When he reached Dryden he took three deep breaths before speaking, then decided to say nothing.

Dryden walked up the path and opened the door with the Yale. Crossing the threshold he breathed in the smell of it, trying to find a trace of his childhood. When they'd moved to London after his father's death he'd noticed one day that their flat – in a block over shops on the Finchley Road – had somehow managed to develop exactly the same smell as the farmhouse at Burnt Fen. What was it? A subtle blend perhaps of diet, washing powder, beverages, furniture, clothes and books. And at the farm there had always been a stock pot gurgling on the range – something his mother contrived to somehow continue in the city. And wood

– the aroma of resin, because they'd only ever had rugs at Burnt Fen, laid over the boards or the quarry tiles, and the flat had polished boards and rugs too. So no carpets, no soft furnishings and no air fresheners. But there was no hint of that here. The house smelt empty, neutral, inert. In fact, now that he thought about it, it smelt antiseptic.

The downstairs rooms were uniformly dull. The property had been rented and was a symphony in beige. Second-hand furniture, generic, tasteless art on the walls. And that was right too, because his father hadn't noticed when his mother had given away a print of Constable's *Hay Wain* which had hung over the fireplace for a decade. The state of repair – efficient, but not loving – suggested a maintenance contract. There were no books to see but a pile of newspapers – several different nationals plus the local evening paper from Cambridge. All of them were open at the puzzle page.

One oddity – there was an internal window between the kitchen and main room and it had been replaced with a stained-glass window. Dryden looked at it for some time trying to work out what was so strange. It was a grid – eight by eight, like a chess board. Each square was one of eight colours. Each line only contained one of each colour – however you 'read' it – up or down, side to side. Clever, mildly disquieting, like a puzzle. Sudoku with colours.

And then there was the kitchen – fitted, a German company, quality. And it was crammed with gadgets, tin-openers, mixers, an iPod dock and a flat-screen TV.

'Liked his toys,' said Humph.

A bottle of beer – Hoegaarden – stood empty on the table. Dryden's father had liked beer, and almost always had a bottle with his evening meal. And he was no Little Englander – so why not a Belgian beer? There were no family or personal pictures on the walls or mantelpiece. If he was indoors, and his father hated being indoors, he'd always had eyes only for the windows. So no curtains except heavy drapes for winter. And that was what was unusual about this house – no net curtains. Everyone on the Jubilee had net curtains.

In the hallway was a notice board with various cards and flyers and a calendar all held in place by red-topped drawing pins. Dryden felt something crunch under his foot and looking down saw two of the pins in the pile of the carpet, which was odd because everywhere else seemed freshly hovered. He moved his finger over some of the flyers: night classes at the college, The Peking's home delivery service, Live Music at The Red, White and Blue – an academic calendar for Ely College.

He eased one of the drawing pins out of a card. 'They weren't looking very hard, were they – the plods.' Underneath the flyer was another, smaller, flyer which had been held up by the same pin.

Ely Singles Club: Divorced or Separated? Ring us, or join us, every Friday evening at The Red, White and Blue. £5 includes first drink and sandwiches.

He handed Humph the card. 'You might need that.'

Humph popped the card in his back pocket, standing at the foot of the stairs and turning 360 degrees.

'I'll check upstairs,' said Dryden. 'You try the kitchen and the yard.'

There was a small hallway at the top of the flight of stairs and the doors to the two bedrooms and the bathroom. Dryden stood for a second thinking it was incredible that someone could live somewhere for six years and leave so little of themselves behind.

He'd clearly slept in the box room. The bed was crumpled, like a nest, with a bedside table and a radio alarm. Dryden hit the PLAY button expecting to hear Radio Four – his parents had listened to nothing else, from *Farming Today* until the *Shipping Forecast*. But it was Star Radio – the local commercial station. Dryden killed the signal. That wasn't right.

The bathroom had more in it than Dryden would have expected – a shelf of men's cosmetics, including aftershave, some skincare creams and a packet of those little brushes dentists sell for cleaning between the teeth. The rest of the bathroom was spotless – there was no bath but a proper shower box, and it was clean, which is difficult to do even if you try hard. Not a single hair against the white tiles.

The main bedroom was in darkness. There were thick curtains, which didn't let any of the sunshine through, until he threw them back. Then he saw the books. Three bookcases, all slightly different sizes and woods, arranged to fill one wall.

He pulled a volume free at random. *The Earth Sciences: An introduction, by Prof J.H.L.Carr.*

'You done?' shouted Humph from downstairs.

'Come up.'

Humph climbed up counting the steps out loud.

'He never had these at the farm – but it's his subject. Natural sciences.'

Looking at the room Dryden could see it was set out for two people. One large chair by the computer screen, then a chair set to one side, as if for an interview. And the computer gear was all top of the range: a new iMac and an iPad on the desk, a wireless airport and a new laptop. Underneath the desk sat one of the latest printers and a scanner.

The doorbell rang.

It was a young girl – maybe fourteen – clutching books. She was halfway over the threshold and already easing one of her black school shoes off the left foot, using her right foot.

Humph, halfway down the stairs, recognized her as a neighbour's daughter on his street. She wore the uniform of the local comprehensive. Her hair had been allowed to grow long, and had been brushed to a sheen so that blonde highlights showed.

'Where's Jack?' she said, then checked her watch.

Dryden touched his lips with the back of his hand and nodded. 'How do you know Jack?'

'He's my tutor. GCSE maths – I'm doing it early. Dad pays.' She looked to Humph and asked, 'Who's he?'

'My name's Dryden too,' said Dryden. 'Philip.'

She went to close the door but left it open. 'Was Jack your Dad?'

'Why'd you say that?'

'Just the name.'

'I don't look like him?'

'Maybe. What's wrong?'

Dryden produced a picture of his father from 1977. 'That's him – thirty-five years ago. Had he changed?' He'd framed the question carefully, and watched her face.

She didn't look puzzled, just quizzical. 'He got way fatter. He looks like you back then.'

'So, just fatter. Otherwise, that's him?'

'You said it was him. I didn't. I'm just saying he looks a bit like you back then. Jack – this Jack – never had a tan. I never saw him – like, *out*, at all. It might be him – but maybe not.' She nodded. 'Maybe not.'

'What's your name?' asked Dryden.

'Cathy Symms,' said Humph when she didn't answer. She gave him a lethal look.

'There's some bad news,' said Dryden quickly. 'There was an accident and Jack was involved – out on the fen. I'm sorry, but Jack was killed.'

'Oh, God,' she said, betraying more interest than grief. She looked at the books in her hand. She's thinking, thought Dryden, if they'll be able to find another tutor. That's the thing about the young, they move on, survive.

'How often did you see him?'

'Twice a week. All this year. He was all right – really good at maths. Like it was a language – right – and he could speak it. Crap at talking, otherwise. Shy. Bit weird.' She shifted her feet. 'There's people like him at school.' She made a little rainbow shape with her index fingers. 'Like on the spectrum.'

'Autistic?'

She shrugged. 'Not bad. Just a bit. Like I said.'

'See any other students?'

'One before me on Tuesday – a boy called O'Brien, from my school. He's A-Level – pure maths. We talked.' She smiled. 'He's cute. There were others – he'd talk about others. Doing science mainly, but he said his special students did maths. So I was special.'

A cat came in from the kitchen calling for food.

'That's Jack's. It's called *Lincoln*. He wouldn't say why. But it made him laugh – like every time he said it. That's like a private joke, right? 'Coz it isn't funny.'

The cat walked out of the front door having made a figure of eight around Dryden's feet. What was Lincoln famous for? he thought. Never telling a lie? Or was that Washington? His father wouldn't have animals in the house at Burnt Fen because in the end you had to kill animals: quickly, deftly, in the barn, with the tools hung from the wall.

'Anyone else ever here with Jack? A woman, friends?'

'No. He drank at The Red, White and Blue,' she said, nodding outside. The Jubilee's other estate pub was two streets away set on a corner. It made the average estate pub look like Café Rouge. 'That's where Dad met him – he wasn't CRB cleared or anything, said he couldn't be bothered with the paperwork. Dad said that was why he was cheap.' She flushed, suddenly and deeply. 'He didn't touch me or nothing.'

'That's a plus,' said Dryden.

'He had a son.'

'Really? He said that, did he?'

'Not straight out. He said his son was crap at maths but that that didn't mean he was stupid. He said he was bright – just not *academic*. That's what people always say when they mean you're thick.'

Dryden was good at maths, good with the abstract, so this mysterious 'son' couldn't be him. His father had gone missing at the age of thirty-five, so there was no reason why he couldn't have had another son. He'd be Dryden's half-brother. The thought made him feel dizzy so that he had to put out a hand and lean on the wall.

The girl's chin came up. 'I liked him.' She'd got her shoe back on and was backing out the door. 'You police?'

'No. Like I said, we were related,' said Dryden.

'No, you didn't. You said you had the same name. That's different.'

'Do you want to look at the picture again – make sure?'

But she'd gone.

FOURTEEN

The town clung to them for half a mile – a market-garden, a single row of old council houses, a water tower; and then they were down to the fen. This was when he felt most at sea, the first mile, because the landscape was so flat the horizon was very close – a mile, maybe two. It was one of the things people got wrong about the Fens – all that space, you can see for miles. You can't. It just feels like you can – the earth you can see is a small circle a few miles across with you at the centre. But if he wanted to see for miles he could – by looking up.

'Nice clouds,' said Dryden. 'Wonder what they're called.'

Humph pretended to ignore him.

Dryden put his head out of the passenger-side window, letting the wind created by the cab's speed cool his face. They were on their way to Buskeybay to see his aunt and uncle. Work was over for the week. He had some time now to delve back, find out more about his father, and the last year of his life, which meant that once Humph had dropped him at the farm the cabbie had nowhere to go until the clubs turned out at midnight.

'Want to know what I think?' asked Dryden.

Humph just about managed to tilt his chin to indicate interest.

'I think someone has cleaned that house from top to bottom and taken away anything which would allow us to see the man's face: pictures, documents. Question is why: did they want to hide the fact it was Jack Dryden, or hide the fact it wasn't? Second question: who took it all away? I'll check with Cherry but I'm pretty certain it's not forensics. He's happy for the DNA to decide it. But if it's not the police, who is it?'

'Was it your Dad's house?'

It was so rare for Humph to ask a straightforward question Dryden took time out to structure his answer.

'The house itself tells two stories: the books could be his, but not the kitchen, not the flat-screen TV, but maybe the garden, the food. The stuff about maths is odd – he loved maths, but not as much as the science. It didn't *feel* right. But then nothing does.'

'Wait for the DNA then,' said Humph.

The cabbie searched his memory banks for some facts about DNA.

'Which Cambridge pub did Crick and Watson celebrate in after their discovery of the double helix structure of DNA?' he asked.

'The Eagle.'

Humph narrowed his eyes and began to whistle as if he hadn't asked the question.

'Aunt Con might know something, or Roger,' said Dryden. 'They knew Dad as well as anyone but Mum. Come in for tea if you like . . .'

Humph's head twitched by way of saying no.

'Maybe there's something in the past,' said Dryden. He looked at Humph in profile. 'Family secrets and all that. Don't they say every family has one?'

Humph shifted in his seat, happier with DNA trivia. 'If you unwrap all the DNA in all your body cells it would stretch to the moon 6,000 times.'

'Useful,' said Dryden.

Humph swung the cab out to overtake a tractor hauling a trailer of sugar beet. The Capri hit a sinuous dip in the road and momentarily took flight, landing with a clatter and a boom from the partly disengaged exhaust pipe. The fluffy dice which hung from the cabbie's rear-view mirror spiralled together like South American bolus, then unspun slowly, as Humph coaxed the engine up to fifty-five mph, employing an urgent posture.

By the last set of level crossing gates a goat had been tethered to trim the grass. As they passed Dryden noted the strange, Lucifer-like, horizontal pupils to the animal's eyes.

The shortwave radio fixed to the cab's dashboard with a speaker phone blared into life. 'Humph – this is Jules, over. Humph – this is Jules, over.'

Dryden knew all the cabs on the Ely rank now. Jules was a woman – at least, he thought she was. Like Humph she appeared to have been welded into her cab. She had forearms like a truck driver and an unruly frizz of red hair. Unlike Humph she had a car with four doors – a Volvo estate. She knew, as did the entire rank, that Humph would either have Dryden on board or be in touch on the mobile, so any news items they spotted en route were relayed into the cruising Capri. It was like being on the news desk at CNN.

'On the back road to Clayhythe,' said Jules, effortlessly bellowing through a burst of static. 'A mile short of the village. There's a house – river authority or summat. Weird place. Round windows. Like Bilbo Baggins' house. God knows what they're up to – coppers, traffic squad cars, the lot. Go see. Go quick. Over.'

'It's on the way,' said Humph, drumming delicate fingers. 'Sort of.'

'Water authority,' said Dryden. He thought of the Eau Fen victim and the withheld address.

At the next junction Humph swung the cab east. Dryden kicked his legs out, frustrated by the cab's limited leg room, as if it should have been designed for the comfort of passengers over six feet tall. The heat seemed suddenly to intensify. Not for the first time he wondered if he had some kind of thermostatic dysfunction. He seemed to spend most of his life cold except for odd, fleeting moments of flaming heat. The Capri didn't help: it was a four-wheel oven, with an air-conditioning unit which redirected engine fumes back into the cab. The air seemed dense, like a steam bath. Despite the open windows the plastic seats were too hot to touch.

A big fat moth hit the windscreen with a crackling of its carapace. Humph despatched it with the wipers, leaving an orange arc. For the cabbie this was back-of-the-hand country, so he switched off the SatNav and expertly tracked a zigzag route to Clayhythe: a cluster of buildings and a pub on the Cam which had once been a wharf for barges serving the main village of Waterbeach up the road. Humph stopped the cab on an old stone bridge. Below them was the river, ink-green here, in the lee of a line of willows. On the far side stood the old water authority building. Jules, Humph's informer, had used the word 'weird' – it was an understatement.

The house was taller than it was wide, like a dovecote with

three stories. The facade on each side came to an elegant Dutch gable pierced by a single oculus window. The pinnacles of the brickwork and leaded roof were decorated with stone figures – Dryden guessed the four winds of Greek mythology. What he could see of the interior was more mundane – a poster in an upstairs room of a Dalek, a kid's mobile, a modern fitted kitchen, a wall-mounted flat-screen TV.

But it wasn't the house that was so unusual. It was what they were doing to it, and what they were doing to it was taking it apart: brick by London brick. Scaffolding covered the facade facing the river. Three building skips were on the riverbank – plastic chutes leading down from the roof and upper storey. Dryden watched as a worker in a Day-Glo green bib carefully dislodged a brick, turned it over, turned it back, then dropped it down the chute. Beside him a uniformed police officer was working his way along the guttering, checking inside and out. The interior of the house crawled with coppers: paper being peeled off walls, carpets being rolled and pushed out of windows, while in the garden individual pieces of furniture were being carefully dismantled. Parts of the roof had been removed, along with several courses of the top bricks, so that the structural beams were left against the sky.

'Skeleton house,' said Dryden.

Humph wasn't listening. He'd got the glove compartment open and was examining an empty miniature bottle of Triple Sec. Dryden got the impression it hadn't been empty very long. Humph's natural curiosity was a fragile, fleeting creature. The police were taking a house apart. Big deal. He slipped on his earphones and pressed the PLAY button on his Estonian language tape.

One of the white-suited coppers in the garden was pointing at Dryden so he got out of the cab and took a quick 360-degree survey of the scene prior to being moved on. Downriver: nothing, just the channel turning gently away in the willows beside a footpath. East: fen, a line of pylons which seemed to diminish with the curvature of the earth. West: fen. Upriver: a boat yard beyond the water authority house, a few river boats, a dredger and a water authority launch, then the lawn in front of the pub with a few drinkers out at the picnic tables. The launch and the dredger were in the water authority livery: orange – that precise shade Dryden had seen the previous day under the fingernails of the man hung from the irrigator.

'Can I help?'

Dryden swung round to find a uniformed PC approaching. His lapel radio crackled. The words buried in the static never sounded like English, but this time Dryden was pretty certain that was because it wasn't English.

'We're closing the road. You'll have to move that.' The PC gestured back at the car. Dryden was certain he hadn't woken up in a police state. Had something happened since breakfast?

'I'd like a word with Detective Inspector Friday.' It was a shot in the dark, but a decent one. Was this Rory Setchey's home? The police had said he worked for the water authority, and the top-level search would explain the lack of home address. For the first time Dryden noticed the house had a name – black stencilled letters on whitewash over the door: Hythe House.

The PC didn't reply but stood back and talked into his radio.

A car came the other way on to the bridge and stopped, almost bumper-to-bumper with the Capri. It was a black BMW and the four men who got out didn't even look at Dryden. They walked away until one of them stopped and produced a packet of cigarettes. A red, chequered packet Dryden had never seen before. Expensive suits, two of them on iPhones, no ties, lots of facial hair shaved for effect: moustaches as thin as eyebrows. The PC appeared to be waiting for a reply on the radio while sweating steadily into his blue collar.

'What about them?' asked Dryden, nodding at the new arrivals.

The PC's eyes narrowed. Behind him, striding up the road, came DI Friday.

'Now we can sort things out,' said Dryden. There was a burst of laughter from the BMW suits and some words on the breeze – again, not English. Humph had slipped off his earphones and wound down the side window to listen.

Friday arrived, lit a cigarette. 'Fuck off,' he said. He took a step closer. 'Now.'

'Strange place,' said Dryden, nodding at the building.

'Water authority-tied cottage. That's it. Now, fuck off.'

'When did he go missing – our man?'

Friday turned to the PC. 'Give him a minute. If he's still here caution him and arrest him for obstruction. The fat bloke too.' He tried to put some venom in the remark but failed. His attention was almost entirely focused on the sharp suits from the BMW.

Humph swung the Capri in a half circle, then a three-point turn, then another three-point turn. It was like watching a merry-go-round.

Dryden climbed aboard. As they pulled away he looked in the rear-view mirror. 'That wasn't English,' he said. 'The characters out of the BMW – foreign language, right?'

'I know.' Humph looked mildly shocked. 'It was Estonian.'

FIFTEEN

I t was an odd illusion but a persistent one: whenever Dryden looked out over the newly created Adventurers' Mere the clouds always appeared as if over a sea. He couldn't see the far shore of the lake, and the sky created the sense that there wasn't a far side, just an ocean.

The Capri tracked the shoreline east creating its own weather, a streak of red peat dust which hung behind the cab. The mere seemed to make its own weather too: a sudden squally wind, so that gusts buffeted the side of the car, and there were a few white horses out on the water. White horses forty miles inland.

'Estonian?' asked Dryden. 'You sure?'

'Yup. I've been studying it for eight months. How sure do you want me to be?'

'And they said?'

'I only caught words. Migrant – certainly, several times, because it was like German – guest-worker. And hotel, and breakfast, and cigarettes. And coffee – they liked the coffee.' Humph's grip on the vocabulary of the Estonian menu appeared first class. Beyond that he was treading water.

'Nothing else?'

'One of them said *milte* and the others whistled.'

'And *milte* means?'

'Million.'

Dryden thought about that but came to no conclusion. 'So – a million. Not millions . . .'

'Singular. The plural sounds different. At least it does on the tape.'

Dryden called *The Crow* and told the news editor to get Mitch out for some pictures of Hythe House. If he brought his telephoto toys he could get some long shots – the house was disappearing, brick by brick. If he made a couple of trips and took the snaps from the same spot they could run a series: *the disappearing house*.

He killed the signal. 'Why, that's the question,' he said to the windscreen. 'Why take a house apart?'

'They're looking for something,' said Humph.

'Brilliant.'

Humph shrugged. 'Drugs?'

'Nah. Drugs squad would rip the place apart – sure. And they'd use dogs – no dogs there. And they wouldn't demolish it. They were taking the roof off – like – *off*.'

'Jewels?'

'It's a bit Famous Five.'

Humph ran a pointed tongue along his plump lips. 'Espionage?'

Dryden shifted in his seat. 'Eh?'

'A microchip? A memory stick? A mobile phone? An iPhone?

'OK, OK . . .'

'Stuff – you know. Secrets. Not *family secrets*. State secrets. Corporate secrets. Information. That's power, right? And they don't take up a lot of space.' Humph eased his T-shirt away from his neck. 'Sometimes, no space at all.'

They came to a T-junction on the bank-top – a drove leading away on the brink of a dyke, a signpost reading Nornea, two miles; the way ahead marked Buskeybay, one mile, running by the new mere.

Dryden had been there the day they'd created Adventurers' Mere – opening the sluice gates at Upware, flooding 2,000 acres in a single day.

It had been the biggest story in the Fens since the floods of 1947. The original plan – put forward by the National Trust – was for a 100-year creeping programme of jigsaw re-flooding – creating marsh, and wildlife habitat, and pasture, with small amounts of open water. But by the mid-1990s global warming had taken sea levels much higher than anticipated while cuts in public expenditure had led to a full halt on drainage work, and on the rebuilding of flood defences. The decision was taken to go instead for an all-out flooding, creating a giant lake. The year-on-year saving for the government was put at £1bn – and a little of the cash was put aside to promote the new water lands as a tourist attraction and a boating area. The National Trust fought the plans, and lost.

When the day came to let the waters back on the land after

an interlude of 350 years the press was invited. Most of the media, dominated by the TV crews, were corralled at Reach, strung along the top of the Devil's Dyke. The Environment Agency, in charge of the re-flooding, had constructed a kind of grandstand for visitors and press – a gantry for the cameras – providing food and cabling for computers and satellite phones. And there'd been lots of media interest – fired-up in part by the fierce local campaign waged by residents to save the fen from the flood. Three small villages – barely hamlets – were due to go under the water, and several farms. The crusade had attracted the usual hangers-on: the police expected rent-a-mob to make an appearance, scuffles, maybe worse. One group of green campaigners had built an 'ark' – a converted Dutch barge with its deck covered with plant pots containing mosses and lichens, ferns and reeds threatened by the rising waters. Overhead a single police helicopter had circled.

Dryden had his own plan that day to get the best story. A story to beat the nationals. He didn't want to watch the fen become a sea, he wanted to be *on* that sea. The Environment Agency was happy to help. They knew him well – he hadn't arrived on a plane from Barcelona, or New York, or – worse – driven up the M11 from London – to watch the great fen flood. He'd covered the story from day one. He'd done them no favours, gave the anti-mere campaigners a fair hearing, but the agency knew he was honest, and serious about the issue, so they helped him on that final day and got him through the security ring they'd had to put in place around the danger area – the 2,000 acres waiting to be flooded.

Humph, a dedicated non-swimmer, had been in a hurry to get back. The cabbie had helped him unload the boat from a trailer attached to the Capri at a spot three miles west of the hamlet of River Bank. According to the OS map that was the lowest spot – twelve feet below mean high tide – and therefore should flood first. Alone, Dryden had scanned the horizon, the distant flood bank of the Cam just in sight, and along it the first signs of demonstrators – placards just visible, thin trails of smoke rising from campfires. The police contingency plan estimated a maximum figure of 4,000. Dryden had rung round and reckoned that by the time the sluices were opened at noon they'd be wrong by a factor of ten. There was also a plan for a mass sit-in the following day at Petit's Fen – the next area scheduled for flooding to the south. Another 1,000 acres, another dozen lonely peatland hamlets.

A distant siren sounded its alarm at 11.45 a.m. – the fifteen-minute warning. On the wind he could hear the distant demonstrators like a faraway football crowd. He heard the blare of megaphones. Somewhere a police siren wailed, adding a note of panic, and from the far side of the river a line of geese, in a rough, elongated V formation, began to cross the sky, honking like vintage cars.

Dryden stood in the boat, looking north, anticipating the sudden percussion of the maroon that would signal the opening of the gates. He watched the geese swing back overhead. It was odd. He loved the landscape, and he loved to see the wildlife set against the landscape, but he'd never really been interested in the wildlife *itself*. The Fens, after all, were essentially to him a lifeless landscape – fixed, no cattle, no sheep, a few horses, perhaps – he liked those, but only when they wandered into town in winter or stood, immobile, in the middle of a drove road. Small deer – the fenland muntjac – were like grey ghosts, and he often felt as if he could see through them they were so slight, so fleeting. They too came to town, and wandered sometimes around the cathedral, but were gone by dawn. So, for him, the landscape was lifeless, which made the sky the most important facet of all, because it was the only moving, living thing.

And so it didn't matter how much water they let through the sluices, the sky would always be there; in fact, there'd be more of it, reflected in the water. Not a sea at all, or even a lake, carrying the inverted outlines of hills or mountains, pine trees, or lakeside homes; but instead just *more* sky.

The maroon went off, the retort echoing twice, three times round the fen. The crowd fell silent as if at the news of a death. And then he heard the water. The Fens are silent, except for the wind, but he could hear from three miles away the spurt of white water through the metal gates. The crowd began to chant again but Dryden felt that even then – just a few seconds after the water began to flow – that the mood had changed: it already sounded like a lament. The demonstrators' leaders had promised a twenty-four-hour vigil but Dryden wondered if they'd just melt away at dusk.

It took an hour for the first signs of rising water to appear: the ditches began to fill first, then the wider dykes, until a new world of water brimmed over into the land. Sitting in his beached boat he ate a packed lunch and tried to enjoy the expectation, imagining what the landscape might look like by the time the moon rose. Smoke made a mazy way into the sky from the distant river bank and he guessed the demonstrators had lit more fires. Through the binoculars he saw occasional tents pitched on the bank side.

He didn't recall lying in the bottom of the boat, or slipping into sleep, or any dreams, but when he woke the sound he heard was like a nightmare: screams, inhuman, and piercing. The water, brimming, was creeping out of the nearest ditch, creating a moat. The source of the sound was harder to find, but eventually he saw them – crowded into a far corner around a single willow. Hares, terrified of the rising water, calling to each other. They weren't the only animals in the field. A small herd of muncjac, about twenty, were standing in the precise centre of the peat, still – as if the scene had been caught in a photograph. They had shadows so Dryden checked his watch: 4.15 p.m.

The moat widened by the minute, edging in like a slow tide, but from four directions. It kissed the boat and he reached down a hand to touch it – warm; and now it was this close he could smell it too, the unmistakable aroma of fresh water – a reedy, dank smell, which made him think of a precise colour: a green, the green of wet moss.

The deer bolted before it was too late – the sound of them running louder than he'd imagined, swinging in an arc across the dry peat and then trying to leap the wide moat, like springbok, but landing short, so that the water was white with them swimming, thrashing, and then they were gone, into a small copse of pollarded willow. But the hares, hypnotized by terror, simply crowded tighter together, the screaming manic and pitiful.

Floating free the boat slipped her temporary mooring at precisely 5.05 p.m. He added the time to his notes so that when he came to write the piece he'd have some solid points of fact in a sea of description. It was an odd moment when it came – the slipping away from the earth – making Dryden grab stupidly for the gunwales, so that the boat rocked and touched the peaty bottom, and then slipped clear. He had an outboard turned up, its blades clear, but he used the paddles, edging out into the water. The screams of the hares had stopped but as he set out towards the hamlet of River Bank he saw one of them in the water, drowned, its angular limbs graceful forward and back, as if running beneath the surface.

He fired the outboard into life at 5.45 p.m. and set out for River Bank. By the time he arrived the village was half-submerged: the little church – *The Little Chapel in the Fen* – and its tower, the sturdy bulk of a large house – *Fenlandia* – with its tall fake-Tudor chimney stacks, all stood clear of the rising waters. But the cluster of farm buildings had gone; the crossroads at the village centre marked only by poplars, their Christmas-tree tops still above water. The chattering of starlings in the trees filled the air. They were in the olive in the churchyard and made it look black and heavy, almost shimmering.

Dryden's camera captured the scene by degrees: the final hours of River Bank. When it was over the only signs of the village that had been would be the trees, the church roof and tower, and the chimney of *Fenlandia*. He tied the boat up to the cedar tree. Lighting a lantern he had some food, and in the cool light of dusk had looked down through the green water to the graveyard six feet below: he could see his mother's headstone, the image buckling slightly in the current. He'd set flowers on the grave itself the day before – sea cabbage, water lilies and samphire which floated now, spreading out green tendrils. Which is when he'd seen the first eel: an adult, maybe three feet long, as thick as a man's arm, moving with that primeval oddity, writing S in the water, over and over again.

SIXTEEN

The farmyard at Buskeybay was protected on three sides by Leylandii hedges twenty-five feet tall, a barrier against the fen winds. The view east, towards the high bank of the mere, was the only one left open. Con sat in the kitchen garden with a bowl of runner beans in her lap, expertly slicing and cutting them into a freezer bag. She radiated a sense of brisk efficiency in whatever she did. She might not be a great enthusiast for the Fens but she never appeared to be a victim of its space and scale. Dryden always thought of her as a typical pioneer, never cowed by nature.

She looked up when Dryden called her name but her eyes went beyond him and he knew she was looking for Laura and the baby.

Disappointed, she tried too hard to smile. 'Philip.'

They didn't embrace or kiss and he couldn't recall when they'd stopped.

'So – what's the mystery? You said something about Jack?' She straightened her shoulders. 'I'll make tea.' She stood quickly, large-boned, the beans held at her hip in a plastic basket.

Dryden stood still, a boy again. He'd played here often with Con and Roger's son Laurie – a year older than him, and long gone to a wife and a new life 'away' – as they said in the Fens. Manchester, Dryden thought. Certainly somewhere crowded and windless. They hadn't been the only children. The tied cottages down by the Isleham Road had been occupied then with families and farm workers. All the summers of his childhood were compressed into a single memory: him, running, across that wide field to the east on a rare windless day, and turning to find each of his footfalls had stirred a miniature red twister of dust, and that beyond that was a whirlwind of amber peat, a fen 'blow', like the one in the *Wizard of Oz*. He hadn't tried to outrun it; he'd just stood there and let it smother him. He could still feel the tiny pinpricks of the dust, the sizzle of the particles, the red light seen through his tightly closed eyes.

His aunt came back with tea: mugs, a saucer of biscuits and a dish of the radish from the garden, with salt and pepper. It was good of her – a kind of peace offering – because she knew he loved them, but she couldn't stand the sound of others eating. Indoors it was intolerable, but out here she'd lose some of the grinding of the teeth against the wind in the trees. That had been one reason she'd survived as a fen farmer's wife – that pressing need to be out under the sky.

'Roger out on the boat?' he asked.

She laughed: 'Always out. You know Roger. In fact, he didn't come back last night. That's routine now.' She searched for the word. 'The latest fad. He goes out and sets the traps for eels – then stays out so he can pull them in at dawn. Apparently they run at night. And it's true, the catch is bigger – and at the full moon too. Old wives' tales turn out to be true. So he stays out a couple of days – two nights – sometimes three. Then drives the catch up to the coastal pubs and restaurants, or into Cambridge. It's crazy because he can earn a fortune. All those years trying to coax a living out of the soil and then there's one on our doorstep just waiting to be enticed into a wicker trap. Your dad always said Roger was like Toad of Toad Hall. But this one pays its way.'

Dryden looked to the distant bank of the mere. 'Where does he sleep?'

'On the boat – he takes a flask, food. Moors up near River Bank – the chapel's still above water.' Her face hardened. 'And whisky. Remember your grandad had a pewter flask?'

He smiled, nodding, but realized he'd been led into a trap.

'That's upstairs on the bookshelf – not big enough. He bought another, stainless steel. Says it keeps him warm.'

'I wanted to speak to him – to you too. About Dad.'

Sipping his tea he told her what had – possibly – happened to Jack: the secret life, the sudden death. He left aside the word betrayal. Then he told her the police thought it was identity theft. That the DNA test would settle the matter.

Con was a still person but she seemed to freeze completely as if the frame had stuck on a DVD. Dryden expected to see her face pixelate then fly apart.

'If it is Dad why would he do that, Connie? Why would he want a different life?'

She put down her mug of tea. 'Well, you don't know he did, do you? You've said the police think it's identity theft, that someone stole his identity. Why are you right, and why are they wrong? The idea that it's him, Philip. It's fanciful. Bizarre.'

'I went to see the body.'

'And did that help?' It was a cruel question and he hated her just a bit for asking.

'Not really. I don't know if it is him or not.' He shook his head: 'I'm *afraid* it's him. I've seen his house – in Ely. It could be Dad's – might be. We'll know when they get the DNA results but they're not in a hurry. Why would they be – it's just a lonely bloke killed in a car crash. They're not overly bothered who it is.'

'You should speak to Roger.'

'I will. But right now I'm speaking to you.' He'd never spoken to her like that before and he was shocked to see the tears start in her eyes.

Dryden's mobile rang, zigzagging across the tin tea tray. He grabbed it, stabbed the call button. 'Dryden.'

His aunt looked away and one of the tears fell.

It was Sam Clarke, Editor-in-Chief of Fenland District Newspapers, the group of local businessmen which had bought *The Crow* just eighteen months earlier. Clarke had an office in March, where the papers were printed. He was a distant figure in more ways than one. His interventions were rare.

'Guess what I've got on my desk, Philip?'

Dryden stood, trying to concentrate. 'A chocolate digestive?'

Clarke had played rugby union for Bedford and was built like a side of beef. Dryden had never seen his desk without food on it.

'Good try. Pasty, actually – chilli beef. And a packet of Doritos. It's the piece of paper I'm talking about.'

'My application for the editor job?'

'Well, yes. I've got that, thank you. You'll get a date and time for the interview. No. I was thinking of something else.'

'A writ?'

'No – worse. A D-Notice. Well, a digital image of one printed up to be exact. Real thing is coming by messenger.'

'Shit.' The Ministry of Defence issued D-Notices – effectively gagging orders, which editors hardly ever ignored, restricting coverage of specific stories or the publication of certain facts or images.

'Shit indeed,' said Clarke. 'And it is hitting my fan at barrister's rates. They get more in an hour than you get in a week. What am I saying – more than I get in a week.'

'One of my stories?'

'Bullseye. Hythe House – you got Mitch to take some pics too. D-Notice is the result.'

'Specifics?'

'Nothing at all about the property, the search, the personnel on site, or any speculation about what they were looking for. We can say, however, that the murder victim lived at that address. But that's it.'

'But it's a DA-Notice right?'

Clarke sniffed, impressed. D-Notices had been phased out in the 1980s. DA-Notices were broader – covering categories of sensitive information.

'DA-Notice 18. National Security.'

Dryden let the words hang in the air. 'What do we do?'

'We don't print the pictures, and we don't write a story telling our readers that the security services – and presumably Scotland Yard – have been crawling all over a house in the middle of the Fens and taking it apart brick by brick. Which is a fucker, given that it's a decent tale. Although – let's look on the bright side – we do have a murder case running. We can still run with that. So what we do is keep on it and wait for our chance. They can't block it forever. And when the DA-Notice gets withdrawn we can go back to the original story. But – in the short term – we keep away. Roads are blocked both ways, and – wait for it – there's an aerial exclusion zone, so I don't want you slipping off to hire a helicopter. Got that?'

Dryden sniffed a laugh.

'We'll speak Monday.' The line went dead.

Dryden turned back to his aunt. The call had given her a vital opportunity to order her thoughts. 'Take the dingy up at the jetty,' she said. 'The key's in the fuel tank on a string, where he always keeps it. Take it. Talk to Roger.' She caught Dryden's waterfall eyes. 'It's not my place.'

She wiped her hands on her apron and walked away.

'*It's not my place.*'

So there *was* a secret. About his own father. She knew it and Roger knew it. He felt a mixture of emotions – curiosity, humiliation and a sense of disorientation, as if he'd lost hold of his anchor. But most of all he felt excluded.

SEVENTEEN

Humph arrived at The Red, White and Blue, collected his free pint of bitter on the grounds that he could sip it and not get up again for the whole meeting, and went and took a seat on the bench behind the table marked:

RESERVED. ELY SINGLES CLUB.

The pub, a fifties roadhouse surrounded by the back streets of the Jubilee Estate, was empty but for a couple playing the one-armed bandit. A digital jukebox churned out the records people had paid for the night before after closing time but had never heard.

Humph drummed his fingers to 'Electric Warrior' by T. Rex. He'd never been to the pub before even though it was the Jubilee Estate's only alternative to the riotous Merry Monk. Give or take a hundred yards he lived a quarter of a mile away. A few more people came in: three teenagers together, close to underage, a couple and two single men. One of the strange side effects of living in a town of fewer than 20,000 people for your entire life was that you end up recognizing everyone – not to put a name to, or a job, or a place, but just in a subliminal way. Everyone is just *slightly* familiar.

This was Jack Dryden's local. Had he come to the singles club having pinned up the card in his hallway – or did he not have the guts for it? Humph didn't have the guts for it. He was only here to be nosy, to try and find that elusive up-to-date picture of Jack Dryden. He was sweating into his Ipswich Town 1961–2 First Division Champions commemorative top.

On the way in he'd passed a set of group photos of the locals on days out each summer to the coast: Lowestoft, Great Yarmouth, Felixstowe. An awayzgoose – a celebration to mark the end of summer. Humph knew that because he'd read it somewhere and he liked the word. One of the pictures had a caption with names taken from the local paper – no sign of a Jack Dryden.

He picked at his chest, lifting the stretched nylon of his top away from his skin, letting some air circulate. The movement woke Boudicca, who tried to force her muzzle between the table edge and his crotch.

The door opened and five women came in. It took them nearly eight minutes to buy five drinks – each one paying alone, each one offering the others to join the round, each one politely declining. Humph tried not to listen. They all seemed distracted, overexcited, but he guessed that they'd seen him. Given he'd just topped eighteen stone he was difficult to miss.

Humph's legs twitched as he fought back the urge to bolt. The music died and there was no more money to keep the entertainment going. In the silence he could hear the sound of a wooden hammer from the cellar and a clock on the wall ticking. He'd read somewhere that clocks don't go tick *tock* at all. They go tick tick. It's just that we can't stand the idea of an infinite series of unchanging sounds – we need a cycle, a beginning and an end – so we hear the tock. The human need for a pattern, and our fascination with mortality, alters our perception – that's what he'd read. He listened, his eyes closed. Bollocks. It was tocking all right.

The publican appeared and placed a plate of sandwiches on the table. Humph had one before anyone looked, and had time to rearrange the rest so the gap didn't show. The women walked over, smiling in a kind of communal rictus.

'Welcome,' said one, holding out a hand. 'I'm Val.'

Humph tried to stand, tipped the table, and they all grabbed their glasses. Subsiding he held up a delicate hand by way of acknowledgement. 'Humph. First time,' he added, taking his hand off the table and leaving behind a damp imprint of his fingers like four slug-trails.

When the men arrived it was better. Six men, then another three women. He listened to other people's conversations. He thought about his wife. When they'd been out together she'd orbited him as if he was a planet, and he'd been able just to be there, because everyone was watching her. Grace had been eight stone and remarkably elfin for a farmer's daughter from Manea. Their daughters had taken after her, at least physically – although he hadn't seen either of them for nearly six months, so who knows. Grace had run off with a postman and they all lived now, as a family, at Witchford, just a few miles away. Humph often drove that way, hoping he'd catch sight of one of his daughters, but he never did. If he caught sight of the postman he'd run the bastard over.

The chairman of the group was called Lionel. He was in his mid-fifties, with one of those faces that's just a single feature short of actually being handsome. In his case it was the chin, which was too big for his small, slightly pouting mouth, and made his grey eyes look weak. The one thing you'd remember if you met Lionel was the birthmark: port wine in colour, round the left eye.

Lionel tapped a glass of white wine with a teaspoon. 'I'm really sorry,' he said. 'I've got a little bad news. I'm afraid it's Paul. He rang. He's moving to Melton Mowbray.'

He'll have upped sticks for the pies, thought Humph, taking a sandwich. 'I came because a friend said it was a good club,' said Humph. 'Jack – Jack Dryden? He lived up the road. Taught kids science at home.'

No one reacted. So he hadn't had the guts.

After that things got worse. They talked about the annual dinner and dance which was held at a pub in the town centre. Humph was asked if he'd like to come and he said he'd love to and Lionel said he'd bring the tickets next time. Which was lucky, because there was no way Humph was coming back. Everyone finished their drinks but no one offered a refill. They sat there for nearly an hour and a half looking at empty glasses. Each time the flagging conversation revived Humph felt another blow to his will to live.

Then Val, clearly the leader of the women, said she had to go, which prompted a general exodus. By the time he heard the cathedral bell chime ten he was alone again at the table. The TV was on showing European football and some kids played pool in the other bar. He got himself a fresh drink and the barman moaned about the singles club.

'We've thought about chucking 'em out,' he said. 'Sat there – a glass of wine or half a bitter – how long?'

'Couple of hours, but it felt longer,' said Humph.

'One of them asked for tap water. That was it. Fucking cheek.'

The door to the loo opened and Lionel walked out. So they hadn't all gone home. 'Drink?' he asked Humph. 'I live round the corner so I'm always last,' said Lionel, his eyes drifting to the football. Something made the birthmark more vivid, alcohol, perhaps, or the heat.

They didn't go back to the singles table but sat at the bar. Lionel rolled up his sleeve revealing tattoos – thick and blue, like a Maori. 'I don't know why I bother,' he said. Now they were alone his accent had coarsened, Estuary English with an edge, and he'd pulled a pale red tie away from his neck. Humph smelt cigarette smoke and guessed that's where he'd been – out the back, topping up the nicotine levels.

'How'd you mean?' asked Humph, his bow-like lips extending to reach the lip of the pint.

'Singles. It's not singles at all – it's loners. We just meet once a week to swap loneliness.' He snorted, as if expelling cigarette smoke.

They drank. The football stopped for half-time adverts which they watched. When the second half started Lionel got a round.

He gave Humph a sly look. 'I didn't say – when you mentioned Jack – but we were friends.'

Humph tried not to jump in, appear too eager. 'You know he's dead?'

'Yeah. Only today – the name's in the paper.' He held up a copy of *The Crow*. Dryden had done a paragraph on the police issuing the name – nothing else.

'I know someone in the family,' said Humph. 'We went out to view the body today. At Manea.'

'Hell,' said Lionel. 'Rather you than me.'

'He didn't come to the club?'

'Nah. Not Jack. You think we're loners. Christ – he was his own man, Jack. He didn't do people. But he did me a favour.'

Humph's emotional intelligence was poor but he knew when to shut up.

'Five years ago I got done – GBH. I hit a kid in the Red Room one night,' said Lionel. The Red Room was Ely's nightclub, an old cinema on Witchford Road, derelict by day, desperate by night. 'Broke his jaw. I'd had a session in here first, then another there. Woke up in the cells. I didn't know what month it was.'

He rubbed the stubble on his chin. 'It's not the first time so they sent me down – six months. Lincoln. Jack wrote – once a week, like clockwork.'

Lincoln. Humph thought about the cat making a figure of eight round Dryden's legs. 'Really?' he said, genuinely impressed. 'Why?' It sounded cruel so he added: 'He must have been a good friend.'

Lionel didn't take it badly, just shrugged. 'That's what I thought. We'd talked a bit – a couple of drinks. He didn't say much. But like I knew nothing about him – 'cept he was smart. Taught kids, you know, like science. When I got the first letter I thought – right off – he's a God-botherer. But it wasn't like that.'

'So why did he write?'

'Second letter he told me. That he'd been in himself – long time ago, but he'd been in. A stretch too.'

Humph looked doubtful.

'No – he had. Believe me. I didn't believe it at first because he was tough, Jack, but not coarse.' He looked around the bar and – for the first time – Humph saw the intelligence in his eyes. 'Or bitter. It wasn't like he didn't care what other people thought of him – it was like he'd didn't know, couldn't imagine. He asked in his letter where I was – the cell, the wing. Return of post he described it – honest, you can't make it up. He knew. Like the corridor from the canteen where you can smoke 'coz they can't see you from the guard room. Or the view from the cell – the old walls, the top of the cathedral, one of those gasometer things. Things had changed sure – but not much. It's a dump, Lincoln – grotty. He'd been in.'

Lionel went to the loo and Humph took the opportunity to ask the barman what his full name was: Lionel Wraight. Ex-railway worker.

Lionel came back, doing up his zip in public. 'Jack knew the ropes all right. Prisons are all different, on the inside. He sent phone cards, fags, mags. You can use them, like a currency. I'd done field work as a kid – picking – so he said I should ask to help out in the gardens. Get out. Get trusted. He played chess. Ended up playing the guvnor. Kept his head down – and didn't do drugs, because if you do that you have to do something for them. And you don't want to know what you have to do.'

Humph knew he'd failed to keep the look of disgust off his face. 'Anyone else write?'

'Me brother – once. He lives in bloody Scunthorpe; he could have come and seen me. It's only twenty miles away. Nobody visited. Jack said he'd had letters – from home – and he said it helped. He said he liked letters, better than visits, because it was up to you when to read them. But if people came to see you, you had to deal with it then – you couldn't put it off. I think he was a bit scared of people.'

'Shy?' prompted Humph.

Lionel stood. 'But one thing had changed.' He leant in close and Humph smelt cigarette ash. 'I didn't say, right. But it was Category A when he was in because he said they was kept in solitary – and that's not Lincoln now. It's Category B. So it was a time ago and he did something a bit choice. Category A is for the dangerous, right – the violent. If you're Category A they don't turn their backs – not once. Me – I'm a puppy dog. But Jack, there was something – cool. No – icy.'

'When did it change?'

'What?'

'From Category A.'

'Why would I know?'

He went out the back to smoke. When he got back Humph was gone.

EIGHTEEN

The submerged hamlet of River Bank lay a mile and a half from the jetty, beneath nearly thirty feet of fresh water, as it had done now for four winters – each of which had been cold enough to seal the ruins under a thin layer of ice. It was the first time Dryden had been back since the day they'd opened the sluices, when he'd seen his mother's grave set in the green water, the newly planted lilies waving in the current. Four winters and four summers during which the flooded woods had rotted, the dead trees falling silently and in slow motion, unheard, while the mud slowly obscured the drove roads and fences, the cottages and the barns. Fish swam where birds had flown.

His uncle ran his nets and traps from the ruins of the village which were still above water, providing a rare fixed point on the great sheet of shifting water. Dryden headed directly for the bell tower of the little chapel. With evening gathering the wind had dropped but it still raised white horses – ragged, random, and stained green by the algae and weed in the mere. And the boat left a wake, a widening V, opening out behind him as if he was unzipping the lake. A mile out he lost sight of the jetty he'd left behind and became the moving centre of a watery world, a disc of blue, darkening to meet the dusk rising in the east.

His right hand reeked of petrol because he'd had to fish the ignition key out of the fuel tank on its line of thread, so he let his fingers trail in the water as he had done on that day when the sluices had first opened. Fresh water to him looked oilier than seawater, less easily creased by wind, thicker, perhaps, even syrupy. He felt the warmth of it too, as it tugged at his hand. Touching it to his lips he tasted how sweet it was.

An oak had stood on the edge of the village on a small island of clay in the peat. Its dead branches still rose from the water in a delicate crown. It alone had survived the four winters, but perhaps not five. He cut the engine to idle and let the boat drift through its shadows, looking down into the water. Below he saw a rooftop – one of the village's outlying cottages, the original sharp lines blurred by a layer of weed and reeds. He'd noted the peculiar quality of mere water: both clear and dense, as if he was peering into solid green glass, into which the ruins of River Bank had been set, like a village in a paperweight.

Another image from *Beowulf* came to him – the monster swimming up from the depths, mud trailing from its webbed feet – and despite himself he had to look away, up through the branches of the oak at the sky. The first faux star, Venus, was just visible.

The boat drifted on, out of the shadows, into the light and towards the chapel. He tried again to recall some detail of this lost place from his childhood and remembered a small garage and petrol station, a lone attendant sat out on a seat, a peaked cap pulled down over his eyes. Opposite, on the empty corner, a patch of grass and a bench. He'd have been ten, cycling past, thinking he could be out on the Great Plains somewhere, a cowboy in search of a waterhole. The memory made him feel like a child again, a physical jolt, as if he was back in the younger body, living in the moment of an everyday adventure.

Only the remnants of River Bank broke the surface of the new mere. The chapel and its tower, the rotting crown of the great oak, the skeleton of a metal grain silo, the single chimney stack of the Victorian villa which had stood at the centre of the village. Dryden recalled the big house's owners, given a bench set aside in honour at the harvest festival in the chapel when he'd gone one year with his parents. Lords, even then, of a manor, now subterranean. A month before the sluice gates had been opened and the village drowned the local museum at Ely had asked permission to remove the Victorian stained glass from the villa's windows. They'd shown the chapel, the great oak and the apostles. Dryden had noticed them on a recent visit when he'd done a story about a new exhibition of local fossils. One of the panes had been emblazoned with the villa's name: *Fenlandia*. And there'd been a black-and-white turn-of-the-century picture of River Bank: the villa dominating even the chapel – four-square, rooted to the spot.

He let the boat drift on towards the chapel. He could see through the west window – the glass gone, just a cave-like opening into the body of the chapel, the water flowing through, constricted, so that the mere seemed to funnel into the body of the ruin. It made Dryden's blood cool – the thought he might be drawn in. He let the boat bump against the brickwork beside the gap.

He splashed his face with the water and the noise of it almost made him miss what he thought was a lone bark of a dog. His uncle had a dog, an obedient sheepdog called Bay. His aunt hadn't mentioned the dog but he hadn't seen him at the farm, or heard him. Dryden examined the silence. A minute passed, then a single bark again, echoing out from the gaping arch of the window.

He called out his uncle's name for the first time and the barking picked up a rhythmic beat – and with it an echo, which rounded the sound, as if the dog was beneath the water. Edging the boat inside the window, using the paddle, he had to duck his head under the pointed neo-Gothic arch. Inside, the watery aisle was lit from the empty narrow windows on either side – their arches just clear of the surface. The roof was wooden, a Victorian barrel design, with pin points of light showing where the lead had been stripped on the outside. As Dryden edged the boat forwards bats swung above his head. It was his imagination, he knew, but he felt he could hear their high-pitched sonar, and he wondered if the dog could hear too.

There was still no sign of Roger's twenty-foot eel boat.

He shouted the name again and the sound seemed to ricochet off the water. The dog barked in reply.

As the boat slipped forward he looked down and saw the gliding forms of eels in the shadows, intertwining. There appeared to be hundreds, thousands, as if there was no water at all, just the eels turning over each other, a living weave, their movement seeming to carry the boat forward. He caught sight of the font below – white stone, the bowl full of slim black eels turning in a circle.

He saw the dog on a set of high stone steps which led up to a door behind the pulpit. His thin paws skittered on the stone at the edge of the water.

'Hi, boy,' said Dryden, bringing the boat in. He didn't like dogs, but they loved him, and Bay licked his hand and jumped aboard. 'Where's Roger, eh, boy? Where's Roger?' The fact that the eel boat was missing too was a comfort because it meant that his uncle had gone somewhere else to lay his traps and would return. But why leave the dog?

Dryden stepped out, taking the rope. Inside the old chapel the temperature seemed almost icy. The little lancet door was on a latch and open. 'One minute,' he said to the dog, which sat down and whimpered.

He climbed the corkscrew stairs. After three twists he passed a narrow doorway into an empty room. A rusted metal frame showed where a clock mechanism had been lodged. Turning away to continue the climb he heard a skittering and caught sight of a rat running at the foot of a wall at a supernatural speed. Breathing deeply he noted that despite its inundation the building retained that peculiar smell that is 'old church' – dust and stone and candle wax.

The room above was the old ringing chamber. The wooden roof had just one hole for a rope. Dryden thought an echo of the bell hung in the air; a kind of audible tension, imprinted now in the walls and flaking plaster.

This, he could see, had been his uncle's refuge. Rather than sleeping on the boat above the eel traps he'd slunk away here. A packing crate table held a china mug; there was a sleeping bag on one of the four pews set against the walls, and a primus stove. On a shelf stood a line of Sunday school primers. On the next his uncle's books – surely; slightly arcane texts on soil science and farm management.

And a volume of *Beowulf*. Dryden picked it up, struck by the coincidence, and by the fact that he'd always felt an empathy with his uncle – one that seemed to go deeper than their blood link.

The chamber had a single window which looked north. From this height you could see the far shore – a low hill with a spire, and to the north the whale's back of the Isle of Ely and the cathedral. The liquid mercury surface of the water was disturbed in the mid-distance by wind, which created a wide oval print of dark grey wavelets and white horses. He couldn't see below the water because the sun was on the horizon now, in the east, and the light just bounced off the surface so that it became a mirror. To the east it was nightrise, the sky darkening like a bruise, the first stars flickering into life. The gathering darkness made him cold at heart.

Nearer at hand stood the lone chimney of the sunken *Fenlandia*. He leant out of the window and looked down into the old grave-yard. The spot where his mother's grave must lie, below the silvered surface, was marked by water lilies, yellow and open.

Beside the window stood a single chair. Kneeling on it he put his head out through the arrow-slit arch and shouted Roger's name into the air. This time there was no echo.

At that moment the setting sun was eclipsed by a single cloud and the surface of the mere dissolved to reveal what lay beneath. And what he saw then he saw completely – not just an object, a story, a tragedy; he saw all of it encompassed in the one image.

The eel boat hung submerged in the green water, keel up, on the bottom of the mere, a rope rising not to the surface, but to the foot of Roger Stutton, who was motionless, a hand reaching for the surface just a few feet above his head. His mouth was open, in mid-gulp, and his eyes – dead and fishlike – caught the light.

The sun slid out from behind its cloud and wiped the image away – but not before he'd noticed a single detail: a series of three neat holes punched in the keel of the boat.

NINETEEN

A police diving unit recovered Roger Stutton's body from the waters at River Bank a few minutes after midnight. He'd been dead – according to the pathologist who attended from Cambridge – between twenty-four and thirty-six hours. Body gases had begun to fill the principal organs, causing the corpse to rise, its ascent restricted by the rope tied to the right foot. Cause of death would have to await the coroner's examination but a working hypothesis was that he drowned: his lungs had discharged fresh water and traces of weed. There were no signs of any external trauma except bruising and cuts to the ankle where the rope had bitten in – and that looked post-mortem. The boat had been lifted clear of the lake by a dredger and crane. The three holes in the starboard keel appeared to have been made with a hammer or blunt instrument – they were in a perfect line. Recovered from the lake bed were Roger's eel traps and gear, a torch and a boat hook.

The policeman who briefed Con on the flood bank had been circumspect. They were treating the death as suspicious. Clearly – a bizarre accident aside – someone had tied Roger Stutton to his boat and then sunk it. He was a plain-clothed DS, from Ely, and unknown to Dryden. He was very clean, as if he'd taken a shower before coming out to monitor the diving unit. He gave Con his card and said they'd talk in the morning, but now – right now – she should tell him if she could think of anyone who might do this. Any enemies, any arguments or violent clashes?

'He was a quiet man,' she said, and they left it at that. It was the perfect description and Dryden considered how often he was drawn to the silent, and the insular. Roger's particular charm had been to combine that silent character with the enthusiasms of a boy. But he must have had an enemy, and that enemy had killed him in the coldest blood. A business partner? A creditor? Because

that's what Roger had in his past – a long line of failed enter-
prises, half-baked attempts to keep the farm afloat.

The body had been taken to the morgue at Peterborough and
an appointment made for an official identification at noon. Dryden
had offered to make the ID but his aunt had insisted that she was
able to do it, in fact, wanted to do it; to see him again. In shock,
but unaware she was in shock, she had asked Dryden to take her
to Flightpath Cottages; she didn't think she could sleep, or rest
at Buskeybay. Then they'd made the call she was dreading – to
Laurie in Manchester. He'd wanted to drive back immediately
but she'd told him to wait. They needed to fix the funeral, get a
date. She hadn't cried until she put the phone down.

Dryden had slept but only after an hour of lying awake. Roger's
death, so soon after that of the man who called himself Jack
Dryden, was profoundly unsettling. It made him anxious, and he
considered getting his baby son from the child's room and setting
the cot at the end of the bed where he could see it. The warmth
of Laura's body was a comfort and he thought for the first time
that was why warmth was so settling, so sleep-inducing. It was
a token of life. A reassurance.

He found Con in the baby's room at six that morning, watching
the wind generator turn its vanes. The child was asleep, so still
it awakened familiar anxieties in Dryden that made him want to
touch his skin, make him move.

'Your father taught science at a big secondary modern – in
Haringey,' she said, her voice a whisper but very clear. 'That
was a matter of principle, of course. He could have got a job in
a private school. But he believed in the state system. That was
his contribution.'

Dryden's arms seemed too heavy to hold up, so he let them
drop by his sides. He hadn't been prepared for this and he didn't
think he wanted to hear it here, in his son's room.

'Look – not now. You're upset. You should rest.'

'Now,' she said. He took her to the kitchen and made coffee
and they took the cups outside and sat at a picnic table. Summer
had become a constant that year and he was not surprised to see
the blue sky and the freshness of the light at that early hour.
There had been no rain overnight so for once the humid oppres-
sion had lifted.

'It's called Kettlebury. He didn't talk about it much. It wasn't for long – two full academic years. Well, nearly two. It wasn't his choice to leave, Philip, but he felt he had to. Maybe – if it hadn't happened – they'd have taken the farm anyway, one day. But I doubt it. They went to Burnt Fen to get away from London – from the school. But he never really got away.'

'Why?' Dryden's throat was dry. The coffee was lukewarm already because the air was cool, the sun only just clear of the horizon.

'It was dropped – eventually. The whole thing. I don't know the details. It was a mess. The police were involved. Your father resigned.' She looked trapped, boxed in despite the fact they were under this huge sky.

'Just tell me.'

'Your father ran field trips. He organized one to the Scottish Highlands. A boy died. A young boy. Jack was blamed by the parents. The school suspended him. I think – talking to your mother – he blamed himself. Always.'

'The police were involved?'

'Yes. There was a chance there'd be charges – criminal negligence. As I say, I never knew the details. It was something your parents kept to themselves.'

There were, she insisted, no other details. All she knew she'd learned from Roger, who'd been told by Dryden's mother. How had the police been involved? Had his father been arrested? Held? How had the boy died?

'You said he never managed to get away from it – what did you mean?'

'It was nothing.' Con looked at him. It was just a fleeting moment but Dryden suddenly knew that if they weren't linked by family they had the capacity – between them – to really dislike each other.

'It's not nothing, is it. It's my father's life.'

'The boy drowned.'

As soon as she said it he knew he'd known, on some level where fears are made, inherited, perhaps.

'Your father was haunted by water. Attracted – then repelled. He couldn't shake the memory of it. After he died your mother talked about it – once, at Buskeybay. You were playing with Laurie in the yard. The first Christmas after Jack died.'

'What did she say?'

'She said she'd been afraid sometimes that he'd take his own life – to stop the memory. It was a thing he had to live with, Philip. But sometimes it was too much and she felt she couldn't help.'

Dryden thought then that he hadn't inherited this fear; he'd somehow taken it in in some form of emotional osmosis. Soaked it up: the lethal attraction of water. And then he knew exactly what his mother had thought the day his father had been swept away. 'She thought he'd given up? Let himself be taken away by the water?'

'She wondered. We'll not know, will we? Ever.'

'Maybe he just wanted to get away – away from the farm, surrounded by water. Maybe he took the chance to leave us before he hurt us. He took the chance to be alone.'

They sat in silence and the pine trees shimmered in the thinnest of breezes.

'Thank you for telling me. It explains a lot.'

'They weren't unhappy.'

'I know. I don't remember any unhappiness. But there was a tension there – and now I know what it was. And that it's in me.'

He looked at the distant bank of the new mere, a mile away, hiding with its glib green facade the mass of water beyond. And another thought insinuated itself into the scheme of how things might have been. What if there was another son, what if he'd been born *before* his father went missing? Had he left one family to be with another?

'I want to bury Roger at Manea – the cemetery there,' she said, not apologizing for distracting him from his memories.

'It's all clay. I just couldn't bear a fen burial. Would you find a plot for me? I don't like to ask – while there's this . . .' She searched for a way forward. 'This uncertainty about Jack – whether this man is him. I know it must be filling your mind – but could you find time for this?'

'Of course.'

'And the view's good and I'll have to visit and it's got a station,' she said. 'The place is desolate but he's not going to be worried – is he? Although it's true he never loved the Fens – not like Jack.'

Dryden thought about telling her to let it be. That she had plenty of time to think about burials. But perhaps it was her way of grieving. Or her way of avoiding more questions about Jack.

The air rumbled across the fen as if there was thunder under a clear sky. They watched a heavy fuel-tanker taking off from Mildenhall – ten miles distant, rising up like a whale surfacing.

She sighed. Dryden remembered then what day it was – the day after this woman's husband had died. He'd already pushed her too far. He got her fresh coffee. Put his arm round her.

She shook her head. 'Roger liked trees too much to love the Fens,' she said. 'Oaks, sycamores, birch, walnut. Trees you don't see here.'

They looked around. Apart from the windbreak of pines the nearest copse was spruce. A lone, shapeless, blackthorn. 'If you can find a nice tree at Manea that would be the spot. Although they're regimented now, cemeteries. Like caravan sites. But we can try. Would you do this for me? He'd have been grateful too.'

She seemed to force herself to look at Dryden. 'He was very fond of you, Philip. You'll know that. I'd like you to have his watch – the compass watch, your father's watch. It was a gift – but now I think it should go back to you.'

Never a materialistic person he considered the watch, the memory of it, and was shocked how much he wanted it on his wrist. He had a craving to touch it as vivid as thirst, or hunger. And to hold it, watching the compass needle swing to the north. But now he recalled that fleeting image of Roger's body, reaching for the surface of the mere, and felt sure the wrist was watch-free.

TWENTY

The railway station which bore the town's name – Manea – was two miles beyond its last house, out on the black soil, a halt marked by a single wooden building. It looked like the set from a western. Tumbleweed Town. Dryden watched the Peterborough train set off west until it slipped from sight. There was silence but for the wind rattling the level-crossing gates. A mile away a goods train trundled towards the station on a spur-line: then stopped, carriages screeching with rusted couplings.

Walking to town he decided he should have rung Humph, despite it being Saturday morning. The cabbie always marked the beginning of the weekend with a lie-in, usually in the cab, parked down by the river in a shady spot, followed by a slap-up Full English. Instead Dryden had let Con run him into town on her way back to Buskeybay. Then he'd got the train. But he should have called Humph because this was going to take half an hour just to walk into the town. And in the Fens half an hour was an eternity of straight lines.

A car swept past at seventy, picking up speed towards the thirty mph sign. A single roadside house flew the Confederate flag. Then he saw it and realized why – subconsciously – he'd chosen to walk. A single bunch of cheap flowers in cellophane tied to a lamp post, the verge still scarred where Jack Dryden's van had slewed off the road and into the ditch, and the grass black, burnt back to the black earth. It was a thought that he'd avoided but now carried its own comfort – it was the ditch that would have killed him, not the fire. That was the point about fen roads. You were belting along at seventy mph, or eighty, and then the road started to buckle under you, a sinuous dip sending the wheels off the ground. Then you lost the road and flew into the ditch – ten feet wide, full of water. And it didn't matter what you hit: the far bank of the ditch or the water itself. The end result was the same. Your body went from seventy mph to zero in less than two seconds, and the forces involved in that tore you apart, not on the outside, but on the inside. He wouldn't even have felt the flames.

The card said: 'In Heaven Now', and was signed 'From No. 135'. There were two houses opposite the crash site – and he could see 134 in big numbers on the off-pink stucco. He thought it was a good thing to do even if they were God-squad. Perhaps he'd leave a tribute too, although he couldn't begin to think what he'd say. In a strange and disturbing way he had come to care less about the identity of this man who had died on a lonely road and more about the identity of his own father *before* the day he'd been washed from the flood bank. What kind of man had he been? The idol that Dryden had made of him as a boy – or an idol with a fatal flaw? How had he failed in his duties as a teacher on that field trip? Dryden had already used his iMac to try to Google up a newspaper report of the story from the time but there had been nothing online. It was nearly forty years ago. He'd have to go back to the borough records, track down dates and times. He'd go to London when this was over, go alone.

Walking, he used the mobile to call Sgt Cherry in the coroner's office. There was still no news on an official cause of death for Roger Stutton or from the lab on the DNA match with the man who'd died right here, on the road to Manea. Dryden said his visit to the victim's house had been inconclusive. Cherry promised he'd text the results when he had them.

Dryden reached the town sign. 'Welcome to Manea,' he said out loud. 'Twinned with Chernobyl.' He'd made the second bit up, but he enjoyed his own jokes, and he took care to pronounce the town name correctly in fen-fashion, so that it rhymed with Ely, the long *ee* a relic of Roman occupation, signifying the town stood on an island.

Manea wasn't ugly just odd, haunted by its own dead-ended-ness. Not a bad place, Dryden thought, to be buried. There was a strange mound in the centre, man-made, egg-shaped, and he recalled a story of some crackpot seventeenth-century plan by the king to turn the place into a port – thirty miles inland, close to the new artificial rivers built by the Dutch. A project, like the town itself, that came to nothing.

There was a Spa shop by the church, partly obscured by a tractor with giant wheels caked with dry peat. There was a video-hire shop that appeared to be closed and a pet parlour which seemed to be open. There was a hairdressers' called Curl Up And Dye. There was a pub whose windows were crowded with DIY signs advertising Happy Hour, vodka chasers and As-Much-As-You-Can-Eat suppers on Mondays. It was one of those buildings which even now, on a blazing hot fen day when you could taste dust on your lips, seemed to radiate the damp of winter.

He walked quickly through the little square and was struck by the idea that if anyone spoke he'd be unable to understand the language. The Fens had that quality of being not here, not now, of providing that small jolt you always get when you wake up in a country that isn't your own.

The cemetery was on the edge of the town, beyond a cluster of farm buildings and a brace of ugly MFI-style warehouses which seemed to be for storing grain. The whole town rested on a spit of clay – the remnants of a fossil river-bed – and the cemetery had taken up the last half-mile. Beyond a neat brick wall he could see neater gravestones, gravel drives, and a backdrop of poplars. Flowers filled a low bank, an arrangement of blooms picking out the word GRANDMA.

The crematorium was fifties built, of a utility design with all the grace of a toilet block on a camp site. But beyond it was what looked like a caretaker's house: stately, late Victorian, but rendered stark by a lack of curtains and an ugly information board showing a plan of the cemetery like a Tube map for the dead. A metal sign stuck in the flower border pointed to the house and said: Office.

Dryden walked in through an open door. There were no carpets and the floor boards were unpolished. The hallway smelt of tomato plants and oil – the source of the latter being obvious: a motorbike stood on the lino blocking the way forward to the kitchen. Dryden knew it was not any old bike but a Harley Davidson, the model spelt out in a fluid gold script: Electra Glide. It was probably second hand but still must have cost a cool £20,000. The bikes were a local fad. William Harley, one of the founders, was the son of a fenman who'd emigrated to the Mid-west in the 1900s. Dryden had covered several of the annual Harley Davidson conventions held in late summer. Strings of bikes roared across the flatlands, the riders trailing greying ponytails.

There were footsteps down the stairs – two at a time – and a man appeared drying his hands with a J-Cloth. He was thirty-five, perhaps forty, with one of those buoyant chests that men get if they do lots of exercise to expand their lungs – running, squash, rugby. Or joining the Army. But he had long, well-brushed black hair and wore jeans and a T-shirt for the Ely Folk Festival. The smell he brought with him was a cliché too: cannabis, an unmistakable earthy tang.

He smiled with the confidence of someone who thinks they have charm. 'She's beautiful, right?' he said, caressing the fuel tank and offering his spare hand. 'Billy Johns.'

'She *is* beautiful,' said Dryden, wondering about the gender, thinking that the object didn't radiate anything feminine to him.

'Yeah. Great thing about the Fens – especially out here. Great bike country.'

Dryden had thought before that the Fens were essentially a US landscape-mathematical, Great Plains-flat. Easy Rider country.

They went into the office which held a single security video screen, a safe, a locked filing cabinet – or rather a cabinet with locks – and an empty swivel chair. Dryden noted a can of Special Brew on the blotter, the tab pulled, and an unopened can of Red Bull.

'How can I help?' said Johns, his hands lose by his side, globes of knuckle on tanned stringy arms. His eyes swam slightly, green, but beneath a milky wash. Dryden wondered if he was always high.

'Philip Dryden – *The Crow* at Ely. I think Mr Dudley-Rice rang?'

'The Yorubas,' he said, looking businesslike. 'The people who lost their baby. I'm Superintendent here. It's all down to me.' He laughed at the pomposity of the title. 'Caretaker, dogsbody.'

Dryden liked him a little bit more for taking responsibility.

'Tea? Or shall we just do it. There's a burial at ten – it's dug, but I need to check things out. There's time either way.'

'Tea's good,' said Dryden because he was a reporter, and it almost always paid to take your time. The Fleet Street foot-in-the-door model was the exception, not the rule. Softly, softly was almost always better.

Johns plugged in a kettle and arranged cups. While they waited for it to boil Dryden asked idle questions. Johns had been at the cemetery for fifteen years since leaving college. His father was an undertaker, his grandfather too. He'd grown up in the business. In his own way he was still in it. He just had more freedom. His own boss, unless someone from the town hall came past, and they hardly ever did. 'Unless they're in a box,' he said. Graveyard humour suited him.

He mashed tea bags and led the way out to a bench in the memorial garden he'd clearly used earlier because there was a small iron ornamental table and that morning's *Guardian* open on the grass beside it, weighted with a piece of stone broken off a memorial – an angel's foot.

'My uncle's just died,' said Dryden. 'He lived out at Buskeybay.'

Johns watched him over the surface of his mug of tea. 'I'm sorry. Illness?'

'He was murdered. Probably.' It was the first time Dryden had used the word and it was a shock. It begged questions: like who and why. He couldn't imagine Roger creating an enemy – not consciously. He'd been so separate from the lives of others.

Johns looked like he wanted to ask a question himself but Dryden said: 'Could he be buried here?'

'Sure. It's a good place. There's no . . .' He searched for the right bureaucratic term: 'Requirements.'

'Best to be dead,' offered Dryden and they both laughed. 'There's space?'

Johns smiled. 'Yeah. Every few years we tidy up the older graves. There's a rolling programme.' He stood. 'I'll let that cool,' he said, setting the mug aside. 'Better get changed for the funeral – I'll be ready in five.'

Dryden looked out over the gravestones to the screen of poplars. Beyond lay the open fen and the levels. There was a lot of space here, and the big sky, and he'd enjoy visiting the gravestone. There might be two: if the body in the morgue *was* Jack Dryden he'd have to bury him as well. They could be close. Was there company after death? In death? He wouldn't come on grey days, when the clouds were low and indistinct. On those days the sky was like a coffin lid.

Johns came back wearing a newly laundered pair of green

overalls and clean boots, a cheap nylon white shirt and black tie, his hair neat under a cap. Aftershave obscured the cannabis.

Dryden stood, pouring the dregs of tea on the roses. 'So – the missing baby.'

They walked towards the screen of poplars and Dryden saw that as they walked the graves got fresher – from early Victorian to present day, from monumental stone to freshly dug, covered in wilting wreaths.

Dryden stopped, panning round in a field of gravestones, thinking he'd never seen so many in one place, except, maybe, for one of the Great War cemeteries in Picardy.

'Nearly 12,000,' said Johns, guessing what he was thinking. 'A lot of the graves are multiples – family graves. So a lot more in terms of the dead.'

'And the Yoruba baby – will she get a stone?'

Johns stopped a few paces ahead and turned back. 'I don't know how much of this you're gonna want. The details.'

'Just tell me everything. Please. I'll decide. Mr Dudley-Rice explained? You need to tell me what you're going to tell them.'

'Right you are. We need to get on the other side of those trees.'

They walked on through the modern section. Gothic-free and regimented. The stones, many of them gaudy modern polished marble, were set in precise rows to allow the gang-mowers through. Some of the stones had an oval picture of the dead – a modern flourish which left Dryden uneasy. It was the contrast which was unsettling, between the favourite picture, and what was beneath. A Nintendo DS had been laid on the stone of a child, the earphones of a weathered Walkman over another nearby.

As they walked Dryden felt an urge to fill the silence which seemed to be thickening, as if the air was getting denser. 'You like this job then?'

'I like peace and quiet. My own company. Yeah – it's a good job.'

Something about the explanation seemed pat. It made him wonder what the real attraction might be.

They passed a grave covered in plastic toys. 'Kids are mixed in?' asked Dryden.

'In the private burials, yeah. You pays your money – no one's bothered about the age. There's one down in the fifties section

that's just hours – two, I think. It's got the times on it like dates
you know – Born ten a.m. Died twelve noon. Parents are still
alive. They come every week. You get to know the regulars. And
the residents.' He laughed warmly, without cynicism. 'That child
was called Alice.'

The curtain wall of poplars was nearly thirty feet high and
apparently impenetrable. But at its centre was a solid iron gate
which Dryden saw was attached to a fence which ran through
the trees. Johns fumbled at a bunch of keys on his belt. The back
of his neck was clean and the skin bore an ugly, fuzzy, tattoo.

'These are the public graves,' said Johns, pushing open the
gate.

Dryden was shocked by what was beyond the trees because
there was virtually nothing: a couple of compost heaps, a few
discarded motor mowers, what looked like a standing fuel tank.
An area the size of half a football pitch, bounded by a ditch and
reeds, with a clear view over the fen. One building: a shed, with
skylights.

'So what's the difference – private – public. There's just no
stones here – that it?'

'All those we've passed are private graves. You buy 'em – well,
lease them, for fifty, hundred years. You get to say who else goes
in the plot and you get memorial rights – you can stick a stone
up. But it costs. When the poor die there's no cash, so the council
has to give 'em a burial. And that's what's in here.'

'Pauper's burial?' asked Dryden.

'We don't use the word any more,' he said, but not in an
unkind way. 'And we don't say open grave either, or common
grave. We say public burial. Euphemism. It's how bureaucrats
talk.' Johns led him over to an area of mown grass with a square,
boarded, centre, like a bit of low garden decking. 'We're replacing
these with iron lids – after what happened. It'll take another
week, maybe less. But for now, this is how it's always been.'

Dryden felt a sliver of anger then, realizing he'd been manipu-
lated by Dudley-Rice. By the time the story came out the council
would be able to say they'd taken action to make sure it couldn't
happen again. By waiting Dryden had got his story, but let them
steal back the initiative.

Johns got a crowbar from a wheelbarrow and used it to lever

up the boards. There was a grave underneath, but not coffin-shaped, this was almost square. Johns held the back of his hand across his nose but Dryden could smell nothing. The hole was dark – deep, but there was something down there. He kept staring until the greys and blacks resolved themselves into some kind of order. He could see three cardboard boxes half covered in earth and what looked like white cement.

'It's lime,' said Johns, without waiting for the question. 'It kills germs – and the smell.'

'Children?' asked Dryden, not believing him. 'There are children in those boxes?'

'Yes. Under one year of age – otherwise they go over with the adults over there.' He pointed to a similar area of decking near the far ditch.

'This is a mass open grave?' persisted Dryden. 'With three children in it?'

'No.' Johns looked at his hand as if he needed the digits to help him count. 'Fifteen so far. Decks of three. We dug it last November. They fill up – it's for the whole district. We stop six feet from the top of the pit – that's the law. Then fill it in with earth.'

'Because?'

'Because it's the digging and filling in which costs money. So we leave it open. Costs bugger all then.'

'And these kids were – what? Like – orphans?'

'Maybe. Either they're unknowns – dumped on doorsteps or waste ground, or the parents and family can't afford it, or just can't face it. So the council takes over. Has to – no choice. Statutory duty. Or they died in childbirth, perhaps, and the parents just ask the hospital to deal with the burial – that's much more common than you think because people are confused, right? They can't face the idea of arranging a funeral when they're at a birth.'

His jaw had set in a line and for the first time Dryden thought he was having trouble maintaining a professional distance from the tragedies around him.

'It's a scandal,' said Dryden. But he didn't make it sound as if it was Johns' fault.

'I guess it is. But it's a public one. It's in the annual council budget. Has been for a century or more, I'd reckon.'

Dryden knew then that Dudley-Rice had briefed him first,

given him that line to spike any idea that there had been a cover-up.

'But you're right – in this day and age. It saves money so nobody makes a fuss. That's the point really – they're here, these children, because nobody *wants* the fuss.'

'But the Yoruba baby? If she's in one of these pits why can't the parents have her back?'

'She was over here,' said Johns, walking to an area which had been turfed, but not watered enough, so that the square showed. 'Last pit. Sometimes, before we fill them in, they get disturbed. Rats. But mainly foxes. End of the winter, when everything's been cropped off the fields they get desperate for food, badgers too. But with the Yoruba's baby it was foxes. They dug round the boards, got in. You could see the prints and we got the police to take some pixs – for the record, in case.'

Dryden shook his head, the vertebra in his neck grating.

'The body was gone?'

'Yeah. Box was chewed through. She'll be out there, on the fen, what's left of her. We tried dogs but no luck.'

'Christ,' said Dryden, thinking it probably happened a lot, but they just never checked, never delved too far, just filled the pit in and moved on. So the Yorubas would never get their grave to visit. He looked round. 'And no one . . .' He wanted to say 'cares' but stopped to find something else. 'Comes?'

'Hardly ever. The pits are marked – numbered. And we've got records of who's in which. But it's not like there's anything personal. I guess people want to forget. It's like the opposite of over there – on the other side. No one comes to remember.'

'But from now on the graves will be secure – with iron covers?'

'Yeah. It'll cost. The press office's got the numbers. It won't happen again.'

So that was the story. But it didn't help the Yorubas.

'But the coffin was left – the little girl's coffin?'

'They're biodegradable. Cardboard. So not much. And a shawl. And a name tag. That's it. The police have got those.' He shook his head. 'There was some hair too – black, wispy, caught in the clasp on the tag.' Johns didn't meet his eyes.

Dryden scanned the graveyard, reluctant to leave. He noticed the shed again. 'What's in that?'

'Old mowers. Crap, really.'

If he'd told the truth so far Dryden thought that was his first lie because the padlock on the shed was catching the light – brand new, silver. And the skylights were clean, moss-free. Someone worked inside, so they needed the light. He filed the thought away.

They walked back towards the gate and out into the cemetery of stones. As Johns struggled with the locks Dryden scanned the view. There were several large, striking trees. A line of willows by the ditch, two oaks, and to one edge a great Cedar of Lebanon.

'Are there any plots left over there?' he asked, pointing at the cedar.

It was a good spot but there was no bench nearby. Johns said Dryden could buy a seat, have his uncle's name inscribed on the little brass plaque. Dryden asked if there was room for two graves and there was. Side by side. It could be a family plot, he thought. And then it occurred to him that one day he might end up here too.

Johns took a note of the code on a little white marker stuck in the grass.

'Thanks for your help,' said Dryden, offering his hand.

Johns shook it, the fingers bony and powerful. Then he took out his wallet. 'I'll give you a card in case there's any more questions – ring anytime.'

Dryden took the card but noted the contents of the wallet – a twenty-pound note behind two fifty-euro notes. 'I guess the undertakers will ring,' he said.

'Sure,' said Johns. 'That's it. And they'll arrange the stone – but there's no hurry. We leave the plot for six months to let it settle. So take your time. You can think of what to put on the stone.'

Dryden tried to imagine it. They'd put some verse from Housmann on his mother's at River Bank because *A Shropshire Lad* was her favourite. Con might want something particular but Dryden thought they could go for a line from *Beowulf* if she wanted poetry. *He crossed over into the Lord's keeping . . .*

TWENTY-ONE

The train back towards town trundled across the fen until it met the edge of the Isle of Ely at the village of Chettisham: a level crossing, a few cottages, and a grain silo topped with a Christmas Tree which stayed in place 365 days a year but was only lit in December, visible from twenty miles, flashing on and off. The station was a single platform which made the one at Manea look like Clapham Junction. Dryden had never known a train actually stop at the lonely halt, so when his did, he presumed they were waiting for the level-crossing gates to close. He dug in his pocket and found a piece of Cornish pasty in a paper bag and some wine gums. Then the internal door opened and the train driver stood aside to let DI Friday into the carriage.

'You should be watching your boys play footie,' said Dryden.

Friday asked Dryden if he wouldn't mind coming with him – they had a car and it wouldn't take long. There was not a trace or recognition, let alone warmth, in this request. Friday said they had some questions: routine, which didn't make sense because he'd just stopped a train in the middle of nowhere to ask them.

Dryden followed him back into the driver's compartment then out through the door. As he walked towards Friday's muddy Volvo he wondered if this is what it felt like being picked up by the SS. They drove off towards Ely at a speed well in excess of the limit. Dryden wouldn't have been surprised to see motorbike outriders.

'I don't suppose there's any point in asking what the fuck's going on,' said Dryden.

'Correct.'

It was an ordinary Saturday in town with the market busy, a momentary traffic jam in Market Street, HGVs lined up at the back of Iceland, but none of that could dispel Dryden's unease.

They slipped into a parking spot by the Job Centre and he followed Friday out into Market Street: a hotchpotch of pubs, two Indian restaurants, a Chinese, barbers, florist; the pavements busy with families heading for Market Square. A few doors from *The Crow* stood a showroom which had sold furniture until it went bust. It had once been The Central Hall – a one-time cinema and meeting room. The shop had been in the old foyer. The hall beyond had been used for St John's Ambulance Brigade meetings, Scouts, the odd jumble sale.

They went down a side alley and Dryden saw that the back car park was full of vehicles, all unmarked, BMWs mostly. Two of them – one of the BMWs and a jet-black Range Rover – had what looked like drivers: chauffeurs out of uniform. One was reading the *Daily Telegraph*, the other a book of crosswords.

The side door was open and led directly into the hall. It had been a very small cinema, even in its heyday. A hundred, maybe a hundred and fifty. The chairs had been ripped out but there was still a stage and some of the original Art Deco plasterwork was in place, and a single circular chandelier flush with the ceiling. It had high windows with chequered green and red glass, and internal shutters.

'Wait,' said Friday.

No heads turned. There were thirty people in the room at desks. Most had laptops open, iPhones sparkled. On the wall were scene-of-crime pictures from Eau Fen. Several officers in one corner were dressed in the green overalls Dryden had seen at Hythe House. At one desk a man in a suit was interviewing Sgt Cherry, the coroner's officer. As Dryden watched the suit tossed a file across the desk so that Cherry had to scramble to stop it falling on the floor. There was something calculated in the action, as if it was designed to humiliate.

Friday was back. 'OK. Into the breach.'

He led the way to a desk in an alcove by the side of the stage. On the far side of it sat two men who didn't get up: one was in a dark suit and tie with short grey hair, cut with the help of a slide rule. He introduced himself as Commander Daniel Mahon of New Scotland Yard, responsible for the Met's liaison with Interpol. The right lapel of his dark suit was scattered with cigarette ash like dandruff.

The other man Dryden had seen at Hythe House. Mahon introduced him as – and Dryden was able to check this with the business card he was handed at the same time – Kapten Jaan Kross of the Central Criminal Police Department of Estonia, based in Tallinn. Kross had an open-necked white shirt showing a gold chain. His hair was almost white, as – presumably – were his eyebrows, which Dryden couldn't really see against his very pale skin. He was a human being almost entirely devoid of colour. Even his blue eyes looked diluted.

Mahon apologized for the 'little drama' on the train. He said they were trying to keep their investigations as low-key as possible and that they had an 'issue' with the railway station at Ely which he said – smoothly – it would be 'tiresome' to explain.

'So – just a few questions,' he said. 'Do you recognize this boat?' It was a colour shot taken at sea of a container ship approaching docks. Dryden didn't think it was possible to identify a container ship due to the fact they were all identical.

'No – but that's Felixstowe, if you're bothered.'

Kross leant forward and seemed to examine his shoes. He had the easy, loose-limbed swagger of a thug.

'In the last few days did your uncle – Roger Stutton – give you anything?' asked Mahon. 'A parcel, a bag, perhaps – for safe keeping?'

Dryden felt his blood pressure alter, a feeling of sudden pressure behind his eyes and nose. 'Why?'

Now Mahon smiled. 'Just answer the question, please.'

'You're not getting any answers until you tell me what's going on. Is Roger's death linked to that . . .' He pointed at one of the scene-of-crime pictures from Eau Fen – the victim's body hung from the irrigator. The shot had been blown up to poster size.

'Yes,' said Mahon. 'We think it is – but we can't say anything else at this stage and anything you do take from this conversation is – I'm afraid – covered by the DA-Notice.'

'No. He didn't give me a package or a bag.'

Another picture, this time of two men standing smoking together on the deck of a white boat, a river cruiser. It was one of the modern pleasure craft that Dryden hated, what the locals called a 'white boat', with patio doors.

'And them?' asked Mahon.

Dryden took his time. He knew he didn't recognize them

but he wanted to clear his head. What they were showing him seemed to imply a narrative thread: a sea voyage by container ship, Felixstowe on the East Anglican coast, then the white boat. And a mysterious package that his uncle appeared to have obtained.

'Did they bring this package for Roger?' he asked. 'Or for him . . .' He pointed at the hanging man, the dripping corpse. 'From Estonia?'

Mahon's hand drifted towards the pocket of his dark suit and Dryden guessed that's where he kept his cigarettes. He sensed a real addict. So the longer this went on the less comfortable he'd be. Mahon took another brown envelope from the file on the desk and slid out a picture.

The smile was stillborn on Dryden's face. It was a white van, the front half a write-off, the interior burnt out. The landscape was flat but there was a one-carriage train approaching from a distance. Dryden's throat went dry. 'Is this the van . . .'

'I'm sorry,' said Mahon. 'You won't have seen this. Yes, this is the van in which Jack Dryden died. Whoever Jack Dryden is.'

Dryden could hear his blood beating now in his left ear. Had it occurred to him there might be a link between Jack Dryden's death and Roger Stutton's? It should have. And now both were connected to the victim of Eau Fen.

'There's a DNA test . . .'

Mahon sat back. 'Yes. We've fast-tracked that so we should know very soon. The case has now been taken forward with the urgency it deserved. A slight hiccough. That has been remedied.'

Dryden glanced at Sgt Cherry who was alone now, with a cup of tea, his head down but his eyes looking round the room.

Kross leant forward and looked past Dryden – or more accurately through him. 'This does not matter to you – I am sure of this. I think this is not your father, this man who dies in the fire. Really – not. I think this man who died took your father's name, and gave himself a new name. This is a valuable . . .' He searched for the word. 'Commodity. A life. Many people will pay for this – perhaps £50,000. So please answer our questions.'

Dryden had thought about someone stealing his father's

identity, but he hadn't thought of that – that someone might have *sold* it.

He looked again at the picture of the burnt-out van. 'Was this an accident?'

The Estonian was nodding and Mahon failed to keep the irritation from registering on his face.

'Yes. An accident. But this begins everything,' said Kross. 'And now it must end. But how?'

Mahon cut in: 'When did you last see your uncle?'

'Sunday – for lunch, at the farm.'

'Not since?'

'I understood the question.'

A smile creased Kross's thin pale lips.

'Why did you take Hythe House apart – was it to find this parcel, this package?' asked Dryden.

'You must be careful, please,' said Kross. 'There are people who want this package we mention very much. If you know anything – at any time – phone us.' He put a finger on his business card. 'The mobile is here. Always.'

'Is that why he died?' asked Dryden, pointing at the picture of the hanging body of Rory Setchey. 'They shot him, why? Because he had this parcel?'

Kross licked his lips, shrugged. 'They shoot this man after he is dead.'

Mahon put a hand over his eyes.

'So how'd he die?' asked Dryden.

Kross touched a hand to his heart.

'He had a heart attack – then they shot him?'

Kross rocked his head from side to side. 'We think maybe one shot – to the knee. First. Perhaps they want an answer to a question. But then the stress . . .' He touched his heart again. 'The pressure. If these men ask you a question they expect an answer very quickly. Silence makes them angry.'

He got up and walked away. Mahon packed up the file.

'Is that it?' asked Dryden.

'Looks like it.'

'How does that work, then? Does an Estonian Kapten outrank a Met Commander these days?'

'I'm doing my bit for EU relations,' said Mahon. Standing,

his width seemed to outrank his height. He gathered his thoughts. 'Thanks for coming in. If we can tell you anything we will. I'm afraid all that's covered by the DA-Notice. Sorry.'

He already had the cigarettes out of his pocket, tapping the filter end on the packet.

'And more bad news. Your aunt, Constance Stutton. She stayed with you last night, I understand. You should go to her farm now. There's been a burglary. Or – what do our American cousins call it – a house invasion. Thank Christ she wasn't there. They did the place over. If you think that house we took apart was bad . . . The farm's a wreck. I think it's pretty clear they thought your uncle had what we're looking for. What we're all looking for.'

TWENTY-TWO

The farmyard at Buskeybay held two police cars, a black Volvo estate and the forensic unit van from Ely. Con was waiting for them, stoic, her hands thrust into an apron. When the car stopped she went to Laura's side and took the child, holding him under her chin, the head cupped.

'You OK?' asked Laura, the nasal tones urgent, frustrated.

She tried to say she was fine but the words wouldn't come so Laura hugged her.

The farmhouse looked like it had been hit by a twister. The curtains in the upstairs bedrooms hung out of open windows. Bedspreads, blankets and duvets were tumbled out in the yard or hanging from sills. Large pieces of old furniture had been dragged out or thrown from upstairs – wood shattered across the yard. The front door was off its hinges and Dryden could see that some of the floorboards were missing from the hall. A safe that his uncle kept in the back office was on the path, split open, the ragged edges scorched by what looked like a welding rod.

The police and forensics officers picked their way amongst the mess.

'You came back to this?' said Laura, rubbing Con's arm.

'I'm all right,' she said, but tears spilt from her eyes. 'But *why?*'

'Inside?' asked Dryden.

'Ransacked. But I can't find anything gone. Broken, ruined, but not gone.'

Her shoulders turned in slightly, as if her chest was hollow, and Dryden realized she'd aged. Not overnight, because he'd seen her at breakfast, but here – now, within a few hours, as if the sight of the house had consolidated all the anguish of what had gone before. Made it real, made it physical.

'I'll make tea,' she said, walking briskly to the side of the house and in through the old conservatory door, with Laura following. The baby cried and the sound, the noise amplified by the glass house, sounded oddly feral.

'I've made a start in here because they said they'd finished,' said Con. The kitchen was Dryden's favourite room. His parents had modernized the one at Burnt Fen but this was still the original. The stone floor was uneven, chilly on the hottest day. The pantry room was still in use, the door open, the floor scattered with tins and jars.

'The burglars looked everywhere?' asked Dryden.

'No.' Con stopped, her back to them, the kettle poised under the tap. 'They didn't. I've been checking – they threw things about, but if they bothered to open something it was this size.' She turned her hands held a foot apart. 'Maybe more.'

'What do they say they're looking for?' asked Laura. Above them they heard something heavy being dragged over the boards.

'They don't. But why – why here, Philip?' It was almost an accusation.

'They think that someone killed Roger to get something – a package, a parcel.' Then, in his memory, he saw something he'd missed out in the yard when Humph had parked the cab: one of the forensic officers working his way along a line of rain butts. He'd called out for someone to help him tip one up. 'Something waterproof,' he said.

'They went up into the attic first,' said Con. 'Cut the water off.'

Dryden nodded. 'Maybe he found it – this package – out on the mere. In his nets?'

The kitchen door edged open and Con looked up and Dryden knew she expected to see Roger and the disappointment, when she saw the white-suited forensic officer, was impossible to hide. They were cutting off the water again, he said, to look in the spare tank.

They discussed the details for Roger's funeral. The inquest, said Con, was scheduled for the Wednesday but they'd told her it would be adjourned. It might be some time before they could issue the paperwork for the death certificate. But they could see the undertakers, start arrangements, and Dryden told them about the burial plot he'd found under the Cedar of Lebanon and how he'd like to buy a bench for the spot.

'Good. I can start on the paperwork,' said Con. 'It'll keep me busy. We'll need his birth certificate – papers. They're in the barn.' She looked at Dryden. 'Would you? They're up in the hayloft with everything else. They had a look out there – the police; they'll search it later, but they said they were pretty sure it hadn't been touched.'

Dryden was going to object, point out that this wasn't the time for paperwork, but she held both hands out, palms down, fingertips up, as if warding away the thought. 'I need to do something Philip, please.'

The old barn wasn't by the yard but separate, about half a mile away, along a narrow causeway raised above the peat. Roger had a theory that the original farm had been out there, on a narrow spit of clay, but that they'd moved to a new clay bank to build the present farmhouse in the 1880s. The old was pitch-black wood, a Dutch gable. Outside Roger had stowed the gear for his market gardening business – polytunnels, propagators, and a small-scale irrigation hose. Everything was neat, in its place. Beyond the barn was the field he'd used for the car-wrecking business. Chasses piled two or three deep and the metal cruncher in the far corner. Dryden didn't like the place because you could always hear the rats. Roger said they bred in the upholstery of the cars.

In the sudden shadows inside the barn Dryden let his eyes piece the familiar images together. In the Second World War Italian PoWs had been billeted at Buskeybay and they'd built a theatre here in the barn – you could still see the remnants of a painted Proscenium Arch under the hayloft. On the far wall was the sketchy outline of a Tuscan landscape – single dark green firs, olive trees and a domed church. Dryden had played here as a boy. The place had held a kind of stage magic, as if all the drama played out within it lingered in the wood. Sadness too – the most enduring kind of sadness – homesickness. It made him shiver even now in the heat of the day, the thought of the Italians huddled in here on a misty fen winter's night.

After Dryden's mother had died and New Farm had been sold, Roger had agreed to store the family's stuff that Dryden couldn't use on the boat – he didn't have much space, so he took a few pictures, an old corkscrew of his father's, his mother's secateurs from the window ledge by the kitchen door. They'd got rid of almost all the rest at auction. The dregs – furniture, books, the papers – they'd put up in the hayloft. Only a week before Roger had said he should come by, see if there was anything they'd like for the new house.

The boards of the half-loft had been swept and two long rolls of roofing material piled along the back wall. But in one corner stood five objects Dryden recognized: a set of golf clubs, a weathered cardboard box that he knew contained a Hornby 00 train set, a kite, a Spanish guitar and a trunk he'd used as a toy box as a child. Opening it now he smelled old paper – it was full of documents and files. He sat back on his heels. It was nearly twenty years since he'd last had a cigarette but he felt the need now, quite urgently, because if he had one he could prolong the moment.

The deeds for Burnt Fen – at least copies – lay on top. He picked up a bundle of papers and they fell from his hands, slewed across the boards.

He saw the edge of a newspaper cutting and pulled it out. It was from the *Barnet Times*.

TEACHER SUSPENDED OVER DEATH OF BOY ON SCIENCE FIELD TRIP

A teacher blamed by parents for the death of their eleven-year-old boy on a field trip to Scotland has been suspended and faces questioning by the Metropolitan Police.

Toby Michaels, of Arkley, Barnet, is understood to have drowned in a lake in the Highlands watched by classmates from Kettlebury Secondary Modern who were unable to save him.

A spokesman for the county council said teacher John Dryden, who organized the trip, was not able to swim.

Strathclyde police confirmed Mr Dryden was airlifted from the scene and is in Blair Athol hospital. A spokesman confirmed he is suffering from shock. The rest of the school party was unharmed and returned home by coach.

It is understood Toby was a keen swimmer but got into difficulties after diving into the lake from rocks. His body was finally recovered by a Search and Rescue diving unit.

Mr Arthur Michaels, Toby's father, said in a statement issued by the family's solicitor: 'We demand an inquiry into the tragic death of our wonderful son.

'In particular we must be told why the boys were left in the care of Mr Dryden – who the school have confirmed was a non-swimmer. He just stood there and watched my son die.'

The accident happened at Black Top Tarn below the summit of Ben Cracken, near Fort William. It is an area visited by school trips studying glaciation. On the day in question a heavy mist had descended on the mountain until late afternoon, when the weather cleared.

A spokesman for the Metropolitan Police said: 'We will be interviewing everyone concerned with this tragic accident on their return to London. Our thoughts are with the family of Toby Michaels.

'Following interviews we will assess the case and consider whether a file should be sent to the Director of Public Prosecutions.'

It is understood the family of the dead boy are pressing for a prosecution for criminal negligence. Mr Michaels is managing director of Barkley Homes, the building firm based in Barnet which employs nearly 150 people.

Dryden's legs had gone to sleep so he stood up, holding the cutting. It was the phrase 'watched my son die' which made him wonder how his father had dealt with the stress, the blame. But the dark heart of the story – the moment when the boy drowned – was still within a black box. Why had Toby Michaels drowned if he was a good swimmer? Why had his father agreed to lead the trip if he couldn't swim?

The newspaper cutting at least gave him a precise date. He was confident he could track down other articles, get a fuller picture; he owed his father that, whether he was the man who died in the floodwaters of 1977 or the man who died in the white van at Manea only last week.

Dryden put the file aside and picked up the next marked ROGER in red capitals. The birth certificate was on the top – all the papers held by a bull-clip. Born April 3, 1951. Hammersmith Hospital. Father's profession listed as school teacher, mother's as office worker. The bull clip slipped and the papers spilt on the floor so he picked them up at random: an HGV licence, an old passport with one corner snipped off, a degree certificate: a 2:1 in natural sciences from Cambridge.

Then he saw his mother's writing, a schoolteacher's hand, clear and unfussy, on a single brown padded envelope which had been sealed but opened. Inside were her own documents and his father's. He held their marriage certificate – the original. And his mother's birth certificate, but not his father's. Had it been in the envelope when sealed? His mother's death certificate was there too: original – the cause of death oblique, lost in Latin.

And then something he didn't expect: his father's death certificate. The original.

'That's not right,' he said, out loud, the noise startling a bird on the roof, which clattered away. If there had been a death certificate there'd have been no life after 1977: no state pension, no medical card, no dental records, no bank account, no driving licence. How could someone have pretended to be Jack Dryden – or indeed – *been* Jack Dryden – after 1977, if there had been a death certificate? The certificate meant he was officially dead.

Dryden smelled the paper: it reeked of the pre-digital age and had been issued at Swaffham Prior Register Office six months after his father had been swept away off Welch's Dam. Five months after he'd first gone with his mother to see the registrar, Philip Trelaw, and been told they had to wait for the body to be found. But the body had never been found. So how could there be a certificate?

And then he thought he remembered something else. That as he'd shook Trelaw's hand that day as a seven-year-old he'd thought: *I shall meet this man again.*

TWENTY-THREE

he Crow's library was called the 'morgue' like all newspaper libraries. The centrepiece was a wooden cabinet with little drawers marked with a single letter of the alphabet. Inside was an index of small brown envelopes, each one a person, each one containing clippings from *The Crow* – or its sister paper the *Ely Express* – or from other local or national newspapers. There was one item for Trelaw. A story taken from *The Crow* for 1979 – two years after Jack Dryden's 'death'. The registrar had complained about the conduct of two families from Littleport who'd turned up for a register office wedding in Swaffham.

In the quiet of the morgue Dryden read out the key paragraph: 'Clearly one gets used to the groom and best man being – possibly – slightly jolly,' said Mr Trelaw. 'I don't suppose a glass of champagne before the event does too much harm. But these people were partying – several brought cans into the ceremony and someone was sick in the civic suite. I like dancing but I think it is inappropriate before the ceremony, let alone during it. We cannot condone this kind of behaviour so I refused to complete the ceremony.'

'Good for you,' said Dryden. Attached to the clipping was a paragraph from *The Sun* based on the same item.

The Crow couldn't afford a librarian – even part-time – to keep things up to date, a problem which undermined its reliability. They had past copies on microfiche and both the papers were now held digitally on a database. But the three systems not only overlapped, they missed each other out, creating blind spots in the record.

He went back to his own desk and flipped open the diary. His only appointment for the weekend was that evening out on Petit Fen to meet Sheila Petit and he could do that on the way home. So he had time – time to dig. He fired up his iMac laptop. He hadn't been in the office for several days so a pile

of post stood two-feet high in his tray, roughly mimicking the
tilt of the Tower of Pisa. It didn't bother him. News arrived by
email these days, or text, or flashed up on to a website. The
post was largely irrelevant except for fat official surveys or
government reports.

The blinds were down on the bay window into Market Street
so he had his desk light on. The office was always locked up on
Saturday but the front counter stayed open and he could hear
voices down below through the floorboards. Outside, close by,
he could hear a busker singing 'Yesterday'.

He fed 'Trelaw' into the digital database for *The Crow* and
got a lot of articles on a local bowls player who'd got through
to the world championships in Preston. A picture appeared across
two columns: a thin man, with weak arms and an old face.
Certainly not the Trelaw he was looking for. The search put up
nearly fifty items and he was on the ninth page when he saw a
one par filler on the appointment of a new registrar at Burwell
to replace Philip Trelaw – who was looking forward to taking
up another appointment with West Fen District Council – the
exact nature of which wasn't specified, which made him think
Trelaw's enthusiasm might be manufactured.

The next item mentioned the same Trelaw – now described
as the 'former registrar of the East Fens'. He stood beside a
gleaming classic Rover – grey, polished like a diamond, with
an AA insignia in the front grille. The story said Trelaw had
set up a club for Rover owners with the P4 model living in
the Fens, and already had 100 members. This was the man
Dryden had seen that day at Swaffham Prior – big, bony, with
sloping shoulders. The article referred to Trelaw as a security
officer for the district council.

The council site had a list of staff and Trelaw was listed under
CCTV unit. There was a direct line so he had a desk job, and
the address was the town hall in Ely. He put CCTV into the
council search engine and got a page which outlined the service.
In Ely there were thirty-six high-definition public cameras: black
globes of glass on posts sprouting spikes to stop offenders snapping up the ultimate souvenir of a drunken night out – a security
camera. The screens were 'live' 24/7 – although the site didn't
claim they were filming 24/7. The pictures were monitored by

staff, one of whom was present at all times. Dryden had an eye for this kind of equivocation – note *present*, so not necessarily viewing the CCTV.

The page stated under 'history' that the unit had opened on January 1, 2008 – just in time to miss any trouble over New Year's Eve. He wound up the microfiche machine and got the *The Crow* for the first week of that year. There was an article on page three showing the unit in operation, a staff of eight, Trelaw in the background.

Dryden went back to his desk to take a note of the number for CCTV. As he did so he saw that the parcel holding up his tower of post had the name and address of the sender on the side in capital letters:

ROGER STUTTON
BUSKEYBAY FARM
NEAR ISLEHAM
ELY
CB6 6GY

It was dated the day before he'd found Roger's body. Posted at Ely.

He couldn't stop himself looking round the room. The window's blinds were shut, the door closed, but he stood to make double sure by locking it from the inside.

Had two people been murdered for this parcel? For what lay inside?

The idea of just taking it to the incident room, to Kross and Mahon, never entered his mind. The extent to which he'd been excluded from the investigation was an insult he found it difficult to forget. After all, it had been his uncle who died out at River Bank, and it might be his father whose death had, according to Kross, triggered the whole series of events. Why shouldn't he look first, then report to Kross? The package was addressed to *him*. And sometimes curiosity is a force of nature.

It was eighteen inches long and otherwise nine-inch square in cross-section, like a CD box set but bigger. Dryden tore the paper off but when he saw the next layer of material – that greasy waterproof pouching fishermen use for wallets – he knew his uncle had probably found it out on Adventurers' Mere when he was laying his traps.

The busker outside had been through his repertoire and was back with 'Yesterday'.

There was a single piece of loose paper in the package with the words FOR SAFE KEEPING written in hurried capitals. And the note triggered a sound – his uncle's voice on the telephone that last time: 'Come to think of it – I have a mystery for you.' He'd tell him when he saw him. But he never saw him.

With a pair of scissors Dryden cut open the oiled plastic package to reveal within a whole series of smaller packages – like the individual DVDs in the box set, but fatter, and supple. He counted them out – twenty-five. Each envelope could be opened like a CD wallet. Each had a name on the front in capital letters in a Gothic black script.

PAUL ROBYNS, JAMES EWART, PETER RADCLIFFE. He flicked on, somehow sensing that this was important, this small act of thoroughness.

Then he saw a name that stopped his fingers moving: SAMUEL SETCHEY.

He thought of Rory Setchey hanging from the irrigator. A rare name, even in the Fens.

He flipped up the envelope lip and slid out the contents on the desk top:

One British passport.

One UK driving licence with no points.

One medical card complete with full National Insurance number.

A debit card issued by NatWest Bank.

A cheque book for the same account.

A Barclaycard.

A birth certificate. September 8, 1986.

All were in the same name: Samuel James Setchey. The picture in the passport showed a middle-aged man with very dark hair and a stubbly beard. Age – working forward from the birth – was twenty-five. Rory Setchey had died aged forty-four.

He put the documents back in the envelope and neatly returned it to the package. There was a life here, a life in paper. An *identity*. He knew it was part of the reason Rory Setchey had ended up as roadkill.

Holding the package he tried to work out what it might be worth. What did a new identity cost? Kross had said £50,000. But this was much more than a new identity; it was everything that went with it. How much would that be worth – times twenty-five?

He recalled the Estonian word for million. *Milte.*

But how? Who were these people? Why didn't they need their lives any more? Were they, had they been real people? Real people like his father. This made him think that he wasn't going to get what he'd always secretly wanted – another thirty years of his father's life. Surely Jack Dryden's life had been stolen too. Did he really need a DNA test to prove it?

There were heavy footsteps on the stairs, the doorknob rattled. Humph's outline was clear through the misted glass panel. Dryden had left the cabbie with his wife and child at a coffee shop off Fore Hill.

He unlocked the door and was shocked by the cabbie's face, which seemed to have succumbed to a greater force of gravity so that his chin and fleshy neck appeared to fall to his chest. Humph was good on his feet, nimble even, but as he stood there he staggered to one side as if the floor had tilted.

'Someone's taken the baby,' he said.

TWENTY-FOUR

The baby had been in his pushchair on Three Cups Alley while Laura and Humph had coffee in the open-air seating area of the little café. Only a low wall and a set of railings stood between them. They could see him, or at least the pushchair, from where they sat. They could almost – Humph had said – touch him; already, Dryden thought, subconsciously starting to prepare a defence. It was a Saturday market day and the path had been crowded with shoppers, strolling between them and the child, breaking the line of vision. They didn't discover he was gone until they'd paid and left: not only the baby was gone, but also the cradle inside the pushchair, the shawl, and a soft toy – a black cat.

'How long?' he asked, standing on the pavement outside *The Crow*.

Humph made a huge effort not to shrug. 'We were there twenty minutes – so that's the worst case. But it might have been seconds. Laura's checking the car parks and the riverside.'

'OK. Go to the taxi rank,' said Dryden, stepping close to Humph. 'Tell them what's happened. See if you can get it out on the radio. Then try the market. I'll do the cathedral grounds – the park. And ring the police – give them my mobile.' They looked at each other and Humph went to speak. 'Go,' said Dryden.

Dryden crossed the road to the Oxfam shop, slipping past the rows of freshly laundered second-hand clothes and up a stair to an office: The Hypothermia Trust. Vee Hilgay was at her desk filling in forms. He told her what had happened and even he could tell his voice was cold, unstressed, almost brutally matter-of-fact.

'Sit down, Philip,' she said.

He didn't even hear her. Vee got up and put on her jacket and said she'd check the bus stops, the bigger shops – Tesco, Waitrose, Wilkinsons, Iceland.

She took Dryden's hands. 'It'll be OK. You're in shock.'

'No, I'm not,' he said, turning away and walking down the carpet-less stairs. But there was something wrong with his hearing because it was a bit like being underwater. Everything was just slightly further away, as if behind glass.

He felt a profound urge to find Laura, as if touching her would close the circle and they'd be all right again. But that wasn't right.

He walked out into the cathedral close and felt his knees give so that he had to sit down on a bench. Tears filled his eyes until he blinked them away. It wasn't grief, or anger – it was frustration. They had a chance, still had a chance, if his son was still in the town, not bundled into a car and gone.

He sent a text to Humph, his fingers vibrating.

RAILWAY STATION RANK. TELL THEM.

If he could find him everything would be all right. Not just today, but forever. It was as if his life, all their lives, hung on these few seconds he was living through. He forced himself to move before the effort became too much.

There was a family on a picnic rug by the Lady chapel, in the pinnacle-shadow. Trying not to sound desperate he asked them if they'd seen a baby in a cradle – one of those modern ones from a pushchair – in green plastic. He'd have been carried by a man, he guessed, but just possibly a woman.

Saying it all out loud made it more real.

The woman looked shocked and covered her mouth but the man was smiling and couldn't stop. 'You're kidding,' he said.

Dryden walked away. He tried everyone on the benches. A group of teenage girls, two pensioners, a young boy struggling with two dogs. Nothing. He followed the path round the apse and found a man examining the gargoyles above with binoculars: a scaly fish, a dragon, and the modern additions – a skinhead, a builder picking his nose. Dryden was about to ask him if he'd seen anything when the mobile buzzed and his body began to celebrate – adrenalin flooded out, making his vision blur.

NOTHING YET. It was from Laura. He sent back a single X. Then Humph: STATION RANK UP TO SPEED. POLICE ON IT.

He turned to go.

'Did you want to ask a question?' said the man with the binoculars.

Another text. POLICE AT THE CAFÉ. From Vee.

'Sorry,' said Dryden, feeling trapped. He thought he had spoken, but clearly not. 'Time's important,' he added. And it was: he knew the statistics even though he was trying to blot them out. Every minute that passed made it less likely they'd find him alive. Less likely they'd find him ever. 'I'm looking for a child in a cradle – someone's taken him.'

'I saw a bloke with a car seat cradle,' he said. 'He went in there.' The man pointed at the South Door of the cathedral.

'You saw him go in?' asked Dryden, distracted by the thought that it didn't sound likely, that you'd watch someone for that long, until they disappeared.

'I was coming out – it's a newborn, right? I've got one too, so I looked.'

Ten seconds later Dryden pushed open the oak portal set in the great door. Inside was part of the old cloister – cool and silent. He walked slowly because he thought quite consciously that this was it – he'd have one chance, one opportunity to avoid a tragedy that would ruin his life. Laura's life.

He wrote a text as he walked: CATHEDRAL, QUICK, then sent it to Humph and Laura.

The second door stood beneath a series of Norman arches, richly decorated, and lit by a spotlight. He pushed it open and stepped over a wooden and iron threshold into the body of the church. He was struck by the contrast: he was searching for a small child in a vast space, echoing and full of light. A group of visitors stood at the West Door by the candles waiting for a tour to begin. But the nave was empty – even the chairs were gone. Under the lantern a stage had been built for a concert. He listened very carefully to the silence, examining it for a cry. Despair washed over him so that he couldn't move his legs.

Then a child's voice, and a toddler suddenly appearing under the lantern and pointing up at the Octagon above. That seemed to unlock Dryden's legs. He walked towards the high altar and the choir. Tombs here, gaudy, Tudor and Georgian, with painted figures of the deceased reclining in stone. A skull, memento mori.

Running now he rounded the end of the chancel, past the chapels to the dead, checking each, searching amongst the stonework. Then on to the altar itself, the tomb of St Etheldreda roped off, between four lit candles. The choir stalls reeking of polish. They were empty too, the misericords up, the wooden animals and demons catching the light.

A woman with a mop and bucket was working on the marble floor. She'd seen nothing. Defeated, he stood still and saw Humph coming down the nave.

Dryden held out both hands, each empty, so the cabbie turned away beneath the Octagon along the transept which led to the Lady Chapel – the only public place left they hadn't searched. Dryden cut through a corridor and got there first; the great cold space was empty, white light glaring, the glass all clear, the walls scarred by iconoclasts. It was like a swimming pool without water.

Humph burst in, almost falling over the threshold.

Dryden's eyes scanned the empty stone chairs of the chapter house. Nothing. Then the medieval altar, restored in gold-and-red-painted stone, and above it the modern Virgin in blue, her hands held up as if she'd held a child which had ascended into heaven. For a second it was an image which threatened to tell the future.

Then Dryden looked down and on the steps leading up to the altar was a cradle, in the open, where it could not be missed. He could feel his pulse in every limb, as if his whole body was his heart. He walked towards the cradle and within two steps saw that there was a child there. But time had stopped, so the baby didn't move. He stood above him and still he didn't move. Dryden unclipped the belt and held him up, the body supple and warm, looking into his son's eyes.

Those eyes blinked; time started again.

There was the sound of someone crying and he realized it was Humph, his face blank but one of his shoulders slumped with the effort of breathing. Laura appeared at the door. Her legs must have folded under her because she just knelt down on the cold stone and held out her hands.

TWENTY-FIVE

K apten Jaan Kross' hotel room was full of steam, billowing out of the en suite bathroom, misting up the Georgian sash windows of The Lamb Hotel. Dryden stood and created a circle of clear glass so that he could look down into High Street. Early Saturday night – a few couples strolling, a man striding past holding a can of Special Brew. The window was directly above the hanging inn sign: a lamb shouldering a crusader's banner above the text:

Agnus Dei – The Lamb of God.

Dryden could see Humph's Capri parked on the edge of Palace Green, Laura in the back with the boy, the dog's face up against the passenger-side window, a police marked squad car behind. Physically he could feel the child, even now, held in his hands, the weight of bone and flesh. The urge to keep him safe was like a colour, tainting everything he saw.

'I'm sorry,' said Kross, coming out in a bathrobe, white and fluffy. Despite the heat of the shower his pale skin was unflushed, his white hair wet and flat to his skull, which was slightly ridged like a bird's. The almost invisible white eyebrows, the white eyelashes, the white goatee (which he hadn't seen first time) gave a false sense of immobility to the detective's face.

There was an empty brown paper package on the bed. When Dryden had gone back to *The Crow* to get the parcel sent by Roger Stutton he'd found only the wrapping. Everything else had gone. Then he'd rung Kapten Kross' mobile, surprised that the policeman had answered in the shower. He told Kross about his son – although he knew already – and that he had something for him.

Kross stood in his robe looking at the wrapping of the package. He examined it, turning it in his long fingers, trying to reconstruct in his mind the shape of the original parcel, reading the sender's address.

'There were cellophane envelopes inside,' said Dryden. 'I could see documents – a passport, driving licence. I didn't get a chance to look at them before I heard my son had been taken. This was all that was left when I got back.'

Kross was very still for twenty seconds, maybe a little more. Dryden wondered if in some way he was able to detect the lie he'd been told.

'You must forget you have seen these things.'

Kross locked the door and rang reception, telling them he didn't wish to be disturbed and that they were on no account to give out his room number to any callers – either by phone or in person. His English was good but he said neither please nor thank you. Then he made another call and talked rapidly – presumably in Estonian – and without pause.

Dryden listened to the stream of guttural syllables and recalled that Estonian – along with Hungarian and, he thought, Finnish – formed a special group of languages unlike any other in Europe. A kind of dinosaur language which had survived meteoric impact to live on in the modern world. Which made him ask himself why he found Kross so unsettling. It was the idea, surely, that he was a foreigner in a foreign land who didn't seemed too interested in following anyone else's rules. And that gave him an aura of easy danger. As if he felt unbound by *any* rules.

Ending the call, Kross sat in an armchair with the mobile on his bare knee.

'Thank you,' he said. 'You have done the right thing. Have you told me everything, please?' Dryden could tell he was struggling to keep a peremptory note out of his voice. Which was a warning in itself, perhaps, that this man's natural instincts were constantly under wraps.

Dryden did not answer. He didn't tell lies – rarely found the need to – but as a journalist he'd learnt to mislead. If he did have to lie he always tried to do it by omission, by not telling the whole truth.

'I've told you what happened,' he said.

'This makes sense,' said Kross, running the brown paper through his fingers. 'Now – *my* job begins. Thank you.' His hands moved to the arms of his chair as if to stand, as if indicating that the interview was over. And that made Dryden briefly angry, like a flame guttering. How dare this man dismiss him? He knew now why he'd not told him the whole truth. Knowledge was power. And this wasn't just another crime statistic. This was the murder of his uncle, and in some way, in all probability, the *theft* of his father's name, of what his father had been. And now, finally, the kidnapping of his son. An elaborate warning, surely, that he should stop asking awkward questions.

'They tried to take my son,' he said. 'I want to know more. I have a right to know more.'

Kross rocked his head from side to side. 'Detective Inspector Friday phoned. I am happy the boy is safe. I don't think they try to take him. It was a warning – a very shocking one, yes. But that only. Now they have what they want: the contents of this package.'

Was the Estonian as cold-blooded as he seemed, or had any empathy been lost in translation? Kross stood and walked to the minibar and took out two cold bottles of beer. Dryden didn't recognize the brand: SUKA. The bottle opener was in the pocket of Kross' robe which made Dryden think it might not be his first bottle of the evening.

He gave one of the bottles to Dryden.

'I can tell you this.' Kross closed his eyes and the white eyelashes meshed. 'We have here a simple thing. A transaction – the sale of a fake ID. There is a customer, there is a supplier, there is the money, there is the ID – the commodity. We know only the name of the customer and the price. The customer is Russian – from Kallingrad, on the Baltic coast. An organization. You would call gang. But it is not like that. It is very . . .' He drank. 'Corporate. They provide these IDs to *their* customers – those wanting entry to the UK and then a new life. If you have the money you can have new life. No questions put.'

Dryden felt the icy beer bottle making his fingers numb.

'They use Estonian intermediaries for this, who come here and pick up the documents and make the payment. This must be done in person, you see. We are very concerned about this trade – but not as concerned as New Scotland Yard. Counter-terrorism is a hard business. London is a target – not Tallinn. And this time it is not one or two IDs but many: so it is not a hard business for New Scotland Yard, it is an impossible business.'

They heard a wave of laughter from the bar below, and a cork popping.

'The men from Tallinn – the intermediaries – come by ship to pick up this package. We show you pictures of the ship. They bring the cash with them. They pay first then go to pick up the package. For this they have a boat which we also show you. They go out by boat to the ruins on the new lake at night. You have words for this place . . .'

'River Bank,' said Dryden.

'Yes. But this night – this last night – there is a moon. Perhaps there is always a moon. By this light they discover that all is not right. The documents are missing. Now we know why, yes? Your uncle has them and has sent them to you.

'They find your uncle there, at the church, I think, in the tower that is left. Watching, perhaps, to see who comes for the package that he has taken. A brave man – but I think this time a stupid thing to do. They ask your uncle to tell them where the package is. He did not tell them. In fact, I think he says that he has no knowledge of this package. We know this now because if he had spoken they would have intercepted the package or come directly to you. This would have been unpleasant. I am sure they try very hard to make your uncle speak. He dies under the water. This we can all call brave. No question.'

He drank then so that Dryden had time to understand what he'd said – that Roger had died rather than tell the Estonians that he'd found the package, that he'd sent it to Dryden.

'The men from Tallinn – we know these men. They are Miiko and Geron Saar and they are brothers. The family is fishermen. A long way back in their childhoods they live on the shore of a lake – Lake Peipus. A vast lake – between my country and Russia. On this lake Alexander Nevsky beats the Teutonic Knights – the Battle on the Ice. You know this?'

'Yes.' He recalled a black-and-white classic film. 'Eisenstein?'

Kross smiled. 'This is the one thing everyone knows of my country. Today this lake can still be a dangerous place. You can cross it at night to Russia – they can cross it the other way. The brothers begin their new careers here as young men. Ferrymen. You say "go betweens". These are the things they are good at:

boats on rivers, boats on lakes, and men with money looking for a new life.

'But now they are in a very difficult position. They have given over the Russian's money but they have no goods to take back. If your uncle does not have the package who does? In the night they come for Rory Setchey. How does this man fit into our picture? I think perhaps he is the suppliers' man – their ferryman. His job is to drop the merchandise at River Bank.'

Kross drank, his Adam's apple sharp in his throat. 'They take Rory from his home to a lonely car park here in your town. We find blood there and broken glass. They make this man very scared. We know the Saar brothers well and they are good at this. A word you have – *adept*.' Kross smiled to himself at how clever that was, to recall the precise word from someone else's language.

'Maybe he cannot talk because he does not know. Or maybe he thinks they bluff and that if he keeps silent they will go home.' Kross smiled bleakly and Dryden noted that even his teeth were colourless. 'And then I think something happens which they did not expect – perhaps Setchey fights back, the gun they use to threaten him goes off – a single wound to his knee – and his heart fails. Now he cannot answer their questions.

'They are very angry – but most of all scared. If not your uncle, if not Rory Setchey, then who has their package? They think, perhaps, it is the migrant workers at Eau Fen. The Poles. We will never know why. But the Saar brothers take Rory's body there to say to the Poles that they know, that they will stop at nothing to get back what is theirs. They hang the body out – bloodied – for all to see.'

'Whoever has the package is close by. So they look for this package, for these people who take it. They ask others to look – many eyes work for them – at the railway station, at the river locks, perhaps even at the police station. Everywhere. You say that money talks. This is true. But more so – it listens. It watches.' Kross smiled again, which made Dryden think he didn't know what smiles were for.

'Today the Saar brothers find the package at last. Perhaps they suspect you have it all the time – and they take the baby so that they can search the office. Or they think you know something so they search your office when they have the chance. Either way, they get lucky. Now the brothers go home with the package, I am sure. We will let them go home because we can track them. For years. Clever people but blind also – they do not know how close we are to them. We watch and wait, learn very much.'

Dryden had to force himself to understand what Kross was saying. 'But they killed my uncle. They tortured my uncle. They can't just go free.'

'This you must accept please and leave to us. To Interpol. This is how we work, how we must work for the good of the many.'

It was the wrong thing to say. Dryden decided then, in a cold-blooded sense, that at some point in the future – not the distant future of wishful-thinking but in the near-future of reality – that the Saar brothers would be brought before a court, a British court, and charged with the murder of Roger Stutton. But for now he listened to Kross talk.

'Our job, Mr Dryden, is now to find the suppliers. We *must* find the suppliers. We need to know the names of those whose IDs are in this package. And then we need to make sure there are no more packages.'

Kross went to the window and wrenched the sash up. Sound flooded in: piped in music from the pub across the road, the bell for evensong from the cathedral. He punched some keys on his mobile and gave it to Dryden to read. 'I should not show you this yet . . . please do not say you have seen this.'

It was an email. The sender's address was CIDfriday@ btopenworld.com.

DNA test on swab taken from Philip Dryden. No match to our victim. We've submitted fingerprints for national database test.

'So,' said Kross. 'As I said – this is not your father.'

What did Dryden feel? Relief, disappointment? In a perverse way part of him had wanted this man to be his father because it held out the opportunity of being closer to him, of extending a life he thought had ended nearly forty years earlier. Now he was left only with the man who disappeared on the flood bank at Welch's Dam – disappeared with questions unanswered about his past. It was an irony which was already haunting him; that in questioning the identity of this unknown man he had uncovered something of the real Jack Dryden. Something that could not be left unexamined.

'I said this,' said Kross. 'Someone stole your father's identity in 1977. The man who has become him dies in the white van with his name, his life. Then we hear in our city a rumour. That the network which provides IDs is to deliver not one, not two or three. This time many IDs – sold together. Coincidence? No. I don't think so. But we do not yet understand why this man's death makes this happen. But your father is important. Someone stole his identity – many years ago – as they have tried to steal these many. Perhaps he was the first. Maybe – if we understand that we will know more. Because there is a problem here. We can see how your father's identity could be stolen: he was swept away, there was no body, no death certificate.'

Dryden bit his tongue.

'But this is very rare. And yet here we have someone selling many IDs. How is this possible? Because we know these IDs are special – like your father's. The customers in Kaliningrad we know have been told that the IDs are special. Do you know how they are special?'

Dryden didn't answer. He objected to the familiarity and he never answered rhetorical questions.

'They are not *fake* at all.' Again the smile, the teeth very small against the faint red blush of the thin lips. 'These are the IDs of people who are dead. The identities of *ghosts*. In Interpol we call them this. And this theft is *ghosting*. We have a word for the people who take on the names of the dead – they are *ghosters*. And here is the problem. It is very difficult to catch the ghoster because the identity is a real one. Not a fiction. And now we must ask how can this be? Are they the identities of the *murdered*? Not one, but many – this cannot be. This is a great question and I must find the answer.'

He finished his beer holding the bottle vertical for a lingering last drop. Dryden set his aside, untouched.

'So maybe this is why you get warning,' said Kross. 'That you should forget your father – or at least the man who took his name. But we will take this up. This is my job.'

Dryden was dismissed with a handshake, but he didn't go. 'And my family – how safe are they?'

'Very – I think, as long as you leave this to us. The Saar brothers have their package – they will go. But the twenty-four-hour surveillance will stay in place. The squad car. And also a unit from Interpol too, I think.'

Another handshake, another dismissal. As Dryden closed the door he heard Kross opening the minibar.

Dryden thought, as Humph drove them home, that for all his clinical intelligence Kross wasn't quite as smart as he thought he was. He hadn't asked, for example, whether Dryden had looked *inside* any of the ID envelopes. And he hadn't asked if he had seen any of the names. The names of the ghosts. Dryden had forgotten most of them – but he remembered Samuel James Setchey. That and the name of the registrar who'd signed *his* birth certificate in 1986: Philip T. Trelaw.

TWENTY-SIX

The journey home took the Capri across Petit Fen – a vast area of peat which encompassed several parishes, criss-crossed by ditches and drains, and scattered hamlets strung out on the flood banks. A bleak landscape, drenched in heat by a late sun. The cab was hot despite the open windows. Laura sat beside the cradle with her hand on the baby's arm, the dog across her feet. Humph kept checking the back seat in his rear-view mirror, as if they might all simply vanish. Each seemed unable to share the sense of shock which they felt. It was little comfort – and Dryden hadn't voiced it – that this was nothing to what they'd all be feeling if they hadn't found the child so quickly and unharmed.

The marked squad car was still in the rear-view.

'I want to know why,' said Laura, touching Dryden's shoulder. 'Why did someone take him?'

He told them what he knew. All he knew – except that he'd seen the name of Samuel Setchey on the documents he'd found in the sealed package from his uncle.

A fresh silence settled on the car.

The road ahead was railroad-straight and passed a small chapel. Looking around Dryden realized where he was and remembered that he had agreed to meet Sheila Petit at six to discuss the next stage of the anti-flooding campaign. Petit had lived her life in the eastern fens; she'd know everything there was to know about the one-time Swaffham registrar Philip Trelaw: the man who'd signed Dryden's father's death certificate, and the Setchey boy's birth certificate. Dryden didn't believe in coincidence; he searched the world for patterns, and Trelaw seemed to occupy a pivotal point in a system which provided new lives for the dead. Lucrative new lives.

Besides, the refuge offered by indulging in work, or returning to everyday life, after what had happened was impossible to resist. It was seven thirty – but he explained to Laura that it would only take a moment to check if Petit was still about. And they didn't want to wake the boy, so a delay did no harm. She closed her eyes by way of answer.

Humph parked in the middle of the single-track road, which ran along a high bank. The sun was touching the horizon – a circle you could look at without pain, the colour of tomato soup in a can. Combine harvesters were out in the distance so that a red cloud of peat was drifting between them and the sunset. Dryden thought there was a word that described the colour of the world at that moment: umber. A burnt landscape. Dryden could taste it on his lips. Hauling himself out of the cab he felt sweat start out on his face, cooling the skin.

'A moment,' he said to Humph, leaving the door open. The cabbie fumbled for his fluffy earphones.

An etched brick over the chapel door read: 1887. The narrow windows were in green glass. The building, Dryden knew, was hired out to various groups but was home to just one. He'd done a story on them the previous summer. A sign, in the style of a hymn board, was nailed to the brickwork and read:

LITTLEPORT HARLEY DAVIDSON SOCIETY.

Artwork included a motorcycle – with long praying-mantis handlebars – and an open road. Dryden had been past on evenings when the bikers met: gleaming machines lined up on the bank top, men with thinning hair drinking tea from flasks. He wondered if Billy Johns, cemetery warden, ever joined them. He doubted it, having sensed a loner who sought private pleasures.

The chapel's biggest crowd turned up on a Sunday for a Catholic Mass. The migrant workers in the fields were mostly Portuguese, Polish, Letts – and most were Roman Catholics, billeted in caravans and mobile homes scattered amongst the farms. A priest came out from Ely to take the service. Dryden had done the story and a picture caption had made the *Guardian*.

There were two cars parked on the hard standing beside the chapel. One was Sheila Petit's Morris Minor – railway green, a polished wooden shooting-break, a Save Petit Fen sticker in the windscreen. The other a four-by-four, a Hyundai, spattered in mud, with a gundog barking in the back.

She was inside drinking coffee from a flask with a young man Dryden didn't recognize: twenty, twenty-five, the outdoor type, with a fen wind-tan and red peat ingrained on his hands.

'It's you,' she said. 'Everyone else has gone. I suppose you do *want* this story?'

Dryden enjoyed her cantankerous nature. Out in the Fens – even in Ely – most people didn't want an argument. You could get someone to agree to two contradictory ideas quite easily, to your face. Only later might you discover, from a third party, that they had their own opinion. Sheila Petit didn't need third parties.

'Hi,' said the young man. 'Edward Petit.'

'My nephew,' said Sheila Petit. 'He runs the Home Farm.' Dryden knew the family still ran the land around the old house but he was pretty sure it was rented now, off one of the big agri-companies.

'I better go. I've got an irrigator running.' He smiled at Dryden and the family resemblance was clear – the strong jaw, the wire-like hair.

Petit didn't watch him go, which was cold of her, but in character. Then she smiled; the smile of the victor.

'Vee will have told you.' She was nodding, looking at Dryden, but already he could sense she was somewhere else. Speaking to an audience, perhaps, hundreds of expectant faces turned to listen.

'I think we've done it, Dryden. Stopped this mad scheme in its tracks. Saved the fen. This is history. *History*. Right now, right here. More than three hundred years ago they created this place out of marsh and reed. Created villages, and farms, and churches, and homes for the people who would work on the land: land won from the water.'

Her voice echoed slightly in the old room, bouncing back off the plastered walls, the wooden-beamed roof.

'This government was going to turn the clock back. What for? To balance the nation's books because some bunch of City whizz kids don't understand the concept of acceptable risk. Bankers, betting billions on a roulette wheel. This was *risk*.' She was almost shouting now, her arms out, encompassing the Fens. 'Giving a fortune to Dutch engineers to drain a swamp. But this was worth it – because when the water finally left the land they'd created thousands of acres of the best farmland in England – in Europe. Peat – rich, black and deep.'

She produced a flask and poured herself tea, realizing, perhaps, that her flight of oratory had gone too far.

'Now we've stopped them,' she said simply. 'Stopped them dead.'

Dryden tried to look impressed but felt uneasy in the presence of a zealot.

She stood, hand on hip, and gave him the details he wanted. It wasn't so much a briefing as a public reading. They were going to stop the proposed re-flooding scheme by buying a crucial strip of land in the middle of the fen. 'I like to think of it as a poison pill, you see. You want to flood this fen you need to buy this strip of land. And – once we've finalized the purchase – we're never going to sell. And they won't be able to buy – ever. It's all wrapped up in a trust. Absolutely no way of freeing it up ever again. It's the perfect solution. A final solution.' It was a mark of the kind of person Sheila Petit was that she could use such a reference without hesitation.

The money for the purchase came from an anonymous donor. 'Local,' said Petit. 'I'm going to be a bit reluctant to provide detail here. There're reasons. How about we say the donation is around £20,000. I'd like to leave the actual extent of the land a bit vague – but the point is that doesn't matter. It could be an inch wide and still be as effective, because they can't flood it unless they own all the land. So you see – it could just as well be a postage stamp.'

'But it's on Petit Fen?'

'Yes.'

Dryden had brought an OS map of the fen with him, with the proposed area to be flooded mapped out.

'The government says this scheme – unlike the one that created Adventurers' Mere – would be different. That there'd be marsh, dry ground and woodland.'

'That's what they said about Adventurers' Mere – look at it,' said Petit. 'I don't blame them entirely – I'm not some flat-earther. I know that global warming exists. Sea levels are rising. Once you let the water on to the land it will get deeper – not now maybe, but one day, then the sea will be back. That's the end game here. The return of the sea. And Ely – an island once again. But that day has not arrived, Dryden. It's decades away, possibly centuries. The fight needs to go on.'

Dryden memorized the quote.

Taking a red pencil she drew a thin line across the map – roughly from north-west to south-east – right across the proposed flooded area. 'That's it – broadly.'

'What if they go for compulsory purchase?'

'Our advice is that's a long shot. We're talking a referral to the Secretary of State. The High Court, maybe. But one of the attractions of this scheme is that we can lock the land up in a very complicated trust system which actually makes it very hard for any purchaser – compulsory or otherwise, or else I could have just used Petit Hall to stop them. But they could have used compulsory purchase on that, and while I'm prepared to fight, I can't vouch for those who come after me – can I?'

It was a rhetorical question. Dryden knew little about Petit's family – only that her husband had died young and there was a son.

'The trust we create will be bound by covenants preventing sale,' said Petit. 'Getting round those will require the full majesty of the law, Dryden. And the great thing about that is it costs the earth and will take years.' She laughed; a kind of hearty bark. 'Even if they got it we'd exact a price. Then we'd have more money to buy land with – we'd get ahead of them every time. Which is why we want the publicity, of course. Once the local landowners know the government isn't the only show in town they'll up their prices. It's perfect.'

She was locking the door when Dryden asked the question he'd come to ask. Humph was out of the cab rolling the ball along the road for Boudicca. Laura stood fifty yards away, her face turned to the setting sun. The local squad car was fifty yards down the road, all the doors open, both occupants apparently asleep in the front seats – heads back, the thin strain of a radio crackling on the hot air.

'Do you remember when the fen had its own registrar – this is back in the seventies? There was an office at Swaffham Prior which would have covered Petit Fen – the back droves.' The back droves was an area of fen crossed by mathematically ruled roads at half-mile intervals. The goods line to Newmarket ran across the landscape creating a series of unmanned level crossings. Remote, backward, it was a byword for rural obscurity.

Petit pocketed the key.

'The registrar was called Trelaw. Philip Trelaw,' said Dryden.

'Yes. Why?' She asked the question but she was already walking away towards her car.

'You met him?'

'I guess. Several times. I think he signed Edward's birth certificate, in fact. And Martyn's.'

'Your son?'

'We had a party at the town hall in Chatteris one Christmas,' she said, ignoring the question. 'We run the registration service locally – births, deaths and marriages, although the data is centralized at Kew, I think.'

It was typical, thought Dryden, that she could refer to West Fen District Council as 'we'.

'So he came – this Trelaw. Shabby man – a giant. Typical in many ways of the fenman – hulking. Poor shoes – brown.'

Dryden nodded. He was always fascinated by the different ways people judged each other. Looking at shoes was a common tic amongst the well-heeled. It was never about how old the shoes were – always the colour, the polish. He looked at his own – leather, battered, red peat dust caked around the laces.

'There was a time when such a position demanded certain attributes,' said Petit. 'Education. Erudition. Still, one shouldn't mock the afflicted . . .'

'Afflicted?'

'It's very rare, you know – out on the fen.' She looked directly at the spot where the sun was just disappearing. 'The demon drink. You'd think – well, I'd think . . .' She laughed at herself and Dryden liked her for a moment. 'I'd think that the boredom of it, the days when then there's no sky, the grey days, that they would drive you to a vice, a vehicle of escape.'

Dryden thought that was an eloquent phrase: vehicle of escape.

'Perhaps it was opium once – that seems to suit the fen character, don't you think, Dryden? Morose, self-contained.'

She smiled, opening her mouth wide so that she revealed the slightly crooked oversized teeth. 'Insular.'

She got in the car, leaving the door open, so that Dryden had to squat down. 'But drink is rare. No pubs out here . . . Not much money in the pocket. Market days were always lively – but other than that . . . So Trelaw stood out.'

Dryden tried to recall Trelaw from the visit he'd made to the register office at Swaffham more than thirty years before. A big man, yes. And she was right about shambling. But the worse for drink? He didn't think he'd have noticed the signs. He'd had a baby-like face, he recalled. So maybe flushed, a little shiny.

'It did for him in the end – or so we thought,' she said. 'Kidneys packed up so he had to go on dialysis. No way he could do that and keep the job. I remember the issue coming up – I was on personnel at the time. No suggestion we'd let him go, of course. Quite rightly in many ways – you have a duty, don't you, to an employee. You shouldn't be able to just walk away. So we found him a job, in Ely, I think – highways? Somewhere close enough to the hospital anyway. Why?'

'I need to talk to him. I thought you'd know some background.'

'He's still alive then?'

'Yes. Probably. Surprised?'

'Yes. Bloody amazed. I think we were given to understand the disease would kill him. Dialysis would help – but in those days fancy transplants were rare. And as I say, he'd given the bottle a pretty good thump. I thought he'd be dead in the year.'

'Who got his job?'

'No one got his job. Well, we named a successor but he never got his feet under the table. We took the chance to centralize – just the office in Chatteris now. So that's his claim to fame, Dryden. He was the fen's last registrar.'

Dryden watched her drive away, the Morris turning on half-a-sixpence and heading east. He recalled that while she still lived in Petit Hall she'd rented most of it out, converted to flats.

As Dryden followed her east he looked in the rear-view mirror but there was nothing behind them but the tracking squad car. The road itself, which the map said was a straight line, buckled in the last tangled folds of the day's heat, like a twisting tail.

TWENTY-SEVEN

Sunday

Dryden had found the webcam by a process of deduction. The FenFishing website showed a view along a stretch of the Little Ouse with a houseboat in the distance, and, on closer examination, there was a single church tower on the horizon – a Dutch-style leaded pinnacle. He'd spread the OS map out on the kitchen floor. The only candidate for the spire was St Mary's Southery – The South Island – a Norfolk village on the edge of the Black Fen. He'd taken a still from the webcam and zoomed in on the spire, looking for something in the foreground which he could match with the lead pinnacle: and there it was, on the far bank, a wooden landing, long disused, but still with three steps – rough wooden planks, and hanging from a post a mooring rope.

He'd tried again to ring Setchey's number at Hythe House, and a mobile number he'd squeezed out of a contact at the water authority, but there'd been no answer on either. So he thought he'd try a long-shot. The spot on the webcam was two miles from Flightpath Cottages. The first time he'd missed it because there was no sign of the lead spire but then he realized that the silvery metal was reflecting the sky perfectly – reflected any sky perfectly, like a shard of mirror. Then he'd seen rooks circling it and realized his mistake. He'd been twice now – at dusk or just after – and each time he'd sent an email to the website, and a time when he'd return. He didn't believe in third time lucky but he'd give it a go. This time at dawn. He left the house at just after four, the air thrillingly cool.

When he reached the spot the sun was rising – like a headlamp, emerging between trees on the edge of Thetford Forest, burning off a water mist. There was an iron sluice gate with a brick footing. The round handle of the sluice meshed to a cog wheel and a vertical piston. The camera, no larger than a watch-face, was bolted to the machinery and had been covered in hessian painted to match the rust. A wire, also camouflaged, ran up the piston which stood proud of the sluice by four or five feet, providing an aerial to transmit the image.

Dryden checked his watch and knelt down so that he was centre-image.

He spoke into the tiny camera. 'Well, I'm here again. I'd like to talk about Rory. I'm not police. But I was there when they found him – like I said in my emails.' He held his watch up to the camera eye. 'I'll be here another hour.' He was going to leave it at that but added: 'I'll be back tomorrow – last time.' He looked into the lens and felt, for a second, a spark of electricity, as if he'd caught someone's eye.

He settled down on the grass and opened his rucksack to retrieve a bottle of water. The scent of the river was almost hypnotic. It made him think of his boat down at Ely, lying awake listening to the ducks, and the occasional oily slop of something slipping into the water off the bank. He drank water, the sunlight catching the upturned bottle.

The FenFishing website was a mystery. He'd been on the site several times a day and it was always updated with the conditions on the river, tides and winds, and bits of news on fishing in East Anglia. And there was a blog with plenty of chatter from fishermen – loads from Sheffield and the industrial north. Nothing about Rory's death, or Eau Fen. Someone clearly thought business as usual was more than a cliché. He doubted it was Setchey's widow. Other fishermen, perhaps? Guides and ghillies who'd worked for Setchey?

Out in mid-river something breached the surface then plopped back into the deep water. The website had been full of pictures of pike, fen monsters at twenty-five pounds, thirty pounds, even more. There was something primeval about the snaggle-toothed fish, as if it wasn't alive today at all, but an artist's impression from the age of the dinosaurs.

The whine of the boat was audible long before it came into sight downriver. He hadn't thought of that – that they could reach all the webcams by water. A small fibreglass dingy with a powerful outboard came towards him leaving a white V in the blue water, slicing an early morning mist into two churning weaves of white vapour.

He tried to put an expression on his face that wasn't threatening, or needy, or desperate. It froze when he realized it was a woman, blonde, no make-up, an attractive face. She cut the engine and threw a heavy line at his feet which he took and slipped round the metal arm of the sluice.

She didn't get out of the boat or look as if she might. 'I don't want to talk about Rory,' she said.

'I'm sorry,' said Dryden, stepping back, hands in pockets.

'You're a reporter. The police said you were there when they got to Rory and that you knew the details. I told them you left the message – they said I should ignore you. That they'd told me everything. But they haven't – have they?' She couldn't stop herself then, letting the emotion register on her face. The muscles around her right eye seemed to jump so that he could sense the tension.

'Have they told you how he died?' he asked. He knew it was cruel, and he knew it was controlling, but she had a right to know. 'His heart.'

'Yes.' She flipped the rope, creating a wave which ran to the sluice. 'That's all they said – and that I couldn't identify the body. Why?'

Dryden sat on the bank. She waited, anchoring stray blonde hair behind on ear. She'd looked fifty, but that was almost certainly the effect of the grief and stress of the last few days. There was an unaffected beauty in her face, a fine brittle jaw, and flying cheekbones.

'Two men took Rory away,' he said. 'They're called Miiko and Geron Saar. Did they tell you that?'

She shook her head.

'They're from Estonia. They work for other – criminals – who specialize in the sale of false identities. They call it *ghosting* – they steal the identities of the dead. It's a very lucrative business. I'm sorry – Rory was involved in this. But not with these men. They were customers. He worked for the suppliers. There's a place out on the mere they used. The documents would be left there. Rory did this for them.'

She sat in the boat.

'He may have done this before, perhaps many times. Some of these documents have photo-ID, details. So they needed a line

of communication between the suppliers and the customers –
two-way. He was part of this.

'But this time someone stole the IDs. The Saar brothers thought
it was Rory. They took him to a car park in their car, the night
before he was found, and tried to make him talk.'

He thought about editing the truth but then he saw a look in
her eye and realized she'd already imagined worse. Much worse.

'They shot him once, probably by accident; there was a fight
in the car. Then his heart failed.'

'It was weak,' she said. 'His heart. His father died young, and
an uncle.' Something about the way she said it made it sound as
if this fault in the mechanism of the heart was something vindictive
in itself, almost a curse.

'When they took Hythe House apart I was there,' said Dryden.
'There was a child's room.'

'The boys.'

'No – they're teenagers, right?' asked Dryden, recalling the
police statement. 'This was a child's room.'

She shook her head as if to dislodge a memory.

'Can you tell me about Samuel?'

'No.' She covered her mouth. Her eyes seemed to lose focus
and for a second Dryden thought she might faint. He took a step
towards the boat and helped her out on to the bank where she
sat down quickly in the grass. She wore felt boots and they
touched Dryden's leg but she didn't pull them back.

'You OK?'

'Yes. Samuel's heart failed. Like Rory's. He was crying in the
night. We tried to ignore the screaming because they say you
should otherwise they never sleep through. I left him – ten
minutes, no more.' She couldn't help looking at him then, trying
to convince him, even after all the years, that it wasn't her fault.

'Then he was quiet but I knew. I ran to the room. He was
already cold. We buried him and came back to Hythe House and
I locked the bedroom and threw the key in the river. I've never
wanted to talk about it, and I don't want to talk about it now.
He was six months old. We never got over it. Rory did, I did,
but together – somehow together we couldn't get past it. Even
when the boys came.'

For a moment Dryden didn't understand, and then he did, and

for the first time he felt a shiver of real fear about uncovering the truth. He'd made the fatal error of *presumption*. He'd thought of them all like his father – their lives lost as adults, the rest stolen. How much better, how much more *lucrative*, to steal a life before it's lived.

Were they all children? All the envelopes containing the lives of people who didn't really exist, people who'd never lived a full life. Like Samuel: dead within a year. And this idea introduced, without warning, a note of genuine evil. Because if you stole the lives of children you'd have to wait, and plan, build their make-believe lives and let them grow up in the world.

He hoped she didn't ask now, why he'd been interested in Samuel, because he didn't want to say any of that out loud. And it would destroy her image of Rory – a father who'd stolen, perhaps, the life of his own child. Did he tell himself it was a victimless crime? You only had to look at this woman's face in profile to realize what an empty phrase that was.

'Was there a death certificate, Mrs Setchey – for Samuel?'

'Yes. We have that – we were very interested in it because it lists the cause of death and we were angry then. It was natural. We wanted someone to blame. But there was no one to blame. It just happened.'

So: an identical case to Jack Dryden. Death, a certificate, but still they stole his life.

'You don't recall the registrar's name?'

She shook her head. 'I don't remember very much – not afterwards. I'm sorry.'

'But it was in Ely?'

'No. Clayhythe fell under Burwell, I think – or Swaffham Prior?'

Dryden nodded. 'I'm sorry to ask so many questions. If I find out more I'll let you know – can I ring? If you've got a mobile.'

He fished out a scrap of paper and a pen. But when she handed it back her movements had slowed down, as if what she was thinking – what she was *daring* to let herself think – was sucking the energy out of her limbs.

'And Rory was involved with these men – the men who stole identities?' she asked.

'Yes. Certainly – but we don't know when, or what he did. It looks like he was just the messenger, the postman if you like. Just a cog in the wheel.'

'There's always been something hidden – since after Samuel died,' she said. 'I thought it was grief that he couldn't share. But it was this, wasn't it – this . . .' Her face had taken on a hardness so that she could use the word: '*trade*.

'I asked once. I knew he went out alone at night, in the boat. And he wouldn't talk about it – just fobbed me off. I didn't think it could be bad – because he wasn't a bad person. And I knew where the money went; it went into the website and the business, and it's a good business – that's why I'm keeping the site running because I can sell it then. That's the words they use, isn't it – the money men. A going concern.

'So I said to him: what do you do at night? No one else who worked for the FRWA went out after dark. He said that I wasn't to worry, that it didn't hurt anyone. He said I could sleep nights.'

Her face seemed to sag, as if someone had just snipped the tendons that held her features in place. 'I think that's a lie. That's what he's left me with – us – a lie.' And then, inevitably, the final question. 'Did they steal Samuel's life – the rest of his life?'

He didn't have the right to deny it. 'Yes. I think they did.'

'I hope they rot in hell.' She covered her mouth but couldn't stop herself finishing the thought: 'All of them.'

TWENTY-EIGHT

Monday

Dobbs Café (no apostrophe), Chequer Lane, just off the High Street, 8.55 a.m. It served coffee in glass cups on glass saucers and had a lino embellished with musical clefs. Starbucks, Costa Coffee and Café Nero were all within 100 yards but Dobbs survived, offering all-day breakfasts and a roast lunch accompanied by the one advertising cliché guaranteed to succeed in the Fens: All You Can Eat. Dobbs had a single table outside. Dryden always took it if he could – if thwarted he'd sit on the low wall by the back of the ironmongers. This morning he'd got the table. A small victory which lifted his mood.

Dryden and Laura had separate appointments to view the body of Roger Stutton at the funeral directors just along Chequer Lane. She'd gone first, and taken their son. Dryden had touched base at *The Crow*, using his own key. Two developments: *The Cambridge News* was reporting that detectives hunting for the killer of Rory Setchey now believed he'd died in a multi-storey car park in Ely the night before his body was found at Eau Fen. They'd asked for information on a black four-by-four seen in the area with shattered windows that night, or in the early hours of the following morning. The report matched Kapten Kross' version of events.

Dryden also had an email from Kross. Interpol had monitored the freighter which had brought the Saar brothers to England as it left Felixstowe for the return journey to Tallinn. Dockside CCTV revealed only one brother on the dockside prior to sailing. Miiko, it appeared, had stayed behind. Kross said he felt there was no cause for concern but confirmed the local police unit would stay with Dryden's family 24/7. Dryden had already decided that wasn't enough. He was no longer prepared to outsource his family's safety to the police.

Dryden sent a text message to DI Friday asking if any progress had been made in identifying the man who had posed as Jack Dryden – successfully – for the best part of thirty-five years. Dryden was perplexed by the details of the case. Someone had stolen the identity of his father: end of story. But not quite. How had they done it? And while he accepted the man who'd died at Manea wasn't his father there were those worrying echoes of his father's life in the house on the Jubilee Estate. This man had become a tutor in natural sciences – his father's degree. Why live in Ely where there would always, surely, be a chance the name would be recognized, if not the face? He'd considered giving Friday the intelligence Humph had gathered on the fake Jack Dryden at The Red, White and Blue – the link to Lincoln Jail – but decided he had a better idea. He had contacts in the prison service; he'd try to trace the link himself.

The cathedral clock struck nine thirty. A crocodile of schoolchildren crossed Back Alley. He saw Laura emerge from the funeral directors on the corner carrying the baby, walking towards him: head down, her face in shadow. He'd bought her a fresh mug of tea which he edged towards her once she'd sat down.

'You all right?' he asked.

She nodded, looking at him for the first time. Her brown eyes were liquid, the whites pink.

'Sure. He looks peaceful. If you can face it go.'

Dryden took the baby.

'In Italy the children see the dead. It is not a big thing,' she said, answering a question he hadn't asked.

'But I had to insist. I said it was his great uncle. That maybe he takes his name.'

'Really?'

'Not Roger – the second name. I saw it on the casket. Eden.'

It *was* a good name. Dryden had once asked his uncle where it had come from. Not the family, not some notable ancestor, just the prime minister in Downing Street when he was born. But still – it spoke of something grander: paradise, peace.

'Maybe,' said Dryden, giving her the child. 'I'll see.' And that was precisely what he meant – that he'd see his uncle and then decide. 'I won't be long,' he said, standing and walking quickly away, his footsteps clattering on cobbles.

Two minutes later he was sitting in a plastic bucket chair in the morgue, by his uncle's body, as if he was visiting him in hospital. Roger's hands had been placed across his chest and the wrists were exposed. There was no watch on the left hand. His aunt had told him his father's compass watch was missing from his body when they'd hauled it out of the water at River Bank. Dryden caught sight of the pale band of skin where it had been, and looked away.

He placed his hand on the edge of the casket and tried to feel some kind of connection with the soul which had inhabited the body. He forced himself to imagine the last minutes of his life: the questions, the lack of answers, the Estonian brothers growing coldly frustrated. And then, for the first time, he thought he knew what had happened to the watch. He saw in his mind's eye one of the brothers slipping it from his uncle's wrist, admiring, joking, setting the needle to north. Then, perhaps, he'd held it up – taunting, using it to count off the last minute of his uncle's life. One minute in which he could have saved himself.

Kross had not spelled out the brothers' precise criminal pedigree but he had said they were dangerous men. Given Kross' own icy authority that counted for a lot. They'd tied Roger's leg by a rope to the rudder of the eel boat, then staved in the hull. How long had it taken for the water to flood in? Maybe a minute was too long. Thirty seconds? However long it had taken he'd had a chance to tell them what they wanted to hear. That he'd taken their precious parcel, posted it to Dryden for safe-keeping.

But the boat had sunk, dragging him down, and when the water had settled they'd have seen his outstretched arm, his fingers vibrating with the effort of trying to touch the surface – the lethal boundary between water and air.

He thought he should touch him now. Fate had robbed him of the chance to touch his father. And, strangely, his nerve had failed him when his mother had died: he'd hovered, wanting to make physical contact, but disturbed by the fact that in death she'd looked nothing like his own flesh and blood. Roger, on the other hand, had seemed to grow more like Dryden's mother now his heart didn't beat: the lean, bony, face; the long, pale fingers, which was a thought he found comforting – that in death the family would grow closer.

He touched his hand and was relieved not to be revolted by the coldness. Taking the fingers almost roughly in his he asked himself if he wanted to name his son after this man: *Eden*. He liked the name but wondered whether, if his son carried it for ever, would he always think of this – a cold room, a casket, and skin like candle wax.

Prayers didn't come so he left him then.

The undertaker who'd ushered him through was working at an iMac laptop in the front office. For the first time he thought of undertakers as part of the system – along with coroner's officers, registrars, gravediggers. The bureaucracy of dying.

'Computers – I guess we're all slaves to them now,' said Dryden.

'Part of the job,' he said. His name was Carney, Matthew Carney, and he was sorry for Dryden's loss.

'But we can't quite do without paper, can we? I once worked in a so-called paperless office in London. There were piles of the stuff.'

Carney smiled. He clearly didn't do laughter. Perhaps it was unprofessional.

'Talking of which,' said Dryden, 'the death certificate. Where do I collect it? My aunt wants me to do that – is that OK?'

'The coroner's office has issued the forms. Then the registrar's your next stop.' The inquest into Roger's death had been adjourned to allow the police investigation to proceed, but Dryden had been told that the police had made no objection to the release of the body.

'You know where the register office is?' asked Carney.

Dryden couldn't help but know it after endless visits to cover local weddings. The driveway was always scattered with confetti.

'And then it's the cemetery at Manea, I think?' asked Carney.

'That's right. I've picked a spot.'

'Funeral service?'

'I'll talk to my aunt.'

He was going to leave; it was sunny outside, and the cool interior was beginning to get to his bones. 'One thing. So I get the death certificate but who tells everyone he's dead – like pensions, Swansea for the licence, that kind of thing. Passport office too. It's registered somewhere central?'

'The GRO – General Register Office. Then they tell everyone else, just about.'

'Where's that then – the GRO? Somerset House. Or Kew?'

'No, no. It's Southport. Lancashire coast. Then I guess they pass info to the National Archives – that's Kew.'

'Southport?' Dryden conjured up an image of Blackpool – the closest he'd ever been. He knew Southport was upmarket. But still – the bleak open sands, the grey Irish Sea, and maybe the Lake District in the distance, blue hills and rain clouds. 'Why Southport?'

'They moved out of London in the early nineties. Before that it was Somerset House. It's a weird place in Southport,' said Carney, brightening up for the first time. 'Smedley Hydro – this huge old school they turned into a spa, like a Victorian health farm.

'In fact, Barnardo worked there – you know, like in the orphans.'

Dryden thought about that – the man who'd saved the lives of children.

'Couple of years ago we had a weekend at Blackpool and I went and had a look. Professional interest. Still looks like a Spa – mind you the security's pretty eye-watering. Cameras every-where – even on the edge of the beach.'

'Who sends them the certificate? The local registrar?'

'That's it. Then someone in the Smedley Hydro puts it on the database. Then it's official. You used to have to tell everyone individually but now it's mostly centralized. Thirty seconds of inputting the details at Southport and then it's there for ever. You're only dead if they say you are.'

TWENTY-NINE

Room 159 was in the sub-basement of the town hall. Dryden had been issued with a security pass on a lanyard and told to go down using the lift to B2. The area was officially restricted to the public but they were short of staff and he'd have to go alone. When the lift doors opened the corridor revealed was in darkness, the only light the soft green of the upward pointing arrow. Then neon tubes flickered on, buzzing like trapped summer flies.

There was a security entry pad on the door marked 159 and when he pressed the red button a voice crackled: 'Mr Dryden?' A man, educated, with a light, tuneful voice.

The door buzzed and pushing it he found himself in a windowless office, a desk lit by a single down-spot, so that an array of computer screens glowed, dominating everything, like mission control.

Philip Trelaw sat at a kidney-shaped desk. The room was hot and the odour sour and earthy. Trelaw didn't get up, an echo of their first meeting nearly thirty-five years ago, but he offered his hand, which was surprisingly small and cold. Even sitting down Dryden could see what a large man he was – what his own father would have described as an 'agricultural' build. His physical shape was such a contrast to the voice he'd heard Dryden looked around the room for someone else, but it was empty.

There wasn't a trace of alcohol in the air but Trelaw's eyes told a different story – the whites distinctly yellow, the baby-like distended skin of his cheeks showing cracked and broken miniature capillaries, like old China.

'I showed Detective Inspector Friday,' said Trelaw. He swung his eyes back to the screens without moving his head. In Dryden's memory he only had a still image of this man behind his desk in that damp, fire-lit office in Swaffham Prior. Now he realized it wasn't a still image at all – it was just that the man maintained an inherent stillness. A hand came up to touch his lips as if rising from under water.

'I know,' said Dryden, taking a seat without an invitation. 'He just thought I might be able to see something. You know – the way someone walks. A habit – a gait – it's one of my special subjects.'

The truth was he'd asked Friday if he could see the film. He wanted to meet Trelaw on a professional basis. Then judge the right moment to look into his past. But most of all he wanted to hear him speak, to see him move, make a judgement on his character.

On the desk was a picture in one of those frames people use for family groups – but this one showed a classic Rover in grey and cream. Dryden recalled the article from the cuttings on the club Trelaw had set up for owners of the Rover P4.

'Nice car,' said Dryden.

Trelaw readjusted the position of the frame but said nothing, returning his eyes to the screens, each of which showed part of Ely town centre bathed in sunshine.

'Here . . .' said Trelaw, his fingers playing with surprising dexterity over a console. His eyes rose to the central screen and stayed there.

Dryden noticed three things: Trelaw had a lunchbox open on the desk top beside him, and a small flask, and his shirt – once white – was grey with repeated washing. Middle-class poverty. Dryden imagined net curtains and threadbare carpets.

An image flickered on the main screen – not a video flicker, but a pixelated digital film.

It was Ely Market Place on Saturday morning. Dryden's flesh cooled rapidly. He hated these images, everyday images, but tainted by the knowledge that something was about to happen, something which meant the day would be remembered for ever. Jamie Bulger's killers in a shopping precinct. The London Tube bombers coming through the ticket barriers. Evil, lethal, but only in retrospect.

'There,' said Trelaw.

A figure crossed over from Fore Hill into the market place carrying a car seat cradle. Relaxed, long-limbed, in shorts, the cot swung confidently, but moving fast. Shorts, showing thick, muscled legs which looked tanned. A T-shirt but the face obscured by a long-peaked US-style cap pulled down. He walked fast, looking at his own feet. The digital time read-out on the screen read 9.08 a.m. Some men look odd in shorts, self-conscious, but this man looked as if he lived in them. They came just below his knees and he slipped a mobile out of one pocket with his free hand and checked it as he walked.

'There's a motif on the cap?' said Dryden.

The image juddered, the magnification jumping once, twice. The cap filled the screen: blurred, but they could read the motif: FedEx.

'Millions of them,' said Trelaw.

The man walked across the screen and into the cathedral grounds through the arched door in the wall of the Almonry Café.

They watched the screen blank out.

'That's it,' said Trelaw. 'I told 'em not to bother you.'

'It wasn't why I came anyway,' said Dryden.

Dryden took out the death certificate he'd found in the hayloft at Buskeybay and slid it along the desk. Issued January 18, 1978.

'That's the original,' said Dryden. 'Your signature.'

Trelaw studied it. 'Yes. It is.' He held it an inch from his eyes, which were large and watery. 'I'm in front of these screens all day. I can read but it takes time to find my range.' He smiled weakly.

'When we met, I was with Mum; we went to your office at Swaffham Prior. You said we couldn't have one of these because there wasn't a body.'

'No. That's right.'

'Except here it is. How did that work?'

'You can apply – the coroner can apply to the Home Office. I think it's the MOJ now – Ministry of Justice. If they're happy to presume the death has taken place they can issue an exemption – that's DDM 67 – it should have been attached.' He pressed a thumb on the double dot of the staple in the corner. 'Here.' He held it up to the light.

Dryden had removed the exemption. He wanted Trelaw to talk him through the process.

'The coroner's verdict is usually left open – that will be on the files. Sometimes, if the circumstances are obvious, they'll go for accidental, or misadventure. Then we sign.'

'It was accidental death,' said Dryden. The inquest, held in the schoolroom at Reach, was as pin-sharp a fragment of memory as he had. It might as well have been framed.

'There were witnesses to the moment of death?'

'Yes,' said Dryden, considering the oddly phrased question. 'But there *is* a problem. This death – Jack Dryden's death – *isn't* registered. There's a certificate, fine. But it doesn't seem to have made any difference. A man claiming to be my father was alive, not far from here, until just a few weeks ago. You see his life had carried on – my father's life – complete with his driving licence, medical card, pension – everything. So I'm going to check but I think it's pretty clear what's happened – The General Register Office – the GRO, was never informed of the death. As far as the state is concerned he was alive and well for thirty-five years after his death. So someone issued this certificate and then didn't inform the GRO. Do you see?'

'And you think that's me – that I did that?'

'No. But I thought you were the first person I should ask. It's a simple question: if you made out this certificate, how is it possible a copy did not get to the GRO?'

The blood in Trelaw's face was blotchy now. 'Why would I do that?'

Trelaw seemed determined to cross-examine himself. But if he was prepared to ask himself the question Dryden was perfectly willing to give him an answer.

'You lost your job because of your drinking problem. It must have been tough. You must have been short of money.' Dryden knew the accusation was implied, and unfair, given he had no idea how the coroner's office worked: who made out the paperwork, who was responsible for the secretarial duties.

'I didn't lose my job. I was transferred to the council offices.'

Dryden hated people who danced along the line between truth and lies and Trelaw's retreat into such detail made him feel better about effectively calling him a fraudster. 'OK. But the registrar's position is a good one – isn't it? You have a certain independence. I would have thought it was better paid than the job you went to Ely for – that was just clerical? But you took it because you needed to be near the hospital. For dialysis.'

'That's right.'

'And they wouldn't consider a transplant because of the heavy drinking. The cost too in those days – the cost to the NHS. There'd be a waiting list and you'd be the last person they'd put on it. A middle-aged alcoholic.'

Trelaw's eyes had filled with water. 'It was a complex decision. My decision. A private decision.'

Trelaw was shaking – Dryden could see that now – very slightly, but at a very high frequency. Buzzing.

Dryden didn't back off. 'So – what I think is – if we're looking for a motive as to why in 1977 you saw fit to sell my father's identity I'd suggest that you had to buy a kidney transplant on the open market. And that's what you did – because I don't think you're teetotal now – are you?

'What did it cost – £10,000? Maybe more if you had to travel. So – for the sake of it – let's say that happened. You sold the ID for £20,000 and got yourself a new kidney. Is that wrong?'

'Yes. I borrowed the money for the operation – £17,000, actually. Although of course it's cost me much more – much, much more. Five times that – six, because I wanted the job back. So I did something very stupid. I went to a loan company. I'm still paying. I'll always still be paying because I didn't read the small print. I have a job but I live the life of a pauper. I pay back every week of my life. If I'd sold your father's identity my life would be very different.'

He straightened his cuffs.

Dryden thought he'd chosen his words carefully. 'I hope you're telling the truth.'

'Why?' asked Trelaw, as if he was speaking to a child.

'Because you're going to have to tell it all again – to the police. I think they'll check the details.'

Trelaw looked at his watch. 'I've already spoken to the police. In fact, it was Detective Inspector Friday I told.' Another weak smile. 'You see, it wasn't my duty to inform the central authorities – the GRO. I was a district registrar for the East Fens. We took all our paperwork by hand into Chatteris once a week. That's HQ for the service – has been since the mid-seventies. The office there dealt with London. If the notification failed to get through it was because someone didn't do their job at Chatteris, or in London, or in Southport. I think that's where

Detective Inspector Friday has taken his questions. It's where you should have taken yours.'

Dryden felt like a fool, which made him angry, and being angry made his brain buzz, and so – with a kind of desperate relief – he saw there was a flaw in Trelaw's logic.

'Right. But what if you didn't send them the paperwork? What if you kept the documents? It was months after my dad's death anyway – I don't expect the office at Chatteris could track all the deaths in the district.'

'There will be records. When we take the certificates in they take a note. Keep a diary.' An emotion finally fought its way on to Trelaw's face: a hint of something devious in his small dark eyes. 'Mind you, back then it was paper records, of course. I've no idea what's been kept.'

Trelaw struggled to his feet. His spine wasn't straight but he still stood six feet tall. 'There's a new system now – I was talking to someone in the department the other week. Digital images – all by computer. But then it was paper, of course. I try to keep up with things. I always read *The Crow* – the death notices, carefully. Roger Stutton – at Buskeybay. His sister was Elizabeth Dryden, at Burnt Fen – that's what it said.'

'Yes,' said Dryden. He couldn't shake off the thought that he'd somehow been threatened in a kind of devious, circular, fashion.

Trelaw held out a hand. 'I'm sorry for your loss.'

THIRTY

A UK Border Agency bus stood outside the small block of flats on Gas Holder Lane. The block was three storeys high, in concrete, with balconies in primary colours which had lost their battle with the fen sun: blazing from dawn to dusk, peeling it back to the wood. The street lay in a small district by the railway station beyond Back Hill. Very few knew about the block, which was used for problem families and short-term accommodation for council tenants. The Yorubas had been given a flat while the Home Office considered David Yoruba's appeal against deportation to his native Niger.

The TEXT from Gill Yoruba's mobile had been short and direct.

HELP, PLEASE.

The bus had barred windows, tinted grey, and was about half full. Dryden could see two faces, one black, one white, but both had exactly the same expression: a combination of exhaustion and resignation. The driver and two men he could only class as guards wore Day-Glo jackets and insignia which read CERTIO. Dryden thought it was a private-sector security company.

Three flights of exterior stairs got him up to the Yorubas' flat. He took them two at a time. Two guards, in the same livery as the men on the bus, were trying to get David Yoruba out through the front door. Dryden didn't like this moment, the one just before violence becomes clear-cut. The security men had him by the arms but in a kind of fake-assistance stance, as if he had trouble walking. And he was resisting, using every muscle in his body to prevent them moving him forward, but controlling his temper, directing all that anger inwards, not outwards. It was the moment just before something snaps.

Behind them, standing in the corridor, was Gill Yoruba, trying not to hold on to her husband, but pawing at his back nonetheless.

'Do you have the right to do that?' asked Dryden. He took out his mobile phone and started pretending to take pictures with it. 'I'm press. I said – do you have the right to do that?'

A third man appeared in the corridor carrying a holdall.

'Can you stand aside, sir.' He flashed an ID wallet at Dryden. 'I have explained to Mr and Mrs Yoruba. Mr Yoruba is required to attend at Yarl's Wood detention centre for the final tribunal into his case. He had twenty-one days' notice of the date. We do have the documentation.'

Dryden didn't see the punch but he saw David Yoruba's head flip back and a sudden flash of red blood. He lost his footing for a second and they had him out on the balcony, and down on his face, in a few seconds. Handcuffs were on swiftly and then they pulled him up again. He looked murderous, and Dryden thought he probably feared that this was it, a bitter goodbye to Britain, to his wife. Through his mind must be running every avenue still open, like a map of hell. Run for it. Head butt one of the security guards. Get back in the flat. Or let them put him on that bus. If he did that, then within a minute, his facial expression would be exactly the same as the bus's other two passengers.

'Go, David,' she said. 'Go. There is still a chance. I'll talk to Mr Dryden. Just trust us, David.'

One of the security guards was nodding and Dryden noticed he had blood on his lip too, but when he cleaned it away there was no cut. 'Yeah. That's it. We might even overlook the assault.'

'I'm a witness,' said Dryden. 'And I'll turn up at court.'

The guards exchanged glances, trying to judge the moment.

They bundled him away and down the stairs. Yoruba looked back at his wife. 'I will call this evening – stay by the phone,' he said, then turned to Dryden. 'If the appeal fails do as we discussed. You will do this?'

'Yes. I will,' said Dryden.

Gill came to the edge of the balcony and she and Dryden watched the bus pull away. She said the lawyer had advised them that if the tribunal did not allow the appeal David would be deported within seventy-two hours.

'Tomorrow I'll go to Yarl's Wood,' said Gill. 'I can't just stay here.'

They went inside and she made him tea. He said he'd contact the UK Border Agency and try and get a statement. If it helped he'd run the story of their missing daughter in the *Ely Express* – but that might be too late. He'd try the local MP, the MEP too. If they could apply any pressure directly on the Home Office it might help.

When he stopped talking they both listened to the silence in the flat.

'I'm sorry – do you remember if Aque was given a death certificate?' asked Dryden. 'You sent the council the birth certificate – a copy. But was there a death certificate?'

Aque's story had been in his mind since he'd spoken to Rory Setchey's widow, the mother of Samuel, whose identity had been stolen after just six months of life. A child, dead tragically young, buried at Manea. If they stole Jack Dryden's identity in 1977, and Samuel Setchey's in 1986, were they still in business?

Gill Yoruba's eyes seemed to brim with tears. 'Yes. I have it. We were going to buy a stone and have it put in the cemetery – not the pauper's graves, with the rest. A memorial stone. They said we could not do this without Aque's body. Instead we can place a plaque in the memorial garden. It's not the same of course, because she's not there. She'll never be there.' She looked to the window which framed a view of a patch of allotments. 'I had to send them the death certificate for that.'

'I'm sorry. I know it's painful. But I need to see it.'

'I have a copy.'

Dryden sat alone, thinking of the memorial plaque for Aque: a brass plate, like the ones you find outside a solicitors' office. A brief comfort to her parents, but little else. They'd always think of her as missing. Placeless. Lost.

Then he remembered a story he'd covered back on his first paper. It had been the 1980s and an IRA bomb had blown up a patrol in Irish border country. One of the soldiers had been local so they'd planned to give the funeral the full treatment: running copy, on press day. He'd been given the job of filing running copy from a spot in the graveyard.

The day before the funeral the news editor read in one of the nationals that the soldier's body had never been found after the blast. Nothing. So what was in the coffin? Dryden, junior reporter, was delegated to find out. He rang the undertaker and learnt a key lesson – that if he was professional in the way he did his job, he'd get answers from other professionals. So he was honest and upfront: if there was no body, what were they going to bury? The answer was common sense: any 'remains' from the scene of the blast would be included in the coffin – scraps of clothing, bloodstained, perhaps, splinters of metal and wood and possibly bone. There were several victims of the blast – so the debris from the scene would be divided between them. Then they'd weight the coffin to match the weight of the deceased. They'd start with his uniform, his medals, his gun, and anything else the family wished to place inside. If it came up light they'd add a lead weight.

They'd covered the funeral service, with its flags and addresses. But he'd kept his distance in the graveyard. Telephoto lenses were lined up beyond a wall to take discreet shots; the Fleet Street boys smoking, not trying too hard to keep their voices down. He'd stood apart, partly shielded by a large Victorian monument to the Boer War. But he'd been struck by the sense in which the burying of the coffin was a cathartic act. Even the widow smiled, clutching her children, leading them away from the grave. And the dead man's comrades, huddled, lighting up once it was over, their voices gaining power after the family had gone, after an hour of whispers.

He'd thought then that the secret of a funeral, its potency, lay in being able to walk away and know that if you ever want to, you can go back, even if you never do. And that's what a gravestone could be: a window on the dead. And that's what the Yorubas had been denied, that connection with their daughter.

Gill Yoruba came back with the death certificate. Dryden took a note of the reference number and went online using his laptop to the GRO site – which he'd explored after his discussion with the undertaker. He went to order a copy of a death certificate and punched in the code: up came the document.

'Right. Well – that's good. All in order.'

He smiled but she didn't smile back.

'I wanted him to disappear,' she said. 'I'd have gone with him. We could have started again, somewhere they didn't know us. The Midlands. He wouldn't do it.'

'He wants to be free, and one day he wants to go home.'

'I know.' Her face changed shape as she seemed to summon up all her bitterness. 'Will I get to bury him there?'

THIRTY-ONE

The Beat Club had initially been a big disappointment to Dryden. He'd had in mind somewhere subterranean, moodily lit, with lava lamps placed ironically in niches above banquet seating. And one of those little cupboard offices on the stairs where a shady character took your coat and gave you a raffle ticket. The building itself gave nothing away: an anonymous town centre two-storey block hidden down an alley by The Lamb Hotel. Just a door with a keypad entrance lock that nobody used because the door was always open.

But when he'd walked in that first time he'd realized his mistake immediately. It wasn't The Beat Club at all, it was The *Beet* Club. How typical of the Fens to name a club after a vegetable. And such a dull vegetable. Mean and moody – no. Just a working man's club with a bar and rooms – snooker, pool, a dart board. At least it had banquet seating, but the lighting was stark, good enough for the legion of domino players who took up most of the tables.

Then he started to like it. The jukebox was retro and he was often the only one feeding in coins so he got to hear his selections. The bar was a decent place to pick up gossip, listen to gossip, or start gossip running. Prices were subsidized, the beer was good, and someone gifted he never saw made wonderful pies which he occasionally asked them to wrap so he could take one to Humph, who was a member, but never set foot over the threshold. Perhaps he was disappointed that having paid his subs he couldn't actually drive the cab into the bar.

The club had originally been set up for the workers at the Ely Beet Factory, down on the river, but its life had gone on beyond its demolition in the 1980s. Black-and-white photos of the factory lined the walls: a glimpse back into a time when working men – and women – had jobs for life, even if they came with an almost lethal dose of boredom. Now the clientele were people who liked the atmosphere of a working man's club: affable, friendly, as down to earth as a sugar beet. The place confirmed Dryden's belief that the east of England had more in common with the north than the south. The flat landscape shouldn't really fool anyone. Or the wide open fields. The people worked hard and were paid little, crowding together where they could, and finding entertainment in small pleasures.

It was dark outside. The blinds were down on the skylights, and a flat-screen TV in the back room was showing BBC 24 on loop. Monday nights were quiet. Even mournful.

Senior Prison Officer Gerry Talbot arrived on time and looked for Dryden because he wasn't a member and couldn't buy a drink – and besides, if he was going to waste an hour of his spare time talking to a reporter the least he could expect was a free pint. Dryden got him one and signed him in as a guest. Talbot was out of uniform and had walked – his neat executive home was half a mile away on an estate – so Dryden bought him a glass of Old Badger at 5.8 per cent alcohol. Dryden nursed a large vodka and tonic – no ice, no lemon. And he'd bought himself a delicacy of the Fens – a packet of cheese and onion crisps with a pickled egg in the bag.

Talbot sat with his back to the wall and kept smiling while letting his eyes flit round the bar.

'Cheers,' said Dryden, drinking, then shaking the egg around in the crisp bag.

'Thanks,' said Talbot, taking two inches off the beer.

'Bad day?'

'It's all over. They're back in their cells.'

Dryden nodded. Talbot was the Prison Officers Association rep. for Whitemoor Prison: a purpose built Category-A facility with 500 inmates, including some of the nastiest people to be found behind bars in Britain, and less than ten miles north-east of the town. It seemed like a lifetime ago that Dryden had written the latest story for *The Crow* – the sit-in at the canteen over the new menu. The nationals had taken a par, but no more, because there were no details. Nothing *juicy*, or even *savoury*.

'The new menu?' prompted Dryden, biting into his pickled egg.

A woman passed their table offering two large aluminium foil trays loaded with the remnants of a wedding buffet which had been served up in the club's function room. Dryden took some slices of pork pie and a sandwich. Talbot declined. 'My dinner's in an hour.' He checked his watch. The prison officer was ex-Navy. Dryden had always been fascinated by the way in which military personnel let their lives be dominated by meal times.

'Makes you laugh,' said Talbot, without a smile. 'A year ago the POA started pushing for a makeover on food. We've had schools – Jamie and all that. Heston What's-His-Name did the Navy. So what about us? We get the same as them – same as the inmates: OK, it's better served, its fresher, hotter. But it's the same meal. So we said we wanted something a bit healthier.'

Talbot was fourteen stone if he was an ounce. 'It's a generation thing – the new lads are fitter. Not so many are Army, Navy. They wanted salads, pasta, fish, a choice of veg. Fresh veg – which is a fair point. The prison's surrounded by half a million acres of carrots. We never see one that isn't shaped like a little fake Christmas tree and comes out of a can.

'So we asked. We all went along with it – 'coz it's national policy too, so you can't rock the boat.' He actually patted his stomach at that, making his own position clear.

A woman in the corner hit the jackpot on the slot machine and it began to pump out coins so loudly they had to stop talking. Momentarily Talbot was distracted by the scene: the woman using her lap to catch her winnings. Dryden didn't understand people like Talbot, people who worked in a place like Whitemoor but seemed to be able to slough it off, like a snake skin, after work. Dryden had been in to the prison once and one image – of a man in a straight jacket in a bare cell – was always with him. He couldn't have worked there, day in, day out, and enjoyed the outside world.

Talbot looked at him as if he'd forgotten what he'd been saying, then picked up the thread: 'So they tried it about a month ago, this new menu. Just a trial – but we were up first, with Bedford. And guess what – prisoners liked it too. First day they grumbled – no chicken tikka on a Wednesday – that's a big deal if you're doing twenty-five years. That's more than 1,000 free takeaways.

'But – *but* – thing was, the food was better. The menu was set on a two week rota so they knew what was coming – they like that. Then we get a note down from the governor's secretary. Home Office says we have to stop – revenue implications: i.e. it costs too much. They reckon an extra five pence a day per prisoner. Yesterday, when they kicked up nasty, it was supposed to be Pollack and Chips, then Fresh Fruit Salad. Fresh fish, not some bit of white cardboard.

'But when they turn up at the canteen it's a roast – which is a fucking euphemism if ever I heard one. That plastic sliced meat. Christ knows what animal it comes from – could be a rat for all the taste you get. Plus steamed pudding and custard.

'That's when they kicked off. One bloke chucked a chair, then the rest started lobbing their roast and two veg into the waste bins from thirty feet away. By the time they'd finished it looked like they'd let the chimps from the zoo have a party.'

Dryden looked away, memorizing the quote. Anonymous source, an eye witness, no names.

'When the officer on duty told 'em to get back to their cells they downed anchors. Every last bastard one of 'em. Which was a bit tricky 'coz they know we were behind the idea in the first place.'

'But they're back in their cells now?'

'Governor came down to the canteen and said he'd go down to Whitehall – personally – to argue for the extra cash. POA thinks he's got no chance – but that's where we are.'

Dryden thought about the story.

PRISON RIOT TO SAVE FRESH FRUIT SALAD.

It wouldn't do the POA's campaign for fresher food any harm.

'OK,' he said. 'Thanks. Decent tale. Very decent.'

He got Talbot another pint. He only ever had two. That was another thing Dryden had noticed about the ex-military: they only seemed to drink in quarts, although he was pretty sure this wasn't the last quart of the day.

'One thing. Small favour,' said Dryden. He'd noted the details down on a blank report card. 'I'm trying to find the name of a prisoner. This is all we know – it's not much, but it's very specific, so I thought it might just be possible.' He looked Talbot in his watery grey eyes – a signal that he *expected* help. Dryden didn't just give Talbot a way into the local press. Dryden could get stuff in the nationals because his copy was trusted on what used to be called Fleet Street.

'What do we know?' asked Talbot, picking up the card.

'Lincoln – pre-1977,' said Dryden. 'He occupied a cell very close to the one later occupied by a man called Lionel Wraight. Very keen chess player, our man – got chummy with the governor. Well-in.'

'Offence?'

'No idea. I've got a morgue shot – but I don't think it would help. They never do. Dark hair, five feet eleven, green eyes. Slim. No fingerprints – victim of a fire.'

'I'll try,' said Talbot.

'Know anyone well at Lincoln?' asked Dryden, pushing, making it clear he wanted him to try hard.

'Yeah – brother. Just transferred. The cell numbers will help – but it might mean you get twenty names. The chess stuff is good – governor's new, but back then they stuck around for years. So that's your best chance. Someone will remember – maybe.'

He sighed. 'Give me a day – or two.' He let two-thirds of a pint slide down his open gullet.

Walking out the bar every pair of eyes watched him go: the slight roll to the shoulders, the unbroken gaze, the set face. That was another thing about the military – and coppers – probably anyone in authority who wore a uniform. They were like spots on dominoes. Ex-Navy stood out even more. Even in jeans and a sweatshirt you could pick them out from a nautical mile.

THIRTY-TWO

Tuesday

'**E**den,' said Laura.
The registrar took a note. 'Eden Gaetano,' said Dryden.
They'd made the final decision over breakfast at home. *Eden* for Roger and because it was an inspiring name, and *Gaetano* for Laura's father and to remind the child of his Italian heritage.

'Could you spell that – the middle name?' The registrar was a woman; neat and businesslike, with some charm Dryden suspected had been learnt on a training course and therefore wasn't charm at all. 'What a wonderful name,' she added, as she laboured over the tricky AE vowels.

Dryden was surprised at the simplicity of the bureaucracy for registering the birth of a child. While the registrar shuffled the paperwork and Laura fed Eden he looked out across the open-plan office. He wondered how Kapten Kross was progressing in trying to track down the official responsible for taking death certificates from district registrars and then failing to notify the GRO in Southport. He guessed he'd start at the council HQ at Chatteris, with separate inquiries in London and Southport. Time frame? Dryden guessed they'd go for 1977 plus ten years.

The registrar added some details to an online form. Dryden had always thought of the registration system: births, deaths and marriages, as a paper system. You still needed certificates. But this must be the digital system Philip Trelaw had described. Electronic certificates flying through the Internet. He wondered then, for the first time, if that would have stopped them stealing identities from the dead. That the Internet age would make it, finally, an impossible crime.

Outside in the corridor Dryden could see movement and then DI Friday's face appeared at the glass porthole. He held up his wrist, pointed at his watch, and indicated 'five' with his fingers.

'We should celebrate,' said Laura. The pupil of her left eye vibrated slightly – one of the lasting side effects of her coma – and an indication that she'd slept badly. Both of them had stayed awake, listening to the noises of the lonely fen: a door banging with maddening infrequency, the Tyler's dog barking a mile away, the swish of the wind turbine towards dawn, and finally the dull percussion of the bird-scaring canon. They hadn't talked but both knew they were sharing the same waking nightmare: the carry-cradle, empty again. Reluctantly, just before dawn, Dryden had told her what he wanted her to do. She'd argued against the plan for an hour, then turned away.

Before falling into a brief sleep she'd said one more thing: 'This house is bringing us bad luck.'

But now the child had a name she seemed upbeat.

'Coffee?' suggested Dryden, wondering now if they'd go through with the plan they'd agreed. In broad daylight the dangers seemed fanciful. 'Stefano's? I'll be a moment – the police want a word. I'll see you there.'

He found DI Friday in the general reception area. He followed him out, across the car park, down the alley to the incident room in the old cinema. There were two CID men working at PCs. Kross sat at a desk on a landline.

Friday looked like he'd been sleeping in his clothes. As he led Dryden into the room his foot dragged badly. He patted his suit pockets searching for cigarettes.

'Still fun and games then?' asked Dryden, in a whisper.

Friday just looked through him.

'Kross seems like a nice bloke,' said Dryden. 'Likes a pint and a fag, does he?'

'Piss off.'

Dryden imagined what it was like working for Kross – the one-way information flow, the peremptory orders, the need-to-know rule ruthlessly imposed.

'Thought they'd have gone home by now, left you to it. Job for the Met now surely – or the regional crime squads. Or are they all off to Blackpool's best hotels for the weekend?'

Friday turned his back so that Kross couldn't see his lips move.

'You're joking. One of the Estonians is still knocking about, along with fifty fake IDs, and you think these fuckers are off back to wherever they came from? On their expenses? Grow up.'

Dryden turned away, shrugging, to conceal his surprise. He knew Kross and Interpol had good contacts. And he knew they'd been alerted to the sale of a large number of fake IDs – but he'd not been told the *number*. Friday had clearly presumed that Kross had given Dryden this detail. A case of bad communications.

In his turn Kross had presumed that the package Dryden had received by post held *all* the IDs. But Dryden had counted only twenty-five. Again, bad communications. Kross' dictatorial style had its limitations.

So – thanks to Friday's simple honesty, he now knew the truth: that Roger had found only half the consignment out at River Bank. Where were the rest? A question the Estonians had no doubt asked themselves, which explained why they had yet to both go home.

Dryden's mobile rang. He looked at the display screen which simply gave an Ely number, so he took the call. It was a man he called Fitz, a regular contact, who worked for the National Farmers' Union as a PR.

'It's this story in the paper,' said Fitz. 'The Petit Fen land sale.'

Dryden had been proud the story had made the splash in the *Ely Express*. And he'd sold it on to the *Guardian* for tomorrow's paper with 850 words of background. So the chance there was something amiss made his skin creep because the last thing he wanted was to get a reputation on Fleet Street for duff tip-offs. Selling two-dimensional stories was a short-cut to being black-listed; becoming one of those names that every news desk shuns.

'It's all fine and dandy,' said Fitz, who was Irish, and occupied a permanent position at the bar of The Bell on Market Square when he wasn't out on some godforsaken stretch of the Fens talking to his members.

'But the price is wrong. Got to be. We've got members out on Petit Fen and it's some of the best seed growing soil in the county. One of 'em said a parcel got sold off to one of the big agri-companies a decade ago and that went for £400,000. Ten years ago. This one's smaller apparently but still – the number's way wrong.'

In the background Dryden heard gulls and a tractor. 'Either way you can check with the Land Register. Just thought I'd say.'

'I owe you,' said Dryden, and cut the line.

He thumb-texted his contact at the *Guardian* and told him to hold the story – update to come. Then he rang the Land Register which was about thirty yards away in the town hall annexe and requested the information on the sale. He'd come by to pick up the information in ten. If the transaction had been registered – and most were, although it was a voluntary system – then they'd have the real number in the time it took to make half-a-dozen key strokes.

Then he tried to work out if it mattered. Sheila Petit had said the £20,000 was just a number plucked from mid-air to protect the donor. But why had she chosen a figure so wildly low? Every reader who knew anything about agricultural land values would spot the mistake, which made him feel like a fool.

Another CID officer, a woman, came in the door with a tray of coffees and gave Dryden one, Kross another.

'Congratulations,' said Kross. 'Your son has a name?'

'Eden,' said Dryden. He thought it sounded better every time he said it.

Some of Kross' calm arrogance had gone to be replaced by a kind of nervous hyperactivity.

'Sit,' he said. 'Drink.' He spilt sugar sachets and milk cartons from his pockets.

'So – found your man yet?' asked Dryden. 'Chatteris – the register office. An inside job?'

'He – or she – will be there, yes. Or, perhaps, was there. If we knew some of the names of those in the package it would be easier for us.'

'I said. I didn't open the individual wallets.'

'You did.'

'How about Trelaw – you ruled him out? He seemed to think the paperwork would put him in the clear.'

Kross smiled. 'Just a few ends are loose,' he said.

Across the over-polished table Kross spread some pictures. 'We take these at the funeral of this man who used your father's name.'

'Funeral? He's been buried – already?'

'Cremated.'

The fresh anger Dryden felt was strangely inappropriate. He wanted to know – wanted to demand to know – why he hadn't been told that they'd released the body. That he hadn't been notified. But he knew the answers: Kross and Friday would have leaned on the coroner to let the funeral take place because they wanted the case forgotten. Submerged, without a trace, beneath the DA-Notice. And they hadn't notified him because he wasn't family, wasn't even related. A man had stolen his father's name. That was it.

'That was quick,' was all he said.

'We thought perhaps the funeral would bring people, people from his past. We need to know who this man was – before he was Jack Dryden. These people attend – you recognize any at all?'

The pictures had been taken out at Manea at the cemetery. The crematorium chimney was in the background, and the small ugly chapel which looked like an electricity booster station.

Six people. He knew none of them. They stood in a small group waiting for the doors of the chapel to open.

'Who are they?' Dryden asked.

'We take names. His friends. Some people from his pub, I think – two pupils, these . . .' Kross dabbed a finger tip on two middle-aged women. 'They do exams.' Dryden studied the faces, which were all looking directly at the camera. Not one of them was disfigured by a birthmark. Where was Jack Dryden's friend Lionel Wraight?

'And this . . .' he added. A big black-and-white portrait picture. 'This is the Jack Dryden they bury – this from his library ticket.'

The picture was much clearer than any he'd seen. This man could never have been his father. The bone structure was too wide at the cheeks, the forehead too shallow, although there was still that unsettling resemblance – a ghost of a likeness, as if he'd been a cousin, long lost.

'If the car accident was just that why are you bothered?' asked Dryden, although he didn't even hear the answer. He was studying the picture taken at Manea again. It wasn't the faces that interested him; it was the cars parked on the tarmac by the Garden of Remembrance.

One was an old Rover, the paintwork almost mirror-like, an AA badge on the front grille. A classic model from the 1960s – the P4. One of Philip Trelaw's beloved P4s. Dryden doubted that the former registrar of the East Fens attended funerals as a hobby. Why had he felt the need to see Jack Dryden turned to ashes?

THIRTY-THREE

When he kissed Laura on the pavement outside *The Crow* he tried not to make it feel like goodbye. Humph studiously ran a chamois leather over the cab's windscreen. He'd told Laura what DI Friday had let slip – the fifty missing IDs, the reason why the Estonians were still on the trail. They both knew what that meant. They had to go through with their plan, and they had to do it now.

'Ring when you get to the coast,' said Dryden. Then he thought about that: the papers were full of stories of mobile phones being hacked into, answerphone messages downloaded. 'Ring on the landline from the B and B – OK? From a call box. *The Crow*, or home. Not the mobile. Humph will text when you're on the train.'

'Families should stay together,' said Laura, the diction particularly syrupy, so Dryden guessed she was close to tears.

'We are together. We're staying together. It's just distance – space on a map – and for a few days.' He'd been close to giving in during the last twenty-four hours – agreeing with her that he was being dramatic, even melodramatic. But now they both knew this had to happen.

Laura's face was a mask, features stiff and pinched. That was the big difference between the worlds they lived in. His was inside his head, so it didn't matter if they were 1,000 miles away. Hers was intensely physical. If she couldn't touch him, he wasn't there.

She checked her bag then threw it in the boot of the Capri. She'd thought he was overreacting, indulging most journalists' tendency to live in a made-up reality where the dangers were darker, the excitement headier. Even now she tried desperately to think of another way.

'Just enjoy the beach,' said Dryden, putting a finger over her lips.

'It'll rain. It's Norfolk. Not Via Reggio.'

Humph was in the cab, and the engine coughed like a smoker.

They put the child on the back seat with the belt through the cradle. She wound down the window and manufactured a smile. 'Please, be careful.'

Then a wave and they were gone in a drifting cloud of blue exhaust, joining the queue of traffic trying to get out of Market Street. He watched until the Capri turned the corner.

He felt a slight uplift in his mood, the almost physical sensation that the weight of responsibility had lessened. He imagined the journey to Norwich, then the little train up the line to Cromer. There was a B&B they'd used the summer before with a view of the sea. It had a sunrise in glass over the door. They'd be safe there, lost in the kiss-me-quick crowds. As long as they weren't followed. That was Humph's job – to zigzag his way to the Norwich line, with an eye on the rear-view mirror.

Dryden took a place in the line of shoppers waiting for the East Fens' bus. When it lurched to a halt he grabbed a seat on the top deck at the front, like a kid, and fished in his pocket for a bag of mushrooms he'd bought on the market. They were out of town in less than two minutes, rocking across the chessboard fens. The bus smelt of cabbage even in summer. Everyone over thirty stayed on the bottom deck, leaving upstairs for holiday kids and moody teenagers.

The bus flew east. On his lap Dryden unfurled the OS map. The price of Sheila Petit's strip of land remained a mystery as neither party to the transaction had registered the transaction: unusual, but not unheard of, according to the official who'd rung him to save him a trip to the town hall annexe. He'd already had two texts from the *Guardian*: the deadline for the inside page slot was three o'clock.

The bus was soon running along the banktop beside Adventurers' Mere. Dryden checked his signal on the mobile and rang the council asking to be put through to CCTV. The man who answered the phone said Philip Trelaw was off sick – off sick 'again'. Dryden rang the office and got Jean on reception to flick through the telephone book. Surprisingly P. F. Trelaw was not ex-directory and he answered at the second ring. Could he answer one or two more questions? Dryden wanted to know why Trelaw had felt the need to attend the funeral of the man who had posed as Jack Dryden, but it was a question he wanted to ask to his face. Trelaw, who sounded like he was lying down, the voice slightly groggy, was reluctant to see him in person. Dryden said it could wait – he was happy to drop in at the CCTV offices the next day. That wasn't what Trelaw had in mind. So he offered to meet Dryden at three at his house: the address, a suburban street on the edge of Ely.

The bus driver shouted 'Middle Pump' as the gears grated and the bus braked. A four-storey Victorian steam pump house, converted to flats by trendy architects who'd gone out of their way to make it uglier, stood at the junction of three roads, a spot celebrated by a post box, three brick cottages, a phone box, a parish notice board and a bench. In fen terms this constituted a 'place' – which is why it had a name at all. Sometimes it was the most memorable thing these places ever had.

Petit Hall stood back from the road a mile south. It was a long mile, like all the rest on the Fens, and walking it was like hiking the wrong way along one of those moving pavements at the airport. At one point Dryden was pretty certain he was getting further away from the stand of trees which stood to the west of the hall's garden. Halfway along he passed Home Farm. Someone was out in the giant field, pacing the boundary, but Dryden's eyesight wasn't keen enough to see if it was Petit's nephew, Edward. There was a small house with the farm itself – no more than a tied cottage, and a child's dress hung from a washing line, cracking in the wind. Finally, he turned into the drive, which was freshly tarmacked and marked with a sign which said:

Petit Hall
Nos. 1–6

The house stood alone, as stark as a standing stone, two storeys plus a row of windows in the attic, a slightly fussy porchere, but otherwise straightforward Victorian solidity. Dryden knew it hid a secret. Sheila Petit told the story to anyone who'd listen, and quite a few more. The Petits had arrived with the Normans at Hastings and been rewarded with estates in Kent. One of them, a Merchant Adventurer of London, had risked everything on the draining of the Fens. A wager that had been handsomely rewarded.

The house behind the facade was late-seventeenth century. As a landscape the Fens was only three hundred and fifty years old. This house was one of the few that had seen it all. Fen aristocracy set in bricks and mortar.

There were five cars parked on raked gravel. All of them freshly polished, including Petit's Morris Minor. The door buzzed when he rang the bell for *S Petit – Flat One*, so he pushed it open to reveal a hall with a black-and-white chequered floor. Doors to either side, a staircase with polished floorboards. Glass cases held fish – pinioned against hand-painted backgrounds of reed and weed. The gold frames held citations to weight and date. A giant pike showed off its snaggle teeth.

A little sign pointed to Flat One where Dryden would have guessed the kitchen had once been – ground floor, at the back.

Sheila Petit answered the door, large glasses on a necklace, a mug of coffee in one hand, *Ely Express* in the other. She blinked several times. 'Dryden.'

'Sorry. I tried the sorting office. They said it was a day off; I had a question . . .' He nodded at the paper. It might be her day off but the helmet of carefully arranged grey hair was as brittle as ever.

'Of course.' She stood aside but Dryden sensed a reluctance to let him in.

A short corridor led past a galley kitchen and a bathroom to the large room that had indeed been the original kitchen: quarry tiled, with a range, the back wall opened up into a half-brick conservatory which gave an uninterrupted view of the fen beyond looking east. Light poured in and seemed to lift the ceiling which was, Dryden noted, decorated with plaster reeds, ducks and eel.

'Wow,' he said.

'Yes. Best room in the house,' she said, her voice suddenly warmer, the usual precise diction softened. 'The rest are flats. It pays the bills. Needs must. Posh bedsits really. But I couldn't face a complete rebuild – all those horrible plaster walls. It makes the place so spooky – so *altered*. At least this way I can dream . . .'

Dryden tilted his head by way of a question.

'Of having it all back. The house. And just me. Bliss.' She drew herself up, arms crossed. 'Still – you had a question.' The voice was louder now and Dryden had the distinct impression there was someone else in the flat.

There was a portrait on one wall, in a swagger gold frame. A couple and a young boy in an informal group by a fireplace.

She followed his gaze. 'That was painted in the drawing room. Flat two now.'

'And that's you?'

She'd be in her twenties, perhaps, a hand on the child's shoulder. A boy, who resembled the man who must have been thirty, with short mousy hair and a heavy agricultural face. She didn't offer an answer but sipped from a mug of tea.

If she was going to decline small chat he'd get down to business. 'I have a problem with the story – just a detail.'

He'd walked to a large oak sideboard crowded with family pictures – mostly the boy again, growing up. There was one with him at the wheel of a tractor, then a university shot – Dryden didn't recognize the buildings – but not Cambridge or Oxford. St Andrew's?

'Fire away – let's take some air,' she said, throwing open French doors in the conservatory and walking out into the sunshine. Dryden thought then that she said it solely to get him out of the house. He took a last look back and noticed that on the kitchen table there were two coffee cups: one a mug with the crest of Cambridge University, the other an espresso cup, unmarked, porcelain.

There was half an acre of lawn leading down to a ditch, then beyond that a field. The sense of free space was almost hypnotic. Dryden couldn't keep his eyes off the horizon, as if he was at sea, on the lookout. In the distance was the bank of the Little Ouse, one of the main river's tributaries, and crouched in its lee what looked like a boat house.

He'd thought about how to play this interview. Originally he'd opted for direct and honest, but now he was at Petit Hall something told him to be more circumspect, even devious. 'I've had some feedback on this land sale. I'm told £20,000 is way off the mark – by a factor of ten, or twenty, or more. Anyone who knows anything about the market would see it was wrong. Sorry, but it makes me look like an idiot.'

'The owner sold at below the market price – he's a member

of the campaign. And I said the price was only ball park.'

'Sorry – you didn't mention that the seller was taking a loss when we talked. I think it would have been honest to have said that, even if it was off the record.'

Petit's eyes hardened, the irises seeming to flatten so that they no longer reflected the light. She always presented herself as of that generation that had risen above dishonesty. 'Did you really think that strips of prime peatland go under the hammer at £20,000?'

Dryden relaxed. He was always constrained by politeness as a reporter, but now the gloves were off he felt at liberty to say what he thought. 'Have you read *Macbeth*?' It was a calculated insult, as he knew Petit had read English at Cambridge.

'That's how the witches operate, isn't it? They tell people things they want to hear but hide the truth by omission. In everyday life we call this lying. Why bother giving me the £20,000 price when the transaction is not based on a market price at all?'

She went to answer but he cut her off.

'I'm angry because I should have checked. I didn't because I trusted you. This appears to have been my mistake.' When he got angry, which was rare and lasted only for a handful of seconds, his voice took on a buzz. It was very effective, and even out here in the garden he thought he heard Petit's mug vibrate on the picnic table.

He was honest enough – with himself – to admit that most of his anger was fuelled by the knowledge that the story was a shoddy piece of work. He believed her because she'd given him what he wanted: the splash.

And he still didn't understand. 'Why sell at all?' he asked. 'If he's on your side to the tune of what – half a million or more – why not just let him sit on the land and refuse to sell to the government?'

She had her hands on the wooden table, the knuckles knotted. 'I said – I think – that we wanted to put the land in trust.' The fact that she hadn't tried to throw him out after being accused of being a liar spoke volumes. 'There has to be a price – it could have been fifty pence. That way we have a legal sale. We needed to transfer the ownership to the trust. Otherwise I could have used this house to stop them – as I said, the last time we spoke. We're anxious about compulsory purchase and we want to make sure that we have a long-term solution. Simply letting him sit on the land was no good at all. What if future heirs to the estate decide they would quite like the purchase price – or even part of it?'

She was on her feet now, pacing, every inch a member of the landed gentry. Turning, she set her jaw. 'I do not intend to see this house – my family's house – under six feet of water. Or the land, for that matter.'

Dryden stood, tired of the lecture. 'And you can't give me the names of either of these two people – the one who is selling below the market price, and the one who is donating the sale money? It's not listed at the Land Registry. I could find out – there must be a way, but I don't have the time. Other people – other papers – want the story.'

'No, I can't. The fact is the deal has been done. Perhaps we should just say the details are private. Which is true. Now – it is a day off for me – but I'm afraid that doesn't mean I have nothing to do. What do you intend to do? Take the nice fat fee for selling the story to Fleet Street or not?'

'Well, as we've descended to the level of plain abuse I think I'll keep that decision to myself.'

He turned to go.

She hadn't finished. 'You can walk back round the house through the trees,' she said. It was a petty, calculated insult; as if she'd demanded he exit by the tradesmen's door even if he'd got in at the front. But when he looked at her face he saw she'd regretted what she'd said.

'I'll amend the story,' he said. He judged she was telling the truth. He had the facts – or at least enough of the facts. He could rewrite for the *Guardian*. 'Land sold by one supporter of your campaign to another for an agreed price, I think – we'll leave out the figure itself.'

She started to speak but stopped. They stood together locked in a confusion of insult and reconciliation.

'You *can* go through the house . . .' she said.

'No. It's fine.'

He walked away at last. Trees were rare out on the open fen and showed that the house must be built on a clay islet in the peat: a vast cedar, a fig, a Douglas pine. He was in the shadows when he saw flowers in the half-light. Walking under the canopy of the cedar he saw a gravestone. Grand in a classy way: a stone edge to the plot, a granite headstone five feet high, with engraved lettering in memory of Sheila Petit's husband. The words and dates were crowded into the top half of the stone, leaving more than enough space, when the time came, for an inscription for his wife.

THIRTY-FOUR

Trelaw's house was a prime example of suburban squalor – if Ely could be said to have a suburb at all. The town tended to just peter out. But there was a thin band of fifties semis on the edge of West Fen, pebble-dashed and bay-windowed. Some had port holes, some didn't, some had stained glass over the front door, some didn't. But all the houses in York Crescent were well painted, with new plastic double-glazed windows, the roofs bristling with Sky dishes. All except Trelaw's. It still had wooden window frames, paint peeling, and the net curtains were grey and torn. The front garden had gone to seed, and the pebble-dashing was disfigured by damp.

Dryden checked his mobile for a message from Humph. Nothing.

The cabbie's instructions were simple. Head north from Ely, make sure he wasn't being followed, then swing around towards the Norwich line, drop Laura and Eden at one of the smaller stations. Then, from Norwich, a local train up to Cromer. Kross might think Dryden was safe, that his family were safe, but Kross didn't know what he knew: that only half the consignment of fake IDs were back in the hands of the Saar brothers.

The mobile trilled: it was a text from Humph and said simply, ON TRAIN. TRAIN ON TIME.

Dryden began to whistle tunelessly. It was late afternoon on York Crescent and nothing moved. He hated suburbia – and if he was honest it was easy to see why. After his father's death he'd been taken away from Burnt Fen, from a world he loved, to the grey streets of North London. It wasn't the uniformity, or the similarity of the houses and the people in them, it was this brittle, dull, silence that really got to him.

A cat crossed the road, leaving that silence unbroken.

At the gate of Trelaw's house Dryden stopped and saw the net curtain twitch in the bedroom. The window was just open and he could hear Bach with adverts: Classic FM. The Rover P4 was parked in front of a wooden garage.

The front door was open too, just an inch, and it swung into the hall when Dryden touched it. There was no carpet. Newspapers covered the boards and in several places oily engine parts were set in drip trays. The hat stand was hung with so many coats and umbrellas it blocked out the light which came from the kitchen – the door to which was open. Dryden saw a wooden table, on which was a carburettor. And two bottles of wine, red, both empty. Food aromas hung in the air: bacon and maybe burnt toast. Definitely something burnt. But the background smell was of oil and petrol. He called out Trelaw's name. Out loud he said he was coming up the stairs. Wallpaper hung down in loops in one corner of the landing but there was a carpet up here which looked new, although it didn't seem to have been fitted, so that there were gaps at the edges where he could see the floorboards. And a mirror – the only decoration he'd seen in the whole house – one of those fifties oval gilt mirrors that distorts the image like a fish-eye lens.

The net curtains had twitched in the front room as he'd approached the house so he knocked on that door, then pushed it open. He stood looking at the bed, the headboard, the pillows. One of the pillows had a bright red circle in the middle of it, and in the middle of that a black circle. Dryden knew instantly that this was where the burnt smell came from. A wisp of smoke rose from the burnt hole. Shock pumped adrenalin into his system and he could hear his heart beat – once, twice, three times. He knew it was a bullet hole in the pillow but he didn't let the words form in his brain.

Time had slowed down. The door was still swinging open to reveal Trelaw's lower body on top of the duvet. He was in a dressing gown – baby blue and clean. His head was missing, but then Dryden realized it was under the pillow. Dryden saw it then – the moment of death – the pillow pressed down, the gun to the linen case, the dull percussion of the bullet fired through the wadding inside the pillow case.

In his right eye he saw movement, reflected sunlight in an old mirror. An arm crooked round his neck and closed across his throat with a mechanical strength, totally irresistible. A knee blow killed the muscle in his left thigh, so that his nervous system seemed to short out like a fuse. He was on his knees in a half-breath, and didn't know how he'd got there.

Then he was standing up because someone had an arm round his neck and had lifted him up. It was extraordinary how helpless he was. It wasn't a matter of panic, or cowardice, or weakness; he was just overcome by what was happening, so he'd become loose, puppet-like. The sound in his ears was distorted, as if he'd been plunged under water. The constriction of his windpipe was complete. He'd lost two seconds of air supply but his body was already anticipating death: his eyes burnt, and his knees had gone, so that all the weight was taken by the arm round his neck.

Two minutes earlier he'd been standing in the street outside looking at a suburban semi-detached house. In another minute he'd be dead. He was swung out into the hallway and dragged to the top of the stairs.

When he considered these few seconds, looking back, he remembered two things: that the man wore gloves – plastic surgical gloves – and that he reeked of marine fuel which has quite a distinct aroma compared to petrol or car oil.

A voice which was so close as to be inside his head said: 'The boy was a warning. Your last warning.'

His feet dragged on the floor as he was edged towards the top step. His eyes were full of water but he caught a glimpse of his face in the fish-eye mirror: the whites of his eyes, bulging, and – at the moment he was thrown – he saw another face revealed behind him. It was Miiko Saar and, despite the mirage-like distortion of the glass, he could see that he was smiling. And see his wrist watch with its wide classic Roman face, and the little compass at the centre.

THIRTY-FIVE

When Dryden opened his eyes he closed them again, immediately – not a conscious act but, he thought later, a defensive one. It gave him time to examine the image he'd seen, and match it to what he could feel. But even then, at that moment, and it could have been no longer than a handful of seconds, he knew he was already trying not to panic, forcing himself to analyse with his mind, rather than react with his emotions, his instincts. If he'd let a primeval response override everything else he'd have screamed. And that would have been the beginning of the spiral, a downward journey, even though he could go no lower.

He'd seen stars. Early evening stars on a light blue canvas. Perhaps the handle of the Plough, but otherwise he could discern no patterns, no pleasing dotted-line Greek heroes or myths: no Orion, or Pegasus. Stars, but not the whole sky, just a rectangle above, surrounded by blackness. What he felt was water. He was lying in water but not floating. An inch, maybe two inches of water. His back, ice cold, on the ground, with – he thought – a pebble or two cutting into his shoulder blade. But that was difficult to isolate because of the other pains.

Pain: at first a dull pulse like a heartbeat, but soon – sickeningly quickly – sharper. Then he remembered the house on York Crescent, the blood on the pillow, the gunshot hole and Saar's face, relishing the moment when he threw Dryden from the top of the stairs. His left hip hurt most and he wondered if it was broken, and his left arm – at the elbow, and most of all – stupidly – the fingers of his left hand, which individually seemed to radiate more pain than the rest of his body: a torch of pain, like a searchlight. He was lying on his arms, which were behind him, and he felt sure that they were tied at the wrists. And possibly his legs as well, at the ankles: his right leg sent him no sensation at all.

Finally – noise. Night noise at first. The single call of an owl, and dogs barking a long way off, and then trees rustling – so pines, shuffling like they do, giving the wind a voice. Then the rhythmic rumble of a goods train, quite clear, and surprisingly close. But otherwise he felt he could hear the open fen – as if he had bat ears, sending out pinging sonar which faded before finding a surface on which to rebound. A great expanse – above – enclosed by a night sky. It made him feel very afraid, so he shut down that emotion, because he could feel a scream rising like a choke.

Then he heard the slightest of sounds: a feathering. If you could hear silence in motion this was it. So he opened his eyes and saw it cross the rectangle above. An owl, a luminous owl, as white as a ghost, its wings motionless, gone in a half-second. So beautiful he was able to keep his eyes open, to let in the image which he'd now constructed through his other senses: the black outer frame of the sky made of four walls of black, damp earth.

He was lying in a grave.

An open grave – not a six by two plot, but one of the public open graves. Admitting it to himself helped quell the next rising scream. One of Manea's open public graves. Unless it was full they wouldn't be filling it in for months. So that helped reverse the spiral of panic because the one thing he feared was a shovel full of earth, thrown against the stars, blotting out his view of the sky.

And then a phone rang. He felt its warm throb in the pocket on his chest. It rang and rang – emitting the clanking sound of an old Bakelite phone. Then it cut off and he imagined the message being left: Laura, perhaps, from Cromer. He imagined her on the little promenade where you could get a signal. The sea white under the pier where the waves had to thread their way through the iron stanchions. The image was so immediate he felt his consciousness slipping, as if he would faint into the dream.

He kicked out instead and the pain made him shout – a thin noise which seemed to get swallowed by the earth walls. His left leg was useless, not broken, but the joint was so painful he wouldn't be able to move it again, knowing it would trigger that electric pulse to his brain.

His eyes were beginning to adapt to the starlight above, which is when he saw the other coffins. The pit was ten feet by ten and he could see four of them, arranged like little jigsaw pieces to save space in one corner. The cardboard coffins were already rotten, sagging. He thought he caught a glimpse of a bone and looked away.

He should shout out. But he felt that if he started to shout he wouldn't be able to stop, that the shout would shift to a scream, that he'd lose control, and that if no one came he'd scream and shout until he'd shredded his vocal cords. But what if he didn't shout? Would he live until morning? Yes. He would live until he was found. His only enemy was himself. If he couldn't control his fears: of the dark, of the grave, of the rats, perhaps, and the insects.

But if he lost his courage his heart might fail. He could feel it now, lurching out of kilter. He'd shout. Once. Then wait. Keeping control.

Filling his lungs he made his ears pop, ready to shout, when he heard a new noise: not so much heard, as felt. A rumble, in the earth under his sore shoulders. And a beam of light, cutting across the stars, then swinging away. A machine, moving in the graveyard, moving closer. He thought about the little digger truck, how it could trundle up to the side of the grave and tip in the spoil, and how that would silence him, how it would be in his eyes and his mouth, and then he'd never see the stars again.

He didn't shout anything coherent, he just started to scream. It started as the word HELP, but then became blurred and wailing. No one came and he tasted blood in his mouth so he stopped, his chest heaving, and realized the mechanical sound was louder, closer; not just the base notes now but the clanging of the machinery, the screeching of a rusty suspension bar.

Then silence, so he shouted again, straining so that he felt a muscle in his throat convulse.

A flashlight stabbed his eyes with pain, which seemed to set off a chain reaction in his body that led to his brain and closed his nervous system down. Just before he lost his sight he saw a figure against the stars, the head lost in a trailing cloud of cigarette smoke.

THIRTY-SIX

He was able to think about what had happened only when Billy Johns lit the fire: coke and a lump of bog oak from the fen. Watching the flames he realized how close fire and life were – how you couldn't have one without the other. Up to that moment his mind was hopelessly entangled with the opposite of fire and life, the coldness of the grave, and the broken rotting coffin boxes which had surrounded him. Standing in the shower block – an institutional addition to the caretaker's Victorian house – the heat had warmed his skin but not his bones. The flesh on those bones seemed oddly bloodless as if – and the thought made him retch – he had in some way been partly dead in the grave, that he'd started to rot, and been brought back in this damaged form. His hip was bruised – blackening – but he didn't think anything was broken, except one of his fingers, crooked from the second joint up. And his arm was lacerated. When he thought about falling down the stairs in Trelaw's house his legs buckled at the knees. He could remember the pain, not the sensation of falling. He didn't think about coming to in the grave: his brain wouldn't let the image form.

Overalls and a jumper added warmth but the shivering – which had begun when he'd come round beside the grave – would not abate. It was a summer's evening, the temperature in the sixties, but the quaking shivers made his jaw ache. So Johns had made the fire. Then he'd gone to the kitchen to make soup, leaving Dryden to stare into the flames. Questions continued to rise in his mind: was it a coincidence that he'd been found by Johns – cemetery keeper, son of an undertaker? Why had he been dumped at Manea? Why had Johns been out after dark working by the open graves?

He got out his mobile and sent a text. Humph replied within thirty seconds: GIVE ME TWENTY MINS.

Dryden had an almost overpowering urge to run from the house. To put miles between his warm body and the cold grave.

But he knew running was a bad idea – his hip was still numb, the joint swelling. He wouldn't get a hundred yards. The bog oak cracked, sending sparks showering on to the wooden floor-boards where they glowed and died.

Johns brought in a mug of soup and took the other seat – a beaten armchair like the one in which Dryden was curled. They both heard a floorboard creak above their heads, someone stirring in a bed.

'I should ring the police,' said Johns. The clock on the mantel-piece said it was nine o'clock. He picked a shred of tobacco from his lip even though he wasn't smoking. The hand that held his mug seemed to envelop it so that it was lost to sight. An institutional phone stood on the floor by the armchair, the landline snaking to the old skirting board. Johns didn't look that keen to use it.

'No – please. I'll talk to them, but not now.' He thought of Trelaw's bedroom. There was nothing he could do for the man now. Had the body been found?

'I probably deserve a bit more information than that,' said Johns, but his voice lacked confidence.

'It's about a boy called Samuel Setchey,' he said.

Johns stiffened.

'The child died four months after he was born in 1986. He's buried here – a private grave, I think. The death certificate was issued within twenty-four hours. But there's almost certainly no central registration of the death – nothing at all on a national database.'

Johns shrugged. 'You think that's unheard of? Someone's slipped up – it's a bureaucracy. A badly paid bureaucracy. They fuck up all the time, Dryden. Believe me. Dad used to despair of the paperwork. I was down there the other day and they're getting ready for computers – digitizing the service. Imagine – it'll get worse, not better.'

'It wasn't the first time, or the last – there's a pattern. Someone has been consistently not reporting deaths. Particular *kinds* of death, I think – the very young. Children.'

'Why?'

Dryden didn't like the tone of the question. Curious, perhaps, but it sounded like a challenge. He decided to ignore it.

'I heard a machine – when I was out there.'

Johns blinked and Dryden thought: he's trying to decide if he should repeat that question or let it go.

'Tipper truck. I was just moving stuff.'

'By starlight?'

'The council's decided to change the layout – because of the Yoruba baby. We'll use the iron covers for a while – six months, then it's all change. They think when you've written the story people will be shocked. They will – I know they will. Open graves, *multiple* open graves. I'd be shocked. So they're going to open up the far end – let some private burials in, landscape it.'

'The coroner's office is going to store bodies in future – we'll wait; when the time is right we'll dig a grave, complete the burials, all on one day.'

Even Johns was struggling with the euphemisms. 'Brass is coming out from Chatteris tomorrow to look at the site. I had to tidy up – it's supposed to be neat down there. So I was out on the tipper. It's got a searchlight.'

Dryden recalled the light in the sky.

'The engine cut out – it does that if I overdo the clutch. I heard you scream,' said Johns.

Dryden felt sick then at the thought that his life had hung on that narrow thread, and that if the tipper hadn't stalled he'd be out there now, in the grave, under the earth. Which meant that if Johns was telling the truth Miiko Saar had meant to kill him, and had devised a neat way to dispose of the body. But how did the Estonian know Johns would be working by searchlight on the paupers' graves? Again, Dryden felt the urge to run.

'I still think you should ring the police,' said Johns. 'Mind you – police are busy.' He sipped his tea. 'The radio says there's been another murder. No name – a house on the edge of Ely. They're not saying if it's linked to that one on Eau Fen.'

Johns looked at him over the top of his mug.

'It's one of those hidden worlds, isn't it?' asked Dryden, not expecting an answer. 'You probably don't realize. You're part of it. A cog. When someone dies it's like a secret society takes over. You're told not to worry, to let the system take over. It's like magic – once you contact the undertaker it all works. There's a grave allocated, a day allotted, the documents filed, the hearse on time, the body . . .'

Dryden leant forward into the heat of the fire.

'The body is the weirdest thing. When my mum died it wasn't till the ambulance took her away I thought – where's she going? Who'll look after her? Where will she be? The undertakers bury her – but when do they pick her up? It's because it's all about death. We don't want to ask, we don't even want to use the word. So we let other people take over. It's painless that way – but maybe, when you look back years later, there's more pain in the end, not less.'

They heard a car beep its horn, then the sound of a door opening on rusty hinges, a single bark.

'My cab,' said Dryden.

THIRTY-SEVEN

Humph was in a good mood because he'd picked up a return fare at Stansted. One of his regulars, an academic – a biotech engineer from MIT – so his passenger knew the ropes and so there was the thirty-five-pound standard fare, plus a five-pound tip, plus eight of those miniature bottles of hooch from the first-class trolley. Four malt whisky – a brand Dryden didn't recognize – and four white rum.

The cabbie's mobile rang twice on the journey but he didn't answer.

'It's that copper – from Eau Fen.'

'Detective Inspector Friday?'

'Right. Wants to know where you are. Keeps ringing. Why does he keep doing that?'

Dryden told him about Trelaw and the gunshot in the pillow. Had someone seen him going into Trelaw's house? Maybe. But more likely they'd simply talked to the CCTV department and been told the reporter had been asking after Trelaw. And Dryden hadn't been wearing gloves, so they'd get his prints eventually.

They drove to the minor injuries unit at Ely in silence. When they got there all the little miniatures were empty. Dryden's mobile had started to ring too. He ignored the phone and told the nurse on duty he'd had an accident. She asked how it had happened, sniffing the alcohol.

'I fell down the stairs,' said Dryden, which was at least only a lie by omission. Two of his fingers were bound together and he declined to show the nurse his hip, which was stiff, so that he hobbled.

'I'd have a very hot bath and go to bed for a week,' said the nurse, which was when she noticed the blood soaking through the sleeve of Dryden's shirt. It took them half an hour to bandage the lacerations.

'Anything else I should see before we set you free?'

'Thanks,' said Dryden, standing up too quickly, so that the room went round.

Back in the Capri Dryden scrabbled through the glove compartment to find a fresh miniature: a Martini this time. They drove to The Red, White and Blue. The effect of the alcohol was magical. A sublime warmth this time, suffusing. That was the word – *suffusing*. The pain, especially the pain in his hip, was a long way away now, almost in another country.

'You realize that you're the witness to a murder?' said the cabbie. 'Maybe you should call Friday?' He took the Capri out of gear and swung it into the car park of The Red, White and Blue.

The car park was empty but the pub was open. It was nearly closing time. They could see two teenagers playing pool through the main window.

'Can I kip at yours?'

Humph nodded. 'Car can stay here.'

They walked into the bar together and Humph saw Lionel Wraight, convener of the Ely Singles Club, sitting down, alone, nursing a pint.

Dryden bought Humph one, himself a tequila, and offered Wraight a refill – he took a double Bells – as Humph introduced them. The name: Dryden, made Wraight's eyes widen.

'I wanted a word,' said Dryden. 'Just give me a sec.' He took out his mobile and sent Laura a text saying all was well. It crossed his mind DI Friday might try to find her. And that was the last thing he wanted. So he should ring Friday – stop the search, end it soon.

They took a seat under the TV which was showing rugby highlights.

'You were a friend of Jack's?'

'You related?' asked Wraight.

'Kind of. He stole my Dad's name. Well – after 1977 he stole his life. I don't have any bones to pick with him – or his mates. I've just got a couple of questions.'

Wraight nodded, drinking the whisky.

'Jack was a friend then?' Dryden prompted.

'Yeah. Good mate, actually. Saved my life when I was inside – I told your man here.'

'Why didn't you make his funeral then? Not very nice. All he did for you.'

Wraight's eyes narrowed and Humph looked up from his crisps.

'What's this about?' asked Wraight.

'Humph tells me you did the odd job for him. I'm perfectly happy to let the DI on the case know that. There's a lot of interest in Jack Dryden's life after 1977. Any information would be gratefully received. But I don't have to do that if you can tell me a little bit about the jobs you did.'

Wraight's eyes flicked to the door. Classic reaction, thought Dryden. Fear and flight.

'Jack worked for someone. I don't know who – he never said. But I got the impression that if they were unhappy with what he did they'd do something about it – something permanent. So I thought, maybe, maybe he didn't die in an accident. And if they were pissed at him they might know about me and come looking for me too. I'm keeping a low profile. I don't want to talk to anyone.'

Dryden let the tequila hit the back of his throat. The door opened, Wraight jumped, and a man in a white coat came in selling sea food. A bloke at the bar asked him if he had crabs and got a laugh.

'Smart plan,' said Dryden, catching the barman's eye for refills. 'Tell me what I want to know and you won't see us again – or DI Friday of Ely CID. No one knows we're here. You're safe.'

Wraight thought about that. You could virtually hear the cogs turning. 'Nah. I'll take my chances with the local plods. But thanks for thinking of me.'

'OK. Only if I don't get what I want here I'll have to ask the same questions elsewhere and then your name might come up. And it's not like the people Jack worked for have gone away. They're still very much about the place. Pretty determined too, from what I'm told.'

Wraight downed the whisky in one, then pushed the empty glass forward.

'There's not much to tell.'

'So tell it,' said Dryden.

'It was random,' he said at last. 'Like, you know, just odd bits and pieces of jobs.' He'd switched back to a pint. 'I took a couple of driving tests.'

'False names?'

He nodded.

Dryden could see it now, the methodical reinvention of a life through the documents you need to live it.

'Pass every time?'

'I've got a HGV licence – advanced driving. I ain't gonna fail.'

'Anything else?'

'Jack would get a flat – Peterborough, Leicester, Newark. I'd go and doss there for a month or two and use the address to apply for stuff.'

'Stuff?'

'Passports. Passports, mainly. Library tickets. Travel cards. Bank accounts.'

Wraight pulled a face, or maybe the face pulled him – because it looked like stress, a sort of twitch which made his mouth curve down at one end. 'Just stuff – stuff we've all got. Get a doctor too, dentist, register with the NHS. Sometimes I had to get a job – just something standard like the local council bins. Then we could use that on the forms with the name. I'd be these people – just for a bit.'

'Did he just use you for this?'

He shook his head but only by a quarter inch.

'I think he had others – others he'd met in Lincoln. Round the country.'

'False names again?'

Dryden could see Wraight struggling with the answer and suddenly realized how bright he was – under the mockney and the bluff. He'd seen a subtlety in Dryden's question. 'Sorry – not *false*. That's the point, isn't it – real names. Not made up at all. The names of the dead.'

'I guess.'

'Where'd he get them? The names?'

'No idea.'

'Not off Billy Johns?'

'Who's he?' He said it just a bit too quickly, but Dryden let him get away with it. Maybe Johns wasn't involved. Or maybe he was, and it wasn't Wraight's job to keep in touch. Maybe it was Jack Dryden's job, and that's why he'd been on the road to Manea the day he died.

Wraight left then. So they had another drink and waited to get thrown out. Walking back through the dark streets Dryden felt his bruised legs beginning to stiffen.

DI Friday was sat on Humph's doorstep. Smoking methodically, a little shower of stub ends around his feet. Humph went to bed and left them talking in the garden: Friday said Trelaw was dead, that a man close to the description of Miiko Saar had been seen in the next street to Trelaw's getting into a four-by-four. The murder weapon – a Russian-made pistol – was found at the scene, free of prints, minus serial number. Six police authorities were now hunting for the Estonian. All ports and airports were on alert. That aside – had Dryden been in the house?

Dryden said he hadn't. He did want to speak to Trelaw – he'd been the registrar who'd signed his father's death certificate – a certificate which had never been registered with the GRO. Now it was too late to ask him any questions.

Friday said forensics were all over the scene of crime like a rash and if it turned out Dryden was lying he'd bang him up just for the fun of it.

Then they wished each other good night: God bless.

The clock beside Humph's spare bed said 10.36 p.m. When he woke up it said 10.41 p.m. He'd lied to DI Friday because he couldn't face a formal interview, a trip to the station, a night in the cells. Tomorrow, maybe, he'd tell him all he knew. But it meant he couldn't sleep. Something told him he was close to something now, something like the truth. So he lay there thinking about what they'd done, men like Lionel Wraight, working for Jack Dryden for years and years, salting away the new IDs, waiting for the ghosts to come of age. Jack Dryden, the spider in the centre of the web. And that left him with the only true puzzle which remained: who *was* the man who became Jack Dryden, the man who'd stolen the lives of children?

THIRTY-EIGHT

Wednesday

T he main entrance hall of the magistrates court was marble – grey-blue pillars, a vaulted roof, mahogany doors. It was cool, a haven from the hot pavements of the town centre. The WRVS had a tea stall and a few of the lawyers stood around talking to their clients. Young men modelled cheap suits, trying to look at ease. On a wooden bench a woman sat with a teenager beside her, holding his hand in a grip which was turning her knuckles white. The doors to the court swung open and Dryden caught a glimpse of the drama within: the magistrates sitting as a tribune beneath the triple-arched window, the accused lounging in the dock, and Vee – alone on the press bench – snapping the pages of her notebook back and forth.

Dryden slipped through a door marked AUTHORISED STAFF ONLY; a cold stone corridor led to a stairwell down to the cells. A uniformed PC at the bottom asked for his name but Senior Prison Officer Gerry Talbot had already seen him and beckoned him through. There were eight cells, four on either side of a wide corridor with benches on both sides.

Talbot checked the spyhole on one of the cells, explaining he'd been detailed to bring in a prisoner from Whitemoor for an appearance before the magistrates. 'Just routine – he'll be for the Crown Court. Still, it's a day out.' He took out a breast pocket notebook: black, flip-back and neat. 'I've got something for you – by way of thanks. The canteen story was a dream.'

Dryden had sold the tale to the *Daily Telegraph* which had run it on the front under the headline: PRISONERS RIOT TO SAVE SALAD DAYS. From there it had gone to *The Today Programme*, which had got the head of the POA in to talk about the union's campaign for better food. The Home Secretary came on live to announce that the new menus had been halted in order to cost a roll-out to all the country's prisons. This would begin in three months, but Whitemoor would get its new menu back immediately. Mr Talbot could have done no better with his press contacts. A fact which will have done his career in the union no harm at all.

In the black notebook Talbot had a prison snapshot: PRISONER 5-FG6. Cell 45. Category A. It was the man who'd lived his life as Jack Dryden, and died in the burnt-out van at Manea. Dryden read the prisoner's name beneath the picture twice – checking he hadn't just conjured the image of the words up out of nothing. It was an oddity of his imagination that he could do that, as if words were objects you could realize in 3D.

Just a name, but it changed everything. His mind raced: building motives, scenarios. And to think, only the night before, he'd lain there unsleeping thinking he'd worked it all out. How the man called Jack Dryden had been the first to steal an ID, then – with Setchey and Johns' help – he'd built a business, a trade, in the lives of others. Now, suddenly, that was only half the story. Jack Dryden hadn't been the spider in the centre of the web at all. 'Tell me about him,' he said, trying to keep his voice flat.

'Chummy? Not much to tell. In for murder – Oxford, 1971. Clever kid – one of those genius types you get in maths. University – Edinburgh. But that summer – 'seventy-one – he was at a summer school in Oxford for high-flyers like him. Prodigies. They'd all got together to talk about something or other . . .' He checked his notebook: 'Latin Squares – whatever they are.'

He stood, checked the cell again, which was silent, and continued: 'Anyway – he may have been a whizz with numbers but he was crap with human beings. There was a girl on the summer school. They got close. They went for a walk by the river. She didn't come back. He said she'd just walked off after they'd had some argument – about sums. Sums with brackets . . .' He flicked through the notebook. 'Factors – that was it. Anyway, her family was distraught. They organized a search. Eight days later they found her in a creek off the main river near Iffley – face down in the mud. She'd been pushed down with enough force to break her neck.

'He changed his story – said she'd gone off to meet a man.

She was local, see. At Keble. Said he'd warned her not to go.
That's what did for him – if he'd stuck to his first story he might
have had a chance, although not much of one. There was plenty
of forensics so the jury only took twenty minutes. He got the
maximum tariff because he'd put the family through those eight
days of waiting.'

'Straight to Lincoln?' asked Dryden. He was asking questions,
listening to answers, but on another level he was putting the
pieces of the jigsaw together. The name was a key which neatly
opened the well-oiled lock of the mystery of his father's death,
the murder on Eau Fen, and his uncle's death at River Bank. In
the end it was all in a name.

'Yup. Straight to Lincoln. Do not pass go. Model prisoner –
didn't do him any good at first. Spent three years in his cell
playing with numbers and running the chess club. Applied for
parole on the due dates but never got a sniff. Last time he was
up – late 'seventy-six – they told him he wasn't going anywhere.
He never coughed to the murder – so that was always going to
make it tricky.

'But they did decide to transfer him – to a Category-B prison
on the Lincolnshire coast. Six weeks later they let him out on a
trip with half a dozen others on good behaviour. A minibus to
the beach, Cleethorpes. One of the three guards on the detail
said he saw him at the water's edge, paddling, just in shorts. This
was August – blue sky, low tide. Then he was gone. Report
concluded he'd just walked into the water. They tried to track
him down, watched the family, friends. Nothing. Body never
turned up. There was never a sniff in the press. Nasty stink
at the prison, mind you. Let's just say they didn't run any trips
to the beach again.'

Talbot turned stiffly on the bench to look at Dryden. 'Presumably
you've found him?'

Dryden nodded. 'I'll be blowing the whistle pretty much today
– but I wouldn't worry. He's dead. Cremated. Your name won't
come up.'

They shook hands and Talbot went to get his prisoner ready
for his brief court appearance.

Dryden went up into the court and took a seat on a bench at
the back. The ceiling of the court was eggshell blue, with gold

decorations of the Royal Standard and the Royal Crest. The glorious roof stretched over the sordid business of the court below like a heavenly sky. He thought about the sky that day off the Lincolnshire coast. The figure on the water's edge walking into the water, out of one life and into another.

THIRTY-NINE

D ryden went back to his desk at *The Crow*. The rest of the morning's routine passed in a trance. He sat tapping out wedding reports, one-paragraph RTAs, and a caption on a flower show at one of the outlying villages. He did a round of calls and got the latest from Ely police on the violent murder of Philip Trelaw at his house in a quiet Ely suburban street. A spokesman refused to deny that detectives were investigating links between the shooting and the death of Rory Setchey on Eau Fen. CID were confident forensic evidence at the scene of crime would lead to a swift arrest. A picture of Miiko Saar was also released, with a warning to the general public not to approach the man if spotted.

At lunch Dryden walked over to The Lamb Hotel. The Morton Suite was booked in the name of Fenland Newspapers. His interview for the post of editor of *The Crow* lasted ninety minutes. A feeling of profound detachment held Dryden in its grip – as if he was watching himself answer questions, watching himself sketch out a strategy for saving *The Crow* from its interminable decline: a new lifestyle magazine on Friday, a website to carry village notes, lots more local News In Briefs – NIBS – dotted through the paper, and a revamp of editorial policy to make the paper a campaigning voice for the Fens, FOR a new Cambridge airport, AGAINST more new towns, FOR a redevelopment of Ely's dilapidated Market Square, AGAINST another supermarket.

He talked them to a standstill. There was time for one question: if he got the job how long would he stay? Answer: for life.

Walking back to the office he had no idea how it had gone. He typed up routine stories from council minutes; his fingers working independently of his brain, which was systematically attempting to analyse what he could do with the knowledge he had – the knowledge, he was sure, he *alone* had: the real name of the man who had become Jack Dryden. A name which was the key to everything. But how to use it to his advantage? And how to use it quickly. Kross – with Friday's help – was on the same trail as he was. And he couldn't be sure he hadn't left a fingerprint at Trelaw's house, on the banister, perhaps, or the bedroom door. If forensics found a single print he was sunk. He'd be in a cell by nightfall.

The solution, finally, came to him in late afternoon. He went out, bought a coffee and sat by the river, thinking it through a second time, a third. Timing was everything, and he had to wait for dusk. He picked up a *Cambridge Evening News* from a newsagent on the High Street and took it to the Fenman. He left Bracken, the news editor, at the bar, and sat outside in the courtyard with Humph, who'd left the cab in the rank with instructions to the driver in front to give him a ring if he ended up in pole position. Above them, over the roof tops, was the West Tower of the cathedral, the dusk gathering around it like the rooks waiting to roost.

At a minute to nine o'clock he left Humph and walked to Palace Green, finding a spot hidden by one of the cathedral's buttresses. To the west stretched the last colours of sunset. To the east was nightrise – the first star clear in the sky.

His mobile showed five bars so he called the number for Laura's Cromer B&B. She was well, Eden was well; they'd been on the beach. She let the conversation lapse into silence.

'It will be over soon. Maybe this time tomorrow,' he said. 'Then I'll come up.'

She let more silence ask the questions.

'I'm sorry,' he said. 'I'm not in danger. Far from it. I've found a way to end it. But I must give the police time. A few hours, no more.'

After he cut the line he waited a minute then rang Kross.

From where he stood he could see the detective's hotel room in The Lamb. A light shone and flickered like a TV.

'Kross,' he said, as if to a subordinate.

First he told Kross the truth – that there had been only twenty-five IDs in the package he'd opened in *The Crow*. Friday had made it clear they had been expecting fifty IDs to come on to the market. Which meant twenty-five were still missing. Which explained why Miiko Saar was still in the country. Then he set out the deal. All Kross had to do was make sure Saar got a message from someone he trusted that the missing twenty-five IDs were for sale. Kross would have to invent the identity of the seller, but Dryden suggested the Polish migrant workforce of Eau Fen was a good place to start. The missing IDs were Saar's for a price: Dryden left it to Kross to pick a figure, but £50,000 was, surely, credible. The sellers would be at River Bank with the IDs from midnight the following evening. They would wait an hour, no longer.

Kross and his men should be in position to arrest Miiko Saar once he appeared at River Bank. Dryden wanted the Estonian charged with the murder of Roger Stutton. Once this had taken place Kross could have the information *he* wanted – the identity of the ID supplier, and the names of others implicated in the network. Dryden had two further small favours to ask. Neither was difficult to grant. Kross had twenty-four hours to organize both.

'Why don't I just arrest *you*, Mr Dryden?' asked Kross.

'I'll say that I made all this up to get Saar arrested. To get what I want. He is here, in Ely, believe me. I saw him at Trelaw's house.'

Dryden let that little confession hang on the line for a few seconds.

'If you don't do this I will not tell you what you want to know. I will not. The Saars will be free to sell the twenty-five IDs they have. And remember – the longer Miiko is at large the greater the chance that he will actually find the missing twenty-five IDs – the whereabouts of which are unknown. I think there has to be a chance he will find them before you do, don't you?'

Kross didn't answer. Dryden saw the figure at the bedroom window tip back a bottle and drink. 'You can do this?' he asked. 'Get a message to Saar that he will trust?'

'Yes. We know his associates. This can be done. You do not have the twenty-five IDs?'

'No.'

The curtain of Kross' window was swept back. Dryden stepped back into the shadows. Kross was in a white shirt, buttons open, the green bottle of beer in his hand.

'And I will be there,' said Dryden. 'At River Bank, where this all began. Midnight. Tomorrow.'

FORTY

The police motor launch created a modest wake as it slipped through the west window of *The Little Chapel in the Fen*, under the pointed Gothic arch. The engine cut out but the echo survived like the last line of a hymn. They'd arrived by starlight but the moon was due to rise at eleven. Kross sat in the prow, while one of the officers from the sub-aqua unit took the tiller, edging forward using a paddle to the foot of the spiral staircase. Dryden peered down into the water, trying to see the entangled eels below.

'It is possible he will not get this message in time,' said Kross. 'I explained – yes? We know people. They are close to the Saar brothers. The message comes from people they trust. But still they will suspect them. Because they trust no one completely. He may never come.'

'Midnight?' asked Dryden.

'Midnight, yes. If he comes.'

They tied up the boat by the altar rail and climbed the stairwell to the chamber above. The mere was oily-flat and motionless. The dead oak tree rose like some ghostly human brain, the nerves twisting and splitting, spreading, reaching for the carapace of an unseen skull. The other landmarks were lit in silver: the chimneys of *Fenlandia*, and the skeleton of the grain silo. The narrow pinnacle of the spire itself threw a moon-shadow on the water.

Kross took first watch and the chair. Dryden descended to the clock chamber, which was windowless, so he could use his wind-up lantern. It was hot – mid-sixties – so he took of his jacket and laid it on a beam and sat with his back to the warm brick.

He opened the file that Kross had given him from the office of the Director of Public Prosecutions: dated November 6, 1974. Pre-digital age, manila cardboard, the front stamped with a blue stencilled label which read: NO FURTHER ACTION.

The summary report was 4,000 words long, and it took him less than half an hour to read it.

The Kettlebury school trip to the Highlands was not organized by the school – or Jack Dryden – but by an outward-bound company called Heather Adventures, of Braemar. They had taken the school party out that morning to the foot of Ben Cracken and despite the poor weather had advised them it was safe to continue. Under the contract signed with the school they should have provided a guide – specifically a guide who could swim, as the school had pointed out that Jack Dryden was a non-swimmer – although he was an experienced climber, Highland walker, and outward-bound leader.

The company informed Jack Dryden at the drop-off point that due to illness they could not provide a guide at that point but that one would join them above Black Top Tarn at three o'clock. All the boys had emergency survival kit and proper clothing. The DPP summary noted that they reached the summit, at 3,009 feet, at five past noon and were in 'cheery mood and fit and well'. The descent was difficult because of the sudden mist which enveloped the mountain in minutes.

Despite almost zero visibility the climb down went well. They reached the rendezvous point above Black Top Tarn just before three. They waited until three thirty but there was no sign of the guide – who, it transpired, never set out. The company had decided that their resources were better placed with a group of teenagers attempting to climb the rockface of the mountain's north slopes. They had attempted a radio message to Jack Dryden but were unable to establish a signal.

The DPP report then noted: 'The incident itself is best described in the statement taken from Mr Dryden at Blair Athol Hospital the day after the tragedy.'

Jack Dryden's statement was just two pages of A4. Its slightly eccentric, mathematical style was a reflection of his father's scientific mind.

'The mist cleared from the sky at just before four o'clock, although traces remained in the rocky stream which is the outfall of Black Top Tarn. The heat in the lee of the mountain was intense – I logged it at eighty-two Fahrenheit as late as four o'clock. The boys were hot and elated that they had finished the climb – the descent stage having been arduous and undertaken almost entirely 'blind'. One of the boys – Paul Windsor – asked if they could swim in the tarn. I said they could paddle. I was not in a position to act as lifeguard and I told them they would be surprised at the temperature of the water – Black Top is a lake formed in a 'cirque': a glacial bowl ground out by the ice. It is fed by streams which descend from the top of the mountain. I told them to paddle and cool down. They could explore the area but were not to enter the water at any other point. I asked them to respect these rules and they said they would. I sat on the beach and sketched the mountain.

'Some of the boys did go paddling and I looked up several times at their cries of alarm as they put their feet in the tarn. I walked to the edge myself and organized six of the boys in a line going out into the water: each took a temperature reading using the thermometers I had brought for the trip. The temperature values began at thirty-seven Fahrenheit at the lake edge and fell to thirty-five Fahrenheit at the furthest extent measured at fifty-one feet: three degrees above freezing. We discussed the physics involved and concluded the water at the back of the tarn – at its deepest – would hold a temperature close to freezing for most of the year, whatever the ambient conditions.

'At approximately 4.15 p.m. I heard a shout and looked across the tarn, to the almost sheer rock face which forms the upper 'lip' of the bowl in which the lake sits. One of the boys was standing on a rock pinnacle in his swimming shorts. As I watched he dived into the water. I heard clapping and saw two other boys amongst the rock scree which fell to the water's edge.

'I climbed a pile of rocks to get a view of the point in the lake where the boy – the boy I now know was Toby – had entered the water. Concentric waves radiated from the spot. I was aware of the phenomenon of time slowing down in a moment of stress and was therefore not concerned at the non-appearance of the boy. I waited. I am unable to say how long the boy was absent from view but it was long enough for me to consider the possibility that he had dived and was attempting to play a joke on his friends in the rocks, and would reappear at the lake edge.

'Then his body surfaced. I knew immediately he was in trouble. He lay almost exactly in the middle of the concentric circle he had created by his dive. His body was floating on his front, legs and arms splayed. He was approximately 100 yards from the spot where I stood.

'The boys opposite were calling his name and edging into the water. Some were swimmers but none were confident and none had received rescue training. I told them to stop. They must not enter the water. By this point several of the other boys had come out of the water and joined me on the rocks. I got one of them – Glen Harrison – to use our radio to call for assistance. Two of the boys assembled the flare gun. I told Roland Timms that in the event that I was to get into trouble in the water he was to be in charge of the group. No one else should go in the water. He should wait with the group for rescue. If necessary they should camp overnight.

'Satisfied that we had done all that was possible I took off my clothes – except for boxer shorts – and waded out towards the body. I had not realized how hot I was sitting amongst the rocks and the temperature was shocking: I could feel my bones instantly aching. I think I was between forty and forty-five yards from Toby's body when I reached my depth. Although I am not a swimmer I thought I should try and reach him.

'I forced myself to float on my back – something I have been able to achieve for short spells in the swimming pool. I tried to get close to the boy using foot strokes. I think I got within a few yards but felt my body bending at the waist – the head coming up to meet the knees – and I swallowed water, which triggered a state of panic. As I twisted in the water I looked towards the spot where I had last seen Toby. I do not recall how I got back into my own depth but suddenly I felt my feet scraping across rock. I stood. I was still unable to breathe due to convulsive movements of my chest. I heard one of the boys saying that it was too late and I should give up. But I felt that I should try again although I could see my feet in the brown tarn water and they were streaked with blood and there was a dull pain in them.

'I floated on my back and used foot strokes again to go into deeper water. Above me in the sky I saw the sudden smudge of the flare and felt the thud of the maroon. The temperature was now making my muscles contract and stiffen. I could hear my heart beat through the water around me. I forced my back to stay straight despite the urge to drop my legs and try to find the bottom.

'The boys were calling from the beach and I did hear the single word, 'Stop!'

'I stopped. I opened my arms out like a snow angel, and then my legs, but I could not see Toby. I was forced to lift my head which unbalanced my body so that I began to sink. Very briefly at this point I saw him. He was perhaps twenty feet below me; I could see his white skin against the deep brown of the tarn water. His face was turned up and very pale so that I could not see his lips although his mouth was open in a nearly perfect O. His arms and legs were askew. As I watched I could see him sinking, the brown water making him less distinct. The downward motion, away from me, was the only motion of his body. I felt powerless. The next thing I recall is waking up in the hospital.'

The DPP report concluded with a note on the inquest held at Barnet Magistrates Court. Toby Michaels was examined by pathologists at Aberdeen Infirmary who concluded that he died of heart failure due to shock. The verdict was *death by misadventure*. The coroner said a file would be sent to the DPP and that it might consider legal action against the organizers – Heather Adventures. He added that the courage shown by the boys' teacher had been exemplary and that he should in no way consider himself to blame for the accident.

Dryden held his head in his hands.

Below, in the flooded nave, he heard a languid slap of water against stone. The noise made his emotions stir: the fear of water, the love of water, never mixing, just existing in dynamic tension to each other. Whatever happened now he knew that at least his uncle's death had brought him this one – unexpected – gift: an understanding of his father, and of himself.

FORTY-ONE

A mechanical sound, a single note, floated down into the room from the ringing chamber above. A marine engine, the shape of the sound clear and sharp, as the noise came to them over the unmoving surface of the mere. By the time Dryden had climbed silently to the upper chamber window the boat was in sight, the pale hull almost luminous in the moonlight, a clear V-shaped wake etched in white on the black water.

It was a river authority boat, a Hereward, Rory Setchey's boat – thought Dryden – missing since the day he died. The forward wheelhouse was lit within and they could see a figure standing, peering forward. The ticking of the engine slowed as the power ebbed then died, and in complete silence the boat drifted forward.

The black-and-white waterscape was shattered by a single burning light: a searchlight, mounted on the wheelhouse of the Hereward, probing the shadows until it locked on the single chimney of the sunken villa of *Fenlandia*. The figure came out on the deck carrying what looked like a billhook, moving with the easy grace of one who has lived on boats – the hook in one hand balanced by a coil of rope in the other hand. Dryden realized he'd seen that loping stride before: the man walking quickly across Market Square, carrying his son in his cradle.

The forward motion of the boat was now almost dissipated so that by the time it reached the chimney the boatman could lean down and snare the brick structure with a loop of the heavy rope. The boat pivoted in slow-motion, the figure turning the searchlight so that it remained on the chimney.

The figure straightened its back. A man, a heavy cloth cap, the light catching a high straight jaw, wide, brutal cheekbones. He sat then, one hand trailing in the water, the other holding a cigarette.

Kross touched Dryden's shoulder. They dropped quickly down the stairs and into the waiting launch. The diver in the prow paddled soundlessly to the arched open window. Out in the moonlight, but still shielded from Saar by the chapel, Kross lifted a mobile to his lips. 'This is Kross. Now.'

Light and noise ripped the night apart. The two police launches beneath the carapace of the old oak tree shot searchlight beams across the water, their engines igniting in a single mechanical wail. Dryden shielded his eyes as their own launch jumped forward, so that he was thrown back off the plank seat and into the bottom of the boat.

By the time he regained his seat they were thirty yards from Saar. He stood pinioned by the lights, both arms thrown up to protect his eyes. The scene stood in stark three-dimensions, so vivid that when Dryden closed his eyes a negative image remained: a white boat on black water, the figure motionless, caught in the moment of recoil.

Kross used a megaphone to broadcast in urgent Estonian.

Saar dropped his arms, thrust both hands into his pockets and looked away from the light.

'Miiko, this is over, please.' English this time. Kross set the megaphone aside. The night was so still his voice carried perfectly. Their boat was drifting towards Saar's on a perfect collision course.

'You must come with us,' said Kross, his voice calm, almost bored. 'There will be a trial. We have your brother too – today, at Maardu. Already he is talking to us.'

Saar squinted into the lights. 'Kross?'

'We have Geron.' Then a long sentence in Estonian.

'That's a lie,' said Saar. The voice surprised Dryden because there was no hint of an accent and it was quite high – not feminine, just sharp and brittle.

Dryden felt Kross stiffen beside him.

'There is no way other than this,' said the detective. 'We cannot undo these things.'

With easy movements Miiko threw his dog-end into the water and produced a packet of cigarettes and a lighter – vivid plastic yellow. From the darkness the sound of a rifle being cocked was pin-sharp. Miiko froze, holding up the cigarette.

'It's OK,' said Kross into the radio.

Saar lit the cigarette, looking around, taking in the three police launches, the searchlights – and then, faintly at first, the thudding rotars of a police helicopter approaching.

'I am not surprised by this,' he said, drawing in the nicotine deeply.

'Then why come?' asked Kross.

'No choice. Our masters demand their money's worth. I cannot go home empty-handed. I must risk everything. I have.' Dryden watched him lick a shred of tobacco from his lip.

They all heard another gun being cocked on board one of the police launches.

'The trial – in Tallinn?' asked Saar. It was a teasing question, almost light-hearted, as if the answer didn't matter. As if no answers mattered any more – let alone questions.

'No. Here,' said Kross. 'There have been murders. There must be justice for those left. Maybe – afterwards – prison will be in Tallinn. One day. But there are no promises.'

The Estonian spat in the water.

Dryden could hear in the tone of this conversation other conversations. He wondered just how close the Estonian CID had got to the Saar brothers. Too close, perhaps, to tell the difference between good and evil.

They were twenty feet apart now. Dryden could see Saar's hands – the hands that had tied a rope round Roger's foot, knotted it to the edge of the eel boat then wielded the hammer, breaking through the clinker-hull. They were smudged with oil and brown grease from the wheelhouse. Dryden thought of Rory Setchey's body hanging on the irrigator on Eau Fen – his hands had been clean, reeking of marine fuel.

'Please,' said Kross again. 'Now – my officers come. Three are armed, Miiko. Remember this.'

They heard the other boats moving forward from the shadows of the great oak tree. A series of three blue lights began to strobe on one of the cabin roofs and the colour took Dryden's attention so that when he looked back he saw that Saar had moved – just a few feet, to a small flip-down wooden seat beside the engine housing.

'A minute?' asked the Estonian, sitting, smoking.

Kross said something into the mobile. The sound of the launch engines died to a murmur.

'Please, Miiko, it's over.'

Saar shrugged, smiling, and pulled up his sleeve so that Dryden saw his father's compass watch, the watch he'd taken from Roger Stutton before he'd killed him. Saar laid it on the edge of the bulwark as if to time his minute. 'Do you have the missing twenty-five packages? No? I wonder where he put them, this man, Setchey. Because we think it was him.' He shrugged. 'An accident. We will never know.'

Saar shook his head, the weight of his skull seeming to over-balance his head so that it fell forward. Then his neck muscles flipped the chin up, and he leaned forward over the metallic casing of the engine, unscrewed the fuel cap in an easy motion, drew on the cigarette, and dropped the butt into the dark hole.

The sound – before any flame – was of steel tearing. The explosion seemed to punch through the darkness of the night, the dense heart of it burning into Dryden's eyes. The sound of the blast was compressed into a single note, trapped in his ears. Ringing. He held an image of Kross, his face contorted into a shout, but no sound of the words.

Then came the fire. A ball of red, with violent edges of amber and blue. All this Dryden saw through tightly closed eyes.

In the water. Without knowing how, he was in the water. He could taste moss, fresh water and marine fuel. A hand grabbed his collar and hauled him back aboard the police launch. The Hereward was still afloat too – but only as a pool of debris, the flames already dying, almost domestic, warming, an open hearth on water.

Dryden was aware that things were falling out of the sky – pieces of wood, rope, and material – linen scraps, tarpaulin. He breathed in and found some shreds of burnt paper in his mouth, sticking to his lips. He held out both hands as if taking communion and caught a piece of cardboard zigzagging down. The breeze blew it away, but another scrap settled on his damp hand. Then more scraps, like two-dimensional snow. The largest piece looked like a banknote, with very subtle blues and reds in complex mathematical designs. Picking it up, he held it in the flickering light and saw the watermark. It was limp with soaked fuel but he knew it for what it was – the first right-hand page of a British passport.

FORTY-TWO

Sheila Petit heard the explosion on Adventurers' Mere from her bed. She'd been lying in the dark thinking, quite systematically, if there was anything else in the flat she should burn in case the police came with a warrant. Miiko Saar had watched her incinerate the master list of the original fifty IDs that she'd supplied. His brother Geron, they knew, was back in Estonia with the twenty-five IDs they'd found on Dryden's desk, the twenty-five IDs Roger Stutton had found lodged in the nets tangled with his own at River Bank. Who had the missing twenty-five IDs? If it had been Rory Setchey, he'd taken the secret of their hiding place to an early grave. They had to hope it hadn't been Rory. It was their only hope. The Russians wanted half their money back, but Sheila Petit didn't have the money because she'd used all of it to buy the parcel of land that would save Petit Fen. So they had to get the missing IDs back, whatever it cost.

Geron had gone back to Tallinn to buy them time with the Russians. Miiko had laid low in the boathouse, waiting, hoping that if someone had the missing package they'd calculate eventually that he was their only buyer – only he could channel the IDs back to the customers whose names and pictures made a match. It had been an agonizing wait. Miiko had hardly spoken since the moment she'd found him sitting arrogantly at her own kitchen table: he was a brutal man, uncivilized, with what she would characterize as base emotions. He ate, she'd noted, like an animal, his fingers sifting through the food on his plate. He'd only hit her once, that first morning after they'd killed Rory. A casual slap which had dislodged a tooth in the back of her mouth. Geron had laughed, picking something from his own teeth.

And then, the evening before, the call had finally come on

Miiko's mobile. Someone they trusted relayed the message: the twenty-five IDs were for sale at £50,000. Rory Setchey's regular midnight voyages to River Bank had, apparently, been noticed. Their intermediary hinted at migrant workers, organized crime, and a Polish connection. It mattered little, as they had no choice but to keep to the deal they had been offered: midnight – at River Bank. She'd helped Miiko get Setchey's boat ready and hauled up the doors for him to slip out into the Lark: the journey ahead sketched on a map, two miles to the sluice at Upware, then out on to Adventurers' Mere, three miles south to River Bank.

She'd gone to her bed, waited, and for the first time in many years, prayed. And then she'd heard the explosion. A dull percussion, but she knew it for what it was. The bedside clock numbers glowed 12.09 a.m. She'd run out on the lawn expecting to see the sky gashed, wounded by fire. But there was just a pale glow, and then a little later a distant siren, then others, zigzagging from the main road out towards Upware. And the helicopter above circling out over the unseen water, a single beam seeming to anchor it to the earth like a gyre.

The explosion meant it was all going to unravel, and that the trail might lead back to her, so she had to be ready: armed, as it were, with a story. She got one of the heavy wooden chairs from the kitchen and took it out to Arthur's graveside where she always went to think. The night sky was still perfect, turning overhead like a planetarium. She sat listening to the whisper in the heavens, as if there was a wind which blew the stars round. After an hour she went back to the house, made tea, brewing it in the mug, and then returned to the graveside.

It would be dawn in an hour but already the sky was lightening, the stars in the east flickering out.

The gravestone only caught the light in the early and dying minutes of the day – and the face, with its inscription, only at dawn. She wouldn't have been able to read the inscription if she hadn't known it by heart.

Raymond Arthur Petit
Born 1930. Died 1970.
Remembered and respected by his wife and son.
He loved this place which was his own.

She smiled, sipping her tea, then bit her lip as the tears came. Being here, at this time, always made her recall the day he'd died, a month short of his fortieth birthday.

When they'd sent Arthur home from hospital she'd put him in the bedroom at the top of the house, in the roof, because it had the best window. It was only later, at the funeral that his sister told her it was the room he'd been born in.

Lying in bed he'd only been able to see the sky, and in clear weather the vanes of the wind farm beyond Wicken, so they'd raised him up and tilted the frame forward so that he could – from the pillow – open his eyes and see *his* land. It had been September 1970, the harvest, and the crop was good. They still had their own farm hands then, and the tied cottages were all full, so the landscape had been alive with people, not just machines.

Even at Cambridge, where they'd met, Arthur had lived for the land that was his. He'd taken natural sciences, specializing in soil science. She'd read English and they shared a passion for Hardy, for Gaskell, the Brontës. Great sagas of the English landscape. He'd brought her home at Easter in their second year. His father – Gerald – had shown her the estate, from the Sixteen Foot Drain to Petit Hill and back to Northern Belt – the line of poplars which marked the land last drained by the Victorians using the new steam engine at Middle Pump. Even then she'd felt that her love of the place, then just a flickering emotion, was dangerous nonetheless.

Arthur had been fatally injured in an accident on a tractor which had tumbled into a roadside ditch. He shouldn't have been doing the work himself but one of the hired hands was off sick and he enjoyed operating the machine. The impact had severed internal arteries and dislodged organs. Eighteen hours of surgery and three months in hospital had failed to rectify the damage. He'd been sent home to die. Their son, Martyn, came home from university at Edinburgh. He wasn't close to his father, or his mother, or to their knowledge, to any other human being. A solitary child who'd lived in his head, at home with facts, and abstractions, and symbols. He hadn't even been close to the land.

The weather had broken the day the boy arrived, snow patches on the fen, and she'd watched him walking from the bus, along the drove, as if it was his own personal *via dolorosa* – his head down, shoulders slumped.

They'd have bought him a car if he'd been able to drive but it was beyond him – almost everything seemed beyond him, except understanding numbers and the patterns they made in his head. At the kitchen table he'd spread out white sheets of paper and spend hours – days – writing in maths. Telling himself stories about numbers.

On the day Arthur died he asked Martyn to open the sash windows and he'd lain there breathing deeply the ice-crystal air off the fen, snowflakes blowing in and lying frozen on the bare boards. Arthur had asked Martyn to hold his hand and Sheila had watched her son's eyes, locked on the grip of the two hands, trying to understand, trying desperately to feel an emotion. A minute, maybe less, then he'd asked them to shut the window and he'd closed his eyes.

The crisis had come at midnight. She'd slept on a divan and woke to hear Arthur calling her name, the precise sound of which she could now recall: not a note of pleading at all, a note of summons. It had been a businesslike hour, the last hour of his life, and she'd always despised him for it, for the cold premeditation of what he'd made her do. After she'd read the will, and a note on dispositions for the farm in the coming year, he'd made her make a simple promise: that she'd never leave Petit Hall, that she'd always farm Petit Fen, and that their son would follow her. Their son, and his sons.

Arthur had slept then but never woken, and so by dawn she was left with the promise, and his cold body, still propped on the pillow so that he could see his land.

Footsteps, suddenly, on the dry leaves beneath the trees.

She tore her eyes away from Arthur's gravestone and looked

up and the first light was in the sky, the stars in the East finally gone. Philip Dryden, the reporter, was walking towards her out of the shadows of the trees, and beside him a man with white hair, and pale skin, who looked bloodless. Both were in white overalls, spotless, but their faces were wet and smudged with oil and what looked like ash.

'I wanted to talk about your son, Martyn,' said Dryden, as he reached the grave. 'He stole my father's life.'

FORTY-THREE

The silence beside Arthur Petit's grave was briefly under-mined by the crackle of a police radio. Two uniformed policemen emerged from the trees and Kross directed them to search the house and to assist the forensic team down at the boathouse. The detective's thin hands, both in SOCO white gloves, hung at his sides. Dryden stood still because he was unsure of his knees, which kept buckling, his nervous system shorting-out. They'd given him SOCO overalls to wear but he didn't seem able to retain his body heat, so that his jaw shivered with cold.

He was going to tell Sheila Petit about Kross and Interpol, and the death of Miiko Saar, but she began to talk: rhythmically, as if imagining herself already on the witness stand.

'The Estonian came three days ago at night. He has guns – not farm guns, military weapons. He said he needed to use the boathouse, and the boat, and that he would stay with me. I was to tell nobody. If I did he'd kill me. I believed him. His name was Miiko. I have no idea why he was here. He left a few hours ago. That's all I know. He slept in the boathouse but he ate in the house.' She turned to Kross. 'Is he dead?'

'Yes. Quite dead,' he said.

'Good.'

Dryden walked forward to the gravestone and ran his fingers over the inscription. He knew he could destroy her version of events because he knew the man who'd been transferred from Lincoln Jail to the Lincolnshire coast and had walked into the sea that day in 1977 was her son, Martyn Petit. And he knew that if they took the DNA sample they'd extracted from the man calling himself Jack Dryden they'd be able to show that it *was* Martyn Petit, aged nearly sixty, and that he'd died in the charred van on the road to Manea.

He chose a place to start telling the truth, and he started with a question.

'Did you plan, one day, to bury Martyn here? With his father? And yet you didn't even go to the funeral.'

She looked up at Dryden and the look in her eyes was close to despairing, which was a relief, because given what this woman had done he'd expected to find only madness or obsession. But the idea that she was sane, that she had made calculations, only seemed to deepen Dryden's sense of the evil which was here, on the Petit land.

'Martyn killed the girl at Oxford – and left the family to hope for eight long days,' he said.

She licked her lips, aching to defend him, perhaps, trying to work out if the story she'd constructed could possibly hold.

Dryden swung round to face Kross. 'Martyn Petit was convicted of murder in 1971. Life – with a minimum tariff of twenty-eight years. Lincoln Jail. Model prisoner, spent most of his time playing chess. Moved to a Category-B facility in 1977 on the coast. Walked into the sea one day – never seen again.'

He turned quickly back to Petit and caught the look of loss in her eyes.

'He came here, didn't he? You gave him my father's identity so that he could live a life – here, near you. There was even a son for him too – so a full life, although he didn't get to bring the child up, did he? Peterborough at the start – then back, nearer home.

'And why steal my father's identity? Did you know him? There were similarities – the build, the face, the degree.'

She seemed to struggle to speak.

Dryden held up a hand. 'Please. It hardly matters. You'd know of his death. Everyone knew. It must have been chaos that winter – the Fens flooded, the Army, the press. All you had to do was stop Trelaw passing on the death certificate. I think that time – just that once – he helped. And you got him a job close to the hospital as a reward. He paid for the kidney transplant himself – that's why he died in debt. You told Miiko that Trelaw had been involved back then, when it all started. The police had asked him questions, I'd asked him questions. Miiko shot him, a pillow pressed over his face to deaden the noise and the blood. Just to make sure he never answered those questions with the truth.'

Dawn was approaching and crows clattered into the trees above them.

'So that was the first time,' said Dryden. 'The first time you stole someone's identity. A victimless crime? Perhaps. Certainly not for money. And I guess it was Martyn who built himself that new life – the new driver's licence, the medical card, all the documents he needed. He was good at that; meticulous, methodical, dispassionate. It wasn't quite perfect, was it – because he had to fit in with Dad's life, and he couldn't really chance anything which needed a picture. But if he was careful he could have a life – a half-life, perhaps.

'And then Rory Setchey's little boy died. I presume he knew your husband – the family. It was the fishing – right? The champion pike. I know Arthur was keen . . .' He touched the gravestone. 'And that's when the thought occurred – which is a dark thought, and not at all obvious – that if you stole the life of someone who hadn't yet lived, then you could build it, construct it, design it, even – for sale.'

'The real question is whose idea was it? And what was the purpose? It's such a cold thing to do. *Mathematical?*'

She looked away then to the house, then up to the sky.

'I thought it was probably Martyn's idea. But then I thought he was *your* son. That there had to be something in you of him – a coldness. But most of all, I think it was your idea because you had the motive. You were struggling here – death duties, taxes, agricultural wages, competition. You had to sell land. Rent land. Then the government announced the plan to re-flood the fen and you needed a lot of money to stop that. So I think you conceived of the plan and Martyn did the work – stealing the lives of the dead. It would take years. But he didn't mind, and neither did you. Years, to let the stolen lives grow and blossom.'

'This is crazy,' she said, moving to stand, but Kross held up his hand.

'It's called ghosting, by the way,' added Dryden. 'Kapten Kross here, and his colleagues in Interpol, can tell you all about it. But maybe you already know. And Rory helped – didn't he? And later, when it was time to start selling the lives, he'd be the ferryman.'

Dryden rearranged his feet, hit by a wave of nausea, the taste of marine fuel in his mouth again. 'Patience, of course, it needed patience. And you had to sell the idea – and I think Martyn knew the people – the right people – from Lincoln, who could find you the customers, or at least the kind of people who'd be able to reach the market. And it was easy for you to intercept the death certificates because you were at the post office. The registrars use registered post. You had access to the 'cage' – all you had to do was request to see certain items at certain times. A package – a dozen forms, who'd miss the odd one that never got to the General Register Office?

'And very soon everyone thought what a good idea this was. An almost *beautiful* idea. Even noble – that's what you told yourself. Because the money was being saved – a fortune building, ready for the day when you'd be able to save Petit Fen. To make the system perfect you needed one more person. Someone to alert you when a child had died – preferably one buried by the council, in the open graves, where no one goes because they just want to forget, not remember. And that's why Billy Johns was recruited. That baffled me for a while – but then, of course, there's the chapel on Petit Fen where the bikers meet. Did you find him there? Seek him out? And he needs money – he grows cannabis, out the back at the cemetery in that shed of his. It's not all for customers, is it? He has his own habit to supply. And then there's the Harleys. So he couldn't have been too hard to tempt. Especially as you no doubt told him, told everyone, it's a victimless crime.'

She actually flinched at that, which gave Dryden some kind of satisfaction.

He spread his arms. 'And so it went on until the unexpected happened. We never think our loved ones will leave us – do we? Until it is too late. Martyn died in that burnt-out van at Manea and suddenly it looked as if you might lose everything. You knew there'd be questions about the true identity of Jack Dryden. One day they'd track him back to Lincoln, to Martyn's cell, and then the truth would be out – or at least part of it. So the assets that you'd been nurturing all those years – the lives of the dead – had to be sold, sold quickly. Everything. A fire sale.'

'This is completely ludicrous,' said Petit, trying to smile, but her lips formed an ugly jagged line.

'In the meantime a parcel of land came up for a quick sale on Petit Fen. So what did you do – borrow the money on short loan rates? High interest. You knew you'd have the Saars' brothers money in your hands within days. So you bought the land with the bank's money. And now you've paid off the banks with the Saar's money. But it's not their money at all – it's the Russians'. So very soon the real trouble will begin.'

'Why?' She'd meant it to sound like a challenge but the word caught in her throat.

Kross stepped forward with a plastic evidence bag and emptied the contents on to the flat stone set in the grave. It was paper, burnt, charred, wet. The air filled with the stench of ash.

'That's what's left of the twenty-five IDs,' said Dryden. 'Setchey hid them in the fuel tank of the boat.'

Dryden caught the sudden electricity in Petit's grey eyes.

'Yes. So near,' he said, realizing that inflicting cruelty was dangerously satisfying. 'Rory kept a spare ignition key in the fuel tank – an old trick – and another in your boathouse. That's where the Saar brothers got theirs. The IDs came in watertight wallets so he popped them in the tank. He thought they were safe – until he found a buyer. I guess they were.

'He would have told them soon enough where they were if his heart hadn't given out. The one shot was a warning? An accident? It hardly matters.'

Dryden knelt on the grass, leaning back to relieve the pain in his back. 'So think on this. The Russians have paid all their money to the Saar brothers who gave it to you – no doubt minus their own cut. But these twenty-five IDs – half your consignment – are gone forever. They're scattered on the surface of Adventurers' Mere. And once we've looked through the records of children buried at Manea over the years – especially the ones in the public graves – we'll know the names of the rest, or most of them. In which case, the batch of twenty-five that they already have will be useless. Especially after Kapten Kross has made it clear through the appropriate channels that we have the names.

'So one day soon you'll be seeing someone. A representative. He'll want their money – the Russians' money. All of it. He'll be terrifically keen. I don't think the Russians do IOUs. You may think – on reflection – that a cell would be the best place to be.'

She looked up at the two-thirds sky. 'Never.'

The final cruelty was too exquisite to be denied.

'And there will be nothing for the boy now. Martyn's son. The heir. By the time the Russians have finished with you I doubt you'll own anything on Petit Fen. You'll be landless, homeless, and so will he.'

She looked at him frankly then, her eyes wide, and he saw some genuine hatred in the light.

'Martyn was never suited for this – for the farm, the land,' said Dryden. 'He lived in his head. He was happy to make you the money you needed. And he got some cash back – for his toys. But what about your grandson?'

And then Dryden knew; the final piece of the Petit family jigsaw falling into place.

'You brought him up, didn't you? But not here – at Petit Hall. That would have prompted too many questions. Boarding schools – abroad, even? Then university. No – because he wasn't academic, was he? That's what Martyn told one of his pupils – that he wasn't good at school. So maybe college, a land economy degree? Yes, that would be perfect. And his reward?'

Dryden pointed down the drove towards Home Farm. The Victorian farmhouse stood on one side of an open square, barns and outhouses on the other two. A yellow John Deere tractor stood in the lee of a few trees, washed clean.

'Edward Petit,' said Dryden. 'Your nephew – running home farm. Really? Sure he's not your *grandson*. Why don't we ask . . .'

Dryden turned to go but she raised a hand.

'Stop,' she said.

'I wonder what he knows?' asked Dryden. 'And there's his child too – a girl? A virtual dynasty.'

Her lips formed a line, murderously straight. 'He knows nothing,' she said. 'Nothing.' The colour flooded out of Sheila Petit's face. Given the calculated dishonesty she'd been capable of Dryden was appalled to feel pity for her.

'Shall I tell him – or will you?'

FORTY-FOUR

Humph brought breakfast to Petit Hall in the Capri: egg and bacon sandwiches wrapped in foil washed down with Russian vodka in little airline bottles marked *Reyka*. He'd brought a flask too, into which he'd got someone to decant half-a-dozen double espressos. They sat in silence, waiting for the moment of dawn, as a small convoy of police vehicles left Petit Hall. Sheila Petit was in the last one, alone in the back seat, and something in her eye caught the morning light as she slid past the parked cab.

Dryden had two cellophane packages in his lap.

He talked Humph through them. One was his father's compass watch, which had been found hooked over the wheel of Rory Setchey's boat when the floating crane had brought its remains to the surface of Adventurers' Mere. The watch was in no better condition than the body of Miiko Saar. The watch face was marbled with cracks, the glass shattered, the little compass needle blown away. There was a slight smear of blood on the inside of the plastic evidence bag in which it lay.

Humph wiped grease from his lips with the back of his hand.

'Kross said I could keep it,' said Dryden.

The other bag contained a metal ID tag and bracelet. The bracelet was minute, and would only encircle three of Dryden's fingers. The clasp was open and the jagged tooth-edge had entangled in it several shreds of very dark hair.

'That's all that's left of the child the Yorubas lost at Manea. To the fox – I told you?'

Humph nodded. 'Why'd he give it to you?'

'I asked for it. It's important.'

'Hey up,' said the cabbie, nodding back towards Petit Hall. Halfway up the drove a police car was parked outside the entrance to the Home Farm. Edward Petit stood with a woman by the gate, a baby girl held between them. Then he got in the car and it crept towards them, past them, to follow the convoy which had already left. Edward waved back at his cottage, but the woman didn't wave back.

'Let's go,' said Dryden.

'Is it over?' asked Humph.

Dryden knew he meant the whole case: Jack Dryden, Martyn Petit and Rory Setchey – and, most of all, Roger Stutton.

'Yes. For us, it is over. We just have to bury Roger. The funeral's next week.'

He checked his watch: it was too early to ring Laura. The pain in his hip was worse now than it had been for hours so he took some of the painkillers he'd been given at the hospital, then asked Humph to put the cab in a lay-by. He was asleep before the hand brake creaked. He didn't so much go to sleep as pass out.

When he woke Humph was banging on the roof of the Capri.

Getting out Dryden saw that something extraordinary had happened to the sky. He couldn't have been asleep for more than ten minutes because it was just a few seconds before the moment of dawn. Above them stretched a high rack of cloud, like a skein, made up of the brightest colours Dryden had ever seen in the sky – not iridescent, brighter than that. Other clouds, scuds, drifted past, but these brighter clouds seemed untouchable.

'That's what I saw,' said Humph. 'I couldn't find them in the book. So I thought . . .' He seemed lost. 'I thought of the Northern Lights but that's crazy – all the books said that was crazy. So I just made up a name.'

'I know what they're called,' said Dryden. His father had seen them on the farm – always at the same times – just before dawn, just after sunset. They were high level, stratospheric, and that was their secret, because they were so high they caught the sun that had not risen, and the sun that had just set. They were the clouds of sunrise and nightrise.

Humph seemed captivated.

'Nacreous – they're called nacreous clouds,' said Dryden. 'It's Latin for mother-of-pearl. They're rare here – exotic. What did you call them?'

The colours were getting brighter so that Dryden made a physical effort to widen his eyes, open them out, to let in the light.

'I see them all the time,' said Humph. 'I call them The Eastern Lights.'

FORTY-FIVE

A week later

A police squad car stood outside the Victorian folly which had been Billy Johns' home. The front door was open and the hall beyond was empty – the Electra Glide long gone, and with it the cemetery caretaker. Money and a Harley Davidson would get Billy Johns a long way – DI Friday had told Dryden they'd had reports of the bike from Spanish customs in the Pyrenees. And there'd been those crisp euro notes in his wallet. But Dryden suspected that was not quite far enough to slip the grasp of Interpol and Scotland Yard. Which was a shame because he suspected that Miiko Saar had ordered Johns to bury Dryden alive the night the Estonian had dumped his body in the open paupers' grave. Johns had disobeyed orders, then fled. If they ever did bring him to trial, Dryden would be more than happy to tell a judge and jury of his act of mercy.

The caretaker's absence, and the police presence, had brought chaos to the orderly running of Manea Cemetery and Crematorium. The interment of Roger Eden Stutton had been delayed two days. Beneath the chosen cedar Dryden and Laura joined the small crowd which had gathered, finally, for the burial, ferried by a cortège of polished black limousines which had zigzagged over the fen from Buskeybay. Eight spotless cars and Humph's Capri. Con stood slightly apart with her son Laurie, holding him by the arm but looking away. Humph sat on a bench on the gravel path in what might have been a suit; but stood when the priest appeared, walking ahead of the coffin.

The service was mercifully brief and might have been for a stranger. No one cried. When it was over Dryden took out the forensic bag Kross had given him and ripped it open, taking out the compass watch. The time said 12.08 a.m. The exact moment Miiko Saar died. He walked to the grave's edge, didn't look down, but dropped the watch. He felt strangely giddy, even weightless, and standing there, trying to think of Roger, he saw instead his father, or rather felt that he *was* his father, floating in that Scottish tarn, reaching out to try and save the boy who was already dead. And then the moment was past and he felt the clay beneath his feet, and locked his eyes on the distant flat horizon, so that he could walk away from the grave's edge. Eden lay in the grass on his back, his eyes full of sky.

Dryden gave Laura an envelope. 'This was on my desk.'

It was from Fenland Newspapers, owners of *The Crow*. They were delighted to inform him that they were able to offer him the position of editor of *The Crow* and the *Ely Express* newspapers and associated website.

'Associated website,' he said. 'We haven't got a bloody website.'

'That's your first job then,' said Laura. 'Well done.' The smile was genuine but brief.

'It's a good job we're moving. You'll need to be nearer.'

They'd made the decision the day Humph ran Dryden up to Cromer. Living in Flightpath Cottages had been a dream. But the reality had been stifling. It was too remote for Laura, too domestic for Dryden. They'd come back from the coast by a boatyard at Denver Sluice and bought a narrow boat to moor beside PK 145 – their old floating home on the river near Ely. They'd sleep in the new boat, live in the old, and teach Eden a life afloat. There was a FOR SALE sign outside the house.

Laura was watching Con, alone, stood beside the grave, which seemed to hold her in a kind of spell.

'They should fill it in,' said Dryden. A mechanical digger stood under the trees, waiting silently, a workman smoking at the wheel.

'It's a good place,' said Laura. 'We can get another bench – over there, nearer the grave. Look.'

Following her pointing finger east Dryden saw the West Tower of Ely Cathedral. It was a fine day and Dryden knew then he'd sit here and try to see it many times in the future but that he'd often fail. The dense, damp fen air was ideal for shrouding distance.

Dryden was glad his father didn't lie in a grave. He thought of him still as being *out there*, washed away into the waterscape, beneath the clouds.

He picked up Eden and showed him the view.

Con walked over and sat with them. Her son, Laurie, was talking to the priest. Laura produced a flask of tea and what looked like sandwiches neatly packaged in tin foil, and a plastic container for biscuits.

Con smiled. 'This is our wake.'

FORTY-SIX

Dryden left them and walked alone to the crematorium chapel. It had a working area, screened off, at the rear. There was a single wooden door, studded in a mock-medieval style, but unlocked. Inside was a waiting area. On a trestle table a small white coffin stood. It made Dryden's blood rush to his heart.

The undertaker he'd met at the funeral parlour appeared from the chapel. 'They're here,' he said.

Dryden recalled the name – Matthew Carney.

'I'll see them at the graveside,' said Dryden.

Carney nodded and then, turning to the small casket, simply lifted the lid.

Dryden looked away. An instinct of self-preservation. It was, after all, a perversion of nature, the child going before the parents.

'Mr Dryden,' prompted Carney.

He turned back and produced the forensic bag with the ID tag inside.

Now they both stood looking into the casket. There was a teddy bear which seemed brand new, a Bible, and a single lead weight marked seven pounds. Dryden held the tag up to the sunlight which streamed in through the stained glass. The jet-black hair glistened. Dryden placed the bracelet at the head of the casket and stood back. Carney screwed the lid on – six screws, arranged at intervals.

Dryden was dismissed with a smile.

Outside the sun fell on the landscape with its full weight. Humph slept in the Capri. Everyone else had gone so that the cemetery seemed muffled in heat, silent, the hot air buckling slightly. Out on the road he could see a bus, the logo faded but discernible: CERTIO. He could see faces inside, pressed to the windows. The driver's door stood open.

He walked away, along a path which led towards the row of pines which shrouded the public graves. There was a spot here, on the edge of the cemetery, where they buried children. Most of the graves held flowers and toys. A single grave lay open, a trestle beside it, artificial turf set around on three sides. A ditch marked the boundary with the fen. Even now, at the end of an arid summer, there was water flowing slowly by, heading north. This spot felt more like the open fen than graveyard, the black soil running into the distance.

Dryden heard them coming and was ready but he hadn't expected David Yoruba to carry the coffin. He set it on the trestle. A Catholic priest stood mouthing prayers to himself, Carney, the undertaker, at his shoulder.

Gill Yoruba came to Dryden and took his hand. 'Thank you. You found her for us. Should I ask how?'

'Trust me,' said Dryden.

They heard gravel scatter behind them and Humph appeared, sweating, a clean handkerchief in one hand.

'They're taking David after we've buried her,' she said. 'The tribunal found against him. They'll go to Brize Norton, then a flight back to Niger. I'll follow. He wants you to deal with the documents he left you?'

Dryden nodded.

'We don't know what will happen. But this is a comfort. It's a place to come back to.'

The shadow of the priest slid over the coffin.

David Yoruba lowered the coffin using linen tapes, and then they sprinkled earth in the grave. Humph rearranged his feet at the edge as if he might fall over. Dryden went last. He held the handful of peaty clay for several seconds then raised it up high, letting the dust slip through his fingers, mixing earth and sky.